WINIFREI
BEWILDERIN

WINIFRED PECK (1882-1962) was born Winifred Frances
Knox in Oxford, the daughter of the future Bishop of
Manchester. Her mother Ellen was the daughter of the Bishop
of Lahore.

A few years after her mother's death, Winifred Peck became one
of the first pupils at Wycombe Abbey School, and later studied
at Lady Margaret Hall, Oxford. Returning to Manchester, and
under the influence of Christian Socialism, she acted as a social
worker in her father's diocese, as well as starting out as a
professional writer.

After writing a biography of Louis IX, she turned to fiction in
her early thirties, writing over twenty novels, including two
detective mysteries.

She married James Peck in 1911, and they had two sons
together. James was knighted in 1938, and it was as Lady Peck
that his wife was known to many contemporary reviewers.

Bewildering Cares, a novel about the perplexing and richly
comic life of a parish priest's wife in the early months of World
War Two, is now available as a Furrowed Middlebrow book.

BY WINIFRED PECK

FICTION

Twelve Birthdays (1918)
The Closing Gates (1922)
A Patchwork Tale (1925)
The King of Melido (1927)
A Change of Master (1928)
The Warrielaw Jewel (1933)
The Skirts of Time (1935)
The Skies Are Falling (1936)
Coming Out (1938)
Let Me Go Back (1939)
*Bewildering Cares: A Week in the Life of
a Clergyman's Wife* (1940)
A Garden Enclosed (1941)
House-Bound (1942)
Tranquillity (1944)
There Is a Fortress (1945)
Through Eastern Windows (1947)
Veiled Destinies (1948)
A Clear Dawn (1949)
Arrest the Bishop? (1949)
Facing South (1950)
Winding Ways (1951)
Unseen Array (1951)

MEMOIR

A Little Learning: A Victorian Childhood (1952)
Home for the Holidays (1955)

HISTORY

The Court of a Saint: Louis IX, King of France, 1226-70 (1909)
They Come, They Go: The Story of an English Rectory (1937)

WINIFRED PECK

BEWILDERING CARES

With an introduction by
Elizabeth Crawford

DEAN STREET PRESS
A Furrowed Middlebrow Book

A Furrowed Middlebrow Book
FM9

Published by Dean Street Press 2016

Cover by DSP
Cover illustration detail from *Village Street* (1936)
by Eric Ravilious

First published in 1940 by Faber & Faber

ISBN 978 1 911413 87 5

www.deanstreetpress.co.uk

"These bewildering cares
Which weigh us down who live and earn our bread"

—WILLIAM MORRIS

INTRODUCTION

'SMALL TROUBLES are a great help in war-time … They fill the foreground of one's mind and enable one to keep a sense of perspective.' Thus observes Arthur, husband of Camilla Lacely, the narrator of *Bewildering Cares* by Winifred Peck (1882-1962), now reissued as a Furrowed Middlebrow novel. Arthur is vicar of St Simon's, a parish in 'Stampfield', a market town in 'North Midlandshire' to which London means little 'though we have a slight respect for Manchester'. St Simon's is one of the churches thrown up in manufacturing districts in the 19th century and was, as Camilla describes, 'of the most dismal Victorian Gothic, with pitch pine pews and pulpit, and a dismal East Window.' The 'small troubles', Camilla Lacely's 'bewildering cares', are those that dominate her life and that of her parish during a week in Lent in 1940. The Second World War has been underway for barely six months, the main news is of Russia's invasion of Finland, the blitz is yet to come, but Stampfield has already accustomed itself to life on the Home Front. The Lacelys' only son, Dick, is with his regiment 'somewhere in the Essex mud' and Camilla has had to accustom herself to running her vicarage, 'a gaunt, big house with a peeling stucco front, three stories high, with a cavernous basement kitchen', with only one maid. Moreover, Camilla tells us that since the beginning of the war 'I have tackled the cooking myself, to prevent waste'. Here, as in so many other ways, the author of *Bewildering Cares* is drawing on her own experience; it was only now that, for the first time in her life, Winifred Peck had had to cook for her household. Moreover, although not a vicar's wife, she knew only too well what it was to live in a clerical household; the *Scotsman*'s reviewer (19 September 1940) particularly remarks that the author 'shows herself a knowledgeable and sympathetic observer of the domestic life of the clergy'.

The third of six children, Winifred was born in Oxford in 1882 at a time when her father, Edmund Knox, who had been ordained ten years earlier, was a fellow of Merton College. However, the family soon moved to Kibworth in Leicestershire where Knox was rector from 1884 until 1891 and where his two youngest sons were born. All four Knox brothers were to have interesting careers: the eldest, as 'E.V. Knox', was to be a renowned editor of *Punch*, and father of the novelist Penelope Fitzgerald, the second, Dillwyn, was a classics scholar and cryptographer whose work in both world wars was essential to the Allied victory, Wilfred was an Anglo-Catholic theologian, and the youngest, Ronald, was ordained as an Anglican but quite soon converted, becoming a Catholic priest, theologian, and writer of detective novels. All the Knox children, except the eldest, Ethel, were demonstrably clever, with Winifred well able to match the intellectual and verbal gymnastics of her brothers.

Edmund Knox had received a dour upbringing from an exacting clerical father but ensured that his children did not suffer a similar fate. Of him Winifred Peck wrote 'My father seemed to me so far removed from the nursery and our schoolroom orbit, and so great, so omnipotent, yet infinitely kind when we were unhappy, that through him the conceptions of an Almighty God was easy to realise.' Their mother, born Ellen French, was the daughter of the saintly bishop of Lahore. Yet, despite what was an overwhelmingly Evangelical clerical inheritance, Winifred reported that 'we had no surfeit of church services or religious admonitions or holy talks.' Life at Kibworth was a time to which all the Knox children looked back as a golden age. But it did not last. In 1891 Edmund Knox felt called to work in what Winifred described as 'a huge slum parish' and the family left their country rectory with its bounteous gardens for the grimmer surroundings of Aston, Birmingham. Very quickly their mother became ill and was taken away to a series of nursing homes. Her children never saw her again. She died in Brighton in August 1892 when she was 38 years old and Winifred was nine.

After an interlude during which a 'fragile and bewildered aunt' attempted to manage the Knox household, the children were divided between various relatives. Winifred was sent with her sister and one of her brothers to board with a decidedly Evangelical great-aunt in Eastbourne. After this experience it was a great relief to return to Birmingham after their father's remarriage in 1895. Winifred's step-mother was also the daughter of a clergyman, but one who had inherited considerable wealth and appreciated the finer things of life. Edmund Knox was appointed suffragan bishop of Coventry and vicar of St Philip's in central Birmingham, allowing the family to move from Aston into a rectory made tasteful and comfortable in a William Morris-ish way by the new Mrs Knox.

After experiencing schools of varying quality in Birmingham and Eastbourne, Winifred Knox was among the first intake at Wycombe Abbey School and completed her education at Lady Margaret Hall, Oxford, where in 1905 she gained a first-class honours in Modern History. She then returned to 'Bishopscourt', a large house set back from Bury New Road, Salford, which had become home since her father's appointment to the bishopric of Manchester in 1903. She continued her research into French history and in 1909 published *The Court of a Saint*, a study of Louis IX of France. She later turned to writing fiction and by the time she wrote *Bewildering Cares* had already published at least nine adult novels as well as contributing many articles to *The Manchester Guardian*.

While at Oxford Winifred Knox had been influenced by 'Christian Socialist ideals' which, 'founded on class-love rather than class-hatred, seemed to offer the prospect of a golden future.' Living at home in Manchester in the years between leaving Oxford and her marriage in December 1911 she tried to give these ideals a practical application and in doing so led a life not dissimilar to that of Camilla Lacely. 'My own poor efforts at social work after I went down, those poor straws of factory girls' clubs, district visiting and committees on which I floated on the vast torrent of human misery, seemed more tolerable because of those dreams of a new Christian social order.' By taking the title of *Bewildering Cares*, slightly misremembered, from the 'Apology' to William Morris's *Earthly Paradise* – 'The heavy trouble, the bewildering care/That weighs us down who live and earn our bread,/These idle verses have no power to bear' – she demonstrated her affection for the work of that socialist revolutionary. Indeed Morris might well have approved of the sermon preached by Arthur Lacely's curate, Herbert Strang, which was to be the most 'bewildering care' of Camilla's week. For on Sunday Strang preached a message of pacifism, lambasting capitalism and even, it was thought, the Empire. Camilla was present but, alas, had slept through his oratory, so worn out was she with her domestic duties. The curate's heresy becomes the talk of Stampfield, having ruffled the feathers of both the leading local businessman and parish committee ladies such as 'Miss Cookes [who] has always suspected Mr Strang of having no interest in missionary work as compared with British social questions'. It took a bout of pneumonia to restore him to the grace of his parishioners.

Camilla is well aware how absorbed she becomes in such 'storms in our Stampfield tea-cup. But tea-cups are important when you live in them.' However, there are plenty of other distractions. As the vicar's wife she is called upon to attend a wide variety of committees, including Comforts for Converts (making 'hundreds of bags of sphagnum moss for Finland'), Warmth for Warriors, the Factory Girls' Club, the District Nursing Association, and a Missionary Society. She visits the dying, listens to various tales of woe, and spends a rather ludicrous 'Quiet Day' organised by the wife of the vicar of Stampfield Parish Church. In addition she is privy to two romances, one of which, involving her own son, prompts her to take out her wedding veil. It is made of Brussels lace, as was the one worn by Winifred Knox at her wedding in Manchester Cathedral.

Throughout the novel Camilla's observes her fellow parishioners with a slightly jaundiced eye, often allowing the ideas of her youthfully acerbic son to float into her mind where she herself might have felt obliged to be more charitable. Of the novel the *Daily Mail* critic wrote, 'It is quite on the cards that before long Winifred Peck will qualify as a modern Anthony Trollope' and indeed Camilla and Arthur are clearly well acquainted with the 'Chronicles of Barsetshire', casually referring in their conversation to Trollopeian characters. Camilla Lacely is also devoted to Charlotte Yonge, E.M. Delafield, Winifred Holtby, Dorothy Whipple, and Angela Thirkell, although for Lent she has been 'trying to do without a library subscription'. However there is little time for reading, except during meals. Camilla is a slave to the work necessary to keep the vicarage and its household in order, even going so far as to unpack the overnight case of the visiting Archdeacon.

When Winifred Peck was writing *Bewildering Cares* her husband held the important position of chief divisional food controller for Scotland. Rationing had been introduced in January 1940 and on the Wednesday of her week one of Camilla Lacely's many tasks is to deal with 'Food Control' in order to get a replacement for a lost ration book for a 'mother [who] drinks, and [whose] children are dirty and verminous'. One imagines that it amused the author to slip in a reference to 'food control', a subject that must have been much discussed at home. James Peck had been knighted in 1938 and it was as 'Lady Peck' that the author was referred to by some reviewers. The *Times Literary Supplement* (28 September 1940) commented 'Lady Peck's wit sparkles on every page. The book is a tonic and she deserves our real gratitude for making us laugh in these troublous [sic] days'. Noting that the book was written before the Blitz, the same reviewer summed up Camilla Lacely thus: '[She] has her hands full without bombs, but she would have stood up to them – probably is at this moment doing so – with the same mixture of courage, humour, slightly acid criticism and sincere faith in God as help her through all the bewildering cares of a poor parish.' In *The Observer* (15 September 1940) L.P. Hartley commended the novel for showing 'us a world in which a multitude of small duties, faithfully discharged, add up to something much greater than themselves'. For, as readers of *Bewildering Cares* will appreciate, Arthur Lacely's observation that 'small troubles enable one to keep a sense of perspective', is as pertinent now as in 1940.

Elizabeth Crawford

PREFACE

This diary was written before the Blitzkrieg began. Part of it appeared, in rather different form, in *The Guardian*; and in thanking the Editor for leave to make use of it, I find myself wondering whether my readers will thank me for taking them back to the spring of 1940. I can only plead that Camilla Lacely will continue to cope with her husband's parish as long as he and she and the parish remain in being. Perhaps the things she cares for are coming to seem more, and not less, precious.

I
MONDAY

MY HUSBAND, Arthur Lacely, is the Vicar of Saint Simon's, Stampfield, North Midlandshire. To the lay mind, the word Vicar conjures up at once, I know, either an image of a thin, fussy, short-sighted fanatic, with bicycle-clips confining his black trousers, or of a stout, bald spheroid in a surplice rising over the top of a pulpit. (Rectors, let me add, have a very different reputation: they may have white, curly hair, infinite charm, and die for their congregations in typhoid epidemics.) So I must insist at once that Arthur, though a Vicar, is tall, dark, as scrupulously clean-shaven as our defective hot-water system allows him to be, and has a delightful way of looking over his spectacles at any acquaintance as if he or she were the one person in the world worth talking to. While I can never admire enough his courage, good-humour and tolerance, I am not sure that he is the right man in the right place in this parish. He took a First in Greats before he served in the ranks, in the Great War, for some months before he got a commission, so that on the one side he is invariably incapable of regarding theological or party problems with anything but detached tolerance, and cannot begin to understand the pettiness or narrowness of the provincial middle-class mind. And on the other, he finds his work among the factory-hands and the out-of-works in the parish so enthralling that I have frequently to remind him that even women have souls to be saved, and that even elderly Church workers need a little attention.

"What it really boils down to," said Dick, our son, when I was making one of my protests, "is that old Mother Weekes happened to plant herself down on the chair where that nice chap, who dropped in on his way back from his factory last night, left a few fancy traces. Well, whose fault was that?"

"You can't expect your Ma or me to wash a chair-cover between ten one night and ten next morning!" put in Kate, unexpectedly, as she flung the potatoes on the table. Kate is our one maid, and I am never sure whether she is a Menace or a Paragon. She breaks china, talks for hours to the tradesmen, comes in late at night, never gets a message right, and is so tall and stout and jolly that Dick always refers to her at the Buccaneer. But she is devoted, usually cheerful, and stays with us; and in any crisis becomes a Treasure at once.

"I admit", said Arthur, "it was unfortunate about the chair, but—"

"Go on, Daddy!" laughed Dick, "But it depends on what meaning you attach to the words 'chair' and 'unfortunate', you're going to say!"

"No, no, I was going to say that Hartly looked in late, at great personal inconvenience, to discuss a serious problem, and Mrs. Weekes interrupted my morning with nothing but some fantastic protest against Miss Boness for putting dahlias in the Church vases in Lent."

"Not dahlias at this time of year!" I had to protest. "And, darling, the point was that you don't have vases in Lent—and a very good idea, too, and I always try to get my name down for March before anyone remembers! The real trouble was that Miss Boness hadn't remembered it was Lent at all, because she didn't often come to church then, and Mrs. Weekes wanted to rub it in!"

"Sweet soul!" said Dick. "Oh, well, she got something else rubbed in all right!"

"It is wholly incredible to me", said Arthur, a little amused yet obviously bewildered, "how any human being in this twentieth century can conceivably attach any importance to such trifles."

I quote this story to show Arthur's point of view. Some clergy wives have to run about making up differences because their husbands are too narrow-minded, but there is almost as much to do when your husband is not narrow-minded enough. I paid the cleaner's bill for what Dick would call "The

Tragedy of the Tail", and had a tea-party for Miss Boness, and that was that.

Dick is our only son. He has neither gone to the bad, like the clergy son of fiction, nor can I pretend to say that he has never given us a moment's anxiety. He broke various limbs in his school-days, and criticized us and the Church fairly severely at the age of fifteen. He took to Communism and was rather extravagant at Oxford, and had a serious affair with a quite horrid little gold-digger. But he is charming, cheerful, adorable to us, and delightfully profane. Riddled though our home has doubtless been with inhibitions, neuroses and Oedipus complexes, we look back to every holiday with memories of happiness and gaiety, only too poignant now that he is with his regiment "somewhere in Essex mud".

As Arthur is a Vicar we naturally live in a Vicarage, and this, again, to the lay mind conjures up a picture either of a country house in embosoming trees, or a Victorian-Gothic villa and church set down in a pocket of asphalt among London streets. Saint Simon's Vicarage is not quite true to any conventional type. It is a gaunt, big house with a peeling stucco front, three stories high, with a cavernous basement kitchen. If it ever had a garden it was sold years ago, and we have a row of little houses on either side, and a very busy brewery yard at the back. The front door opens upon a flight of stone steps, a strip of gravel behind a stucco balustrade and a gate, into a narrow—and much frequented—street. The porch, rails and gate have all subsided a little into the ground at different angles, so that, as Dick says, the old home looks as if it had been having "a bit of a night out". It has seven bed., three sit., bath (h. & c., but not much h. without vast expenditure of coal) and the usual offices, all inconvenient. It can never be sold or exchanged, as country rectories so often are, as it belongs wholly to a past age of cheap coal and cheap domestic labour. Until the War, I managed it easily with two hereditary treasures. We had a little money of our own in industrial shares then, and those

6 | WINIFRED PECK

of course we can count on no more. So Kate and I manage together, and I know I am very lucky to have her.

I began writing this after waking up on Monday morning with a Presentiment.

This, I admit, was often the case while I had my two Treasures, and I attributed it to the diet of cold beef and colder blancmange which they looked upon as the orthodox Sunday supper. Since they went Kate, of course, takes every Sunday afternoon off, and I cook a cosy supper myself for Arthur, so that cause for superstitious fears is removed. It was surely enough to reflect that it was a wet morning, the first Monday in Lent and the Washing. Still I felt unreasonably anxious as I took the letters out of the post-box. However, there was nothing for me but one from my old friend, Lucy Day, who may perhaps be tactless but cannot be tragic.

"It's such ages since I heard from you," she wrote, "but I came across Clover Field the other day, and we were talking about you, and how sad it was that you and I had drifted apart," (Lucy has drifted to a charming little place on the Cornish coast, and we have drifted, or, I should say, been called to Stampfield.) "Do write and tell me all your news, not just outer happenings but about the inner *you*, the YOU that is YOURSELF." (Has Lucy been reading Queen Victoria's letters, I wonder?) "It's always hard to imagine you a parson's wife, and I long to know what you *really* think about our dear funny old Church. You used to write such amusing letters. Do sit down and give me a picture of yourself and of your daily life. Clover and I wonder what you look like. She's shockingly stout and rather *raddled*-looking. I must say I do find myself veering to seats with their backs to the light, don't you? But, thank Heaven, *I've* kept my figure and most of my hair. Is yours curly still, and *have* you bleached it? Clover and I remember that you had *good* bones (chin-line, etc., I mean), and I do trust you use Elizabeth Forest's preparations—the *only* hope at our age. Now *do* write and answer all my questions …"

As Lucy went on to reflections on the War, which she finds very dull and tiresome, and inquiries about Dick, I put her letter away and got to work. Every morning I "do" the study, sacred to Arthur, while Kate bounces about the dining-room, leaving a good deal of dust, though never failing to switch every picture crooked. Having run the carpet-sweeper safely round the holes in the faded Turkey carpet (a relic from Arthur's old rectory home) and dusted the furniture, I turned to the mantelpiece. It is surmounted by a walnut-framed mirror (also inherited from the Rectory), and, peeping over the black marble clock (presented by last Parish), the photographs of Arthur's parents and of college friends he can hardly remember, I took a good look at my reflection, with special reference to Lucy's queries. I should like to assure her that I have no need to bleach my hair yet, and have kept my figure; but truth compels me to acknowledge that the words "scraggy" and "grizzled" are those which leap to my mind. I shall reply candidly that my hair is still curly, most fortunately, and that no Forest preparations would make any difference to the lines on my face. But I won't add that Dick considers "cos", as he calls cosmetics, repulsive in any woman over fifty! I was just peering over a china cat creeping out of a vase (an early present of Dick's) to wonder what, if any, good bones I possessed, when I found Kate at the door, and dropped some sixteen Notices (mostly of past date) out of the side of the overmantel in confusion.

"Shall I do the bacon now?" Since the War began, and my other maid went away, I have tackled the cooking myself, to prevent waste, and though I am now, really, far more efficient than Kate, she still looks upon my activities as rather a joke, and tries to forestall me. "And I got the stock-pot on already—there's some good bones from yesterday!"

That the best use for my good bones would be to make good nourishing soup seems the only conclusion I can draw from this coincidence. My dear old mother-in-law once summed up the case for the traditional, and too often accurate, representation of a parson's wife as a tired, plain, dowdy little lady, by saying: "Remember, my dear, what a congregation likes is that one should look as if one *had* seen better days!" And here and now I wish to make my protest on behalf of the dress of my sex, age and profession. Every woman knows that to be well-dressed you must either have plenty of money, and place yourself in the hands of experts; or plenty of time, in which your own skill and taste can achieve the same result; or, failing these, a cast-iron resolution to buy little and buy it really good. The last is what many of us in the Church aim at. We save for months or years so as to order a really good tailor-made coat and skirt (our badge of office), and then at the last moment, some heart-rending appeal from Chinese Lepers or Indian Blind or African Hospitals or Country Holidays arrives to cut our hearts. We send off a cheque to the good cause, and assure ourselves that a cheap ready-made will look as well and last as long. Of course the answer is that it doesn't. Personally I am lucky just now, as I hardened my heart and got some really good tweeds for Dick's last School Sports, so that the middle of me, at any rate, comes up to my mother-in-law's standard, and looks as if I had seen Better Days.

Arthur came in to interrupt these useless reflections, looking so thin and pale, and so disappointed to find no letter from Dick, that I had to read him Lucy's letter at breakfast to make him laugh.

"And as I am trying to do without a library subscription in Lent," I said, "and there are no evening meetings owing to this blessed black-out, I shall just write down for her what the life of a parson's wife is like. Just one week to show her how everything happens and nothing happens!"

"And it will keep you from thinking," agreed Arthur, and then we were both silent. For, like everyone else in Europe, we have lived for these last two years as people who know a thunderstorm is coming, and now the storm is raging all the time, though the lightning has not struck Dick nor ruined our cities yet, and the only thing to do is to turn away from the windows at odd moments and try to forget, as best you may, if you wish to keep your reason.

"And by the end of it", I said, dragging myself away from that window again, "I may have discovered the answer to that old problem, whether the clergy should have wives or not."

It is part of Arthur's charm that he makes a sympathetic answer to fatuous remarks like that. Although, he added, he doubted if Lucy would really be interested in a treatise on the celibacy of the clergy.

"Oh no! One must take the clergy and Church of England as they are, a compromise like the British Constitution! Now I won't say another word, for you've eaten enough to earn your newspaper!" (Yes, I have been a bully since the War, and have persuaded Arthur to eat something always before he faces the news.)

"But I only hope nothing will happen this week," he added, as he settled down with his pipe in the arm-chair. "I gather from something Weekes said, when he passed me outside the church just now, that there is going to be some trouble over Strang's sermon last night. I wish I'd been there instead of at the Mission. What was he talking about?"

Mr. Strang is our Curate. He only came when our dear John Hay was called up with his battalion and left us. We are doing our best to like Mr. Strang and his wife just as much, though I confess I should find it easier if he didn't speak of the church as "the Chuch", and wasn't such a firebrand about Pacifism and almost every other "ism". As I cast my mind back to last afternoon's service (we have to have Evensong at five because of the lights) I was horrified to realize that I could remember nothing but that I thought Mr. Strang looked very ill with a horrible cold, that his text, "Can these dry bones live?" had special reference to the non-attendance at the parochial guild—and a peculiarly vivid dream which supervened

immediately, in which Dick was teaching Mr. Strang an eight-
some reel to the tune of "Onward Christian Soldiers", while
Arthur and I watched them from a boat, in which we had
gone out to look for submarines. I only hope I did not really
call, "There!" as I woke with a jerk behind my pillar. Anyhow,
the sound would have been drowned as everyone was standing up. I foresaw at once that this sad failure of mine, both
as a Christian and a detective, might prove very awkward if
there was going to be any fuss over Mr. Strang's tiresome effort at oratory. It will be a storm in a tea-cup, of course, but
then we happen to live in a tea-cup! Stampfield (pop. 60,000:
Market-day Thursday) would not recognize itself as that, and
only those who have lived in a northern county-town can
realize how self-sufficient such a unit can be. Geographically
it is quite a fair comparison, for the old town lay in a hollow,
and from the market-square, with its Georgian Church and
big portico, trams and motor-buses strike out through narrow,
winding little streets up the hills in every direction. Our parish embraces several streets of "period" back-to-back Victorian
slums, a brewery, three rubber factories, and a fringe of large
residential villas in small, well-manicured gardens on the out-
skirts. Our aristocracy consists of the owners of the factories
and businesses, and a small professional class, who are opposed
bitterly in the town council by the Labour Party, supported by
the Non-conformists and most of the operatives. The County,
consisting mostly of impoverished hunting people, means very
little to us, and London even less, though we have a slight respect for Manchester. In short, Balzac would feel at home with
us, and the Montagues and Capulets would pass, in municipal
elections, as kind, friendly old couples.

Mr. and Mrs. Weekes are undoubtedly the leaders of this
aristocracy for us, for he is our churchwarden, and secretary
of the parish benevolent fund, and she is self-appointed war-
den-in-chief of all our committees and charities, and it would

be useless to try to describe our lives without giving them a ceremonious introduction.

"Pa Weekes", says Dick, "always reminds me of a grumpy, kind-hearted walrus, and Ma Weekes of a rather arrogant cod-fish," and I can see the justice of both descriptions. For they are both stout and inclined to baldness, but there the resemblance ends. For Mr. Weekes atones for want of hair on the top by a drooping white moustache, and Mrs. Weekes by a vast erection of white curls from the Manchester hairdresser, known rather unfortunately as "my coiffurze"; and while Mr. Weekes long ago bade good-bye to the carpet slippers (which live under the coalscuttle in his "den") Mrs. Weekes entrusts her figure to the sort of corsetiere who only allows any exuberance above the waist in front, and below it at the back, lo that her ankles and small feet seem little less likely to support her weight than a fish-tail.

I believe walruses are fundamentally amiable creatures and so, we well know, is Mr. Weekes if he is taken in that tortuous way described as "right". He has worked his way up from the smallest beginnings to the ownership of the big rubber factory, of which he is the kindest and most generous master. He has therefore a proper sense of the value of money, and would look at a stranger very coldly if he tried to borrow half-a-crown or interest him in an investment; but if he once trusts anyone, as he does trust Arthur, his generosity is wonderful. I can't say boundless, as he has very definite political views and disapproves of most of the social legislation of the last thirty years as molly-coddling. Sometimes we feel that such people are the real obstacle to social progress, for he is convinced that anyone with thrift and initiative can succeed as he has done, and the thought of free milk or meals for school-children, and even workmen's compensation or housing-schemes, drives him to fury. At the same time, given an Agag-approach, he is kind-hearted to the point of sentimentality over any individual misfortune, or any charity which his wife urges him to rescue from want of funds.

His Church views were adopted for life at the Sunday School of his youth, and his ignorance of Church affairs and theology is so great that Arthur always says he could preach the Immaculate Conception to him without a protest, in a black gown, whereas the introduction of the Cross into Arthur's processions with the choir round our streets on Sunday evenings in summer proved indeed a stumbling-block. "It's not that I mind a Cross as such, mark you," he said, "but I call it the thin edge of the wedge." I am afraid I choked slightly over this novel view of the Symbol of our Redemption, but luckily he only asked if "the wife felt that window". Nothing in the training of the clergy helps them to make contact with this type of mind, so alien to our universities, and I think, if I may humbly say so, that diplomacy rather than sacerdotalism is greatly to be desired. On this occasion, Arthur said so warmly that he would rather sacrifice his own wish to remind our less Christian streets of the great sign of Christianity than offend so true a Churchman as his Vicar's Warden, that Mr. Weekes hummed and hawed, and eventually presented a new Cross to the church. There must be points of conscience always where the clergy cannot yield, but on all others I do believe in compromise. The mind of a Weekes moves slowly and, in the lightning reforms of the last fifty years, too many of such old, suspicious, true-hearted people have been alienated, and when they lost the habit of church-going their children lost it too. "Just for a handful of ribbons they left us", is the obituary of too many honest, narrow-minded, invaluable laymen in the Church of England.

Mrs. Weekes is a less complex character. Beneath her fat, faintly supercilious exterior lies, I am sure, a vast inferiority complex. She is afraid of her servants and her social inferiors and superiors alike, and is therefore always asserting herself. She is more socially aspiring than her husband, and has a great respect for Birth which isn't easily gratified in Stampfield. But she too has the kindest heart in the world, and it shows their fundamental goodness that their daughter Ida, who went to a fashionable girls' school only laughs at their oddities and adores them both. Still, in view of the Weekes' character and position we not unnaturally felt some anxiety, this morning, about the probable effects of a Labour Pacifist address from the pulpit on Sunday night.

At this point Kate put her head in round the door to say that Mr. Elgin was coming up the steps and did the master want to see him or not before he rang the bell? This rather cryptic inquiry was quite clear to Arthur, who recognizes it as part of Kate's plan for guarding him maternally, and he said, "Yes, that's all right," and I went off upstairs.

"And I hope", said Kate, when she joined me to make the bed, "that the Vicar'll give him a hint to have something a bit less mouldy in the way of chunes. Private Jenkins and I dropped in to church last night, and, as he says, when you want a bit of a rousing singsong, why go bleat-bleat about Mercy in fancy dress, and such like."

Arthur has, I know, some sympathy with Kate's point of view. Mr. Elgin is one of those rather pathetic, emaciated, long-haired musicians who began life, I feel sure, with a vision of conducting his own symphonies in the Queen's Hall, and, after thirty years, is reduced to playing our organ (£70 a year), giving music-lessons at the High School, and writing bitter letters to the local press about the crimes of the B.B.C., and the shocking musical taste of the British public. He finds his only consolation in playing austere fugues of Bach as voluntaries, and condemning us to a diet of almost exclusively plain-song tunes to the hymns in church. And though there is nothing more beautiful than Gregorians sung in such a church as that of the Cowley Fathers, our choir is not of a nature to endear them to the congregation. For the one ambition of the six men who take the tenor and the two who roll out the very deepest bass, is to present anthems and chants of the Stamp-field variety with special reference to men's voices. The choir is paid, but a tradition of the parish makes it very difficult to look outside it for musical talent; so our eight little choir-boys are often selected rather for the church-going habits of their parents than their musical ability. Arthur has done his best to form a voluntary choir to help them, as the services of the paid choir are only available on Sundays, or, of course, at much higher rates, for weddings and funerals. The good ladies who make up the former admire Mr. Elgin, and urge him forward in his plain-song ways, while the regular choir maintain an un-regenerate preference for ordinary Anglican melodies. "And I defy even a diplomat", says Arthur, "to find a *modus vivendi* be-tween J. B. Dykes and Saint Ambrose."

At the moment, however, I was more interested in Kate's criticism of the service, because I recognized that her unusual attendance at church was introduced chiefly to forestall any comment of mine about the lateness of her return to the vic-arage. Another sign of this was her extreme gloom when we went down to the kitchen together.

"The butter's short," she said, "and sugar's low, and the greengrocer passed the remark that veg. are very awkward just now."

"Wasn't your bus very late last night, Kate?" I felt it my duty to ask, though well did we both know that the last bus was off duty long, long before Kate slammed the back door on her return home.

"I don't know what happened to the time last night, as you may say," replied Kate more gloomily than ever. "I only know I couldn't sleep a wink for thinking of dear Master Dick and my boy friend and all our boys. Private Jenkins" (Kate has a martial love for any military title, however lowly) "says that the reports all say that they're to be off to France next week."

As Kate began to sniff at this point I had to yield about the bus, even though Private Jenkins had held this sword over

Kate's head (with a considerable addition to the number of her nights-out) ever since the beginning of September. As I could not contemplate being left alone again, after Saturday and Sunday afternoons, with all the work to do, I hastily suggested that she should bake a nice cake for Dick and for Jenkins this afternoon, because there is plenty of black treacle and syrup for gingerbread. This suggestion was so popular that it appeared at once that we have plenty of sugar and butter. "And that," added Kate, inexplicably, "that'll give me plenty of time to peel the potatoes and manage the bedrooms and the breakfast, if you'll give a hand to clearing 'em."

This admirable change of front enabled me to settle down to prepare the meals of the day, and I turned my attention to soup for the evening and one of those dainty war-time supper dishes which begin with onions and end with lentils, however original they pretend to be. I often wonder if other women who are taking to their own work in war-time are filled with the same stupefied admiration for domestic servants which I feel now. Unruffled, they seem to be able to leave milk on the boil while they answer the Laundry and oblige with 3s. 6¾d., wipe the flour off their hands while they respond to the Rubbish, break off in whipping up an egg to polish and take up the shoes, and keep a kindly eye on the soup even while, at the basement gate, a gentleman is imploring them to view the writing-paper in his attaché-case.

"It's all a question of *Method*," Mrs. Weekes says to me, impressively, but what method is there about these amiable visitors? And if Kate were downstairs (instead of upstairs at the back at that moment) she would have a lingering conversation with every one of them, scrub the kitchen as well and turn out a passable meal. But she is so wasteful and extravagant, and careless about her utensils, that I feel it better to keep her as only second-in-command in the kitchen, now that it is a national duty to be careful. "You don't tell me Hitler'll get what he's asking for if you fiddle about with those scraps of cold mutton," is her attitude on this question.

"Miss Croft at the gate," called Kate, in a stentorian whisper down the stairs. "I thought she'd be popping in when I saw Mr. Elgin coming along. Shall I say you'll see her or that you've not cleaned yourself yet?"

"Oh, yes, I'll come," I said, horrified at the alternative suggestion. "I've finished but for grating the cheese—if you could do that and add it as this recipe tells you, Kate."

"That I will. It fair makes me smile to see you working on at that grater by the hour when I gets it done in five minutes. And as for recipes, a stew's a stew whether you fill it with odds and ends and call it Raggout Victory or not, I say!" And I must admit that after many experiments with New War-time Suggestions I couldn't help feeling that Kate had right on her side.

One of the depressing parts of provincial life is a remark like my omniscient Kate's on poor Miss Croft's visit. Sometimes I had vaguely imagined that there might be a faint lavender-scented whisper of a romance (musical, in D sharp) between Mr. Elgin and my visitor, but it had seemed to me to have such a vague, touching, twilight atmosphere that I had never even mentioned it to Arthur. I had no idea that anyone but myself might have wondered if Miss Croft's regular attendance in the voluntary choir, and Mr. Elgin's regular appearances for a cup of coffee in her "Olde Teapot" café (his chief meal in the day, I sadly fear) pointed in that direction, but I had no idea that Kate's all-seeing eye had perceived the drama, and I sincerely hoped that Miss Croft didn't guess it as I hurried upstairs, trying to get flour off my dress and out of my nails, and hoping the best for my hair.

I am fond of little Miss Croft, partly because I first discovered her when I was a little lonely and alien on my arrival, and learnt much really from her rather highly-coloured picture of what life in the provinces meant to her. When she first came here, as a girl of twenty in 1910, in a cretonne overall, bead chains and a volume (I feel sure) of Henry James in her suit-case, she rented a low two-fronted little old shop off the Market Square, and started a library for semi-highbrow books, an "Olde Teapot Room" with home-made cakes and jams, hand-made pottery and little beaten brass objects with special reference to the Lincoln Imp. Girls and young men *flocked* to her, she says, and before the War she and the one apostle of culture she found in Stampfield, named, not very appropriately, Sarah Stump, started a Browning Society, a "musical gathering", and a small amateur theatrical society. "Where", asks Miss Croft, dramatically, "are they now?"

It was not the Great War which broke up this Society—though Sarah's elopement with a Private was a terrible blow—as much as the wireless, the films, motors and the cocktail habit. These agents have standardized, she says with some truth, the lowest type of Main Street civilization in the provinces. "Where", she asks, "are the earnest girls with long skirts who found interest and culture in their homes, and only left them to plod on foot, or cycle anxiously, to 'Ye Olde Teapot Room' in search of books and guidance?" Their place is taken by gay young things who slip, in huge fur coats and infinitesimal guinea frocks, out of their boy friends' cars into the picture houses, or to the bar of the Midland in Manchester for drinks. If they have to endure an evening at home, do they read or play the piano? No, they turn on the wireless dance bands.

There is not, she declares, 'one person in Stampfield who has heard of Virginia Woolf or Gertrude Stein or T. S. Eliot, and she thinks these authors ought to *know* about it. "And their mothers are no better," she says, drawing the worn, faded cretonne curtains across her windows, with wizened hands on which her silver and amethyst rings hang so loosely. They laugh at her and say they took up Culture when they were young because they'd nothing better to do, and now they drift off to the pictures to *wallow* in stories of women of forty and fifty who still Find Love in the most unexpected places.

It was at this moment of cultural depression that I persuaded Miss Croft, after joining her library (2s. 6d. deposit, and 2d. a week for such a new volume as the last but one Aldous Huxley) to come to Saint Simon's and join the voluntary choir. In a month or so she had joined the Parochial Guild, and was busy getting up a Mystery Play.

"And never again, if I can help it," she told me after three months of internecine warfare in the parish. "What with persuading the Archangel Gabriel that she was not meant to look like the Principal Boy in the Pantomime, and all that cattiness about the part of the Madonna, and the way the Angels' haloes would slip to one side, and their wings get broken through sheer carelessness, I think we'll keep to Shakespeare's readings in the future, Mrs. Lacely."

But, alas, Shakespeare's readings and Browning societies and Old English Madrigals are all lying under the blight of the War now, and Miss Croft gives all her energy to the choir, the church, and various committees, and is not proposing, as Dick naughtily suggests, to go off as a Vivandière with "Ye Olde Teapot" slung on her back. She was looking tired and dispirited this morning, I thought, and indeed I don't suppose the twopenny books and threepenny cups of coffee really manage to cover the rent of the little rooms off the Market Square.

"I am so sorry to bother you," she said, "but I just looked in about the work-party this afternoon."

The working-party is another of the minor disturbances created in Stampfield by the War. It was devoted to garments for our Mission in India, and held every Monday afternoon; but with the outbreak of hostilities a strong, patriotic party, led by Miss Boness and Miss Grieve, demanded that we should leave the Indian hospital patients to clothe themselves (which I cannot help feeling they might prefer to do) while we gave all our energies to Warmth for Warriors. Weight was lent to the Opposition by Mrs. Weekes (thirteen stone of it) with no better motive, I sometimes fear, than an ever-simmering rival-

ry with Miss Boness, and Miss Croft cast in her lot with our
churchwarden's wife, partly because she is always on the side
of church officials, and partly, I fear, because one of the major
pleasures of her life are the Royal Commands for afternoon
tea which she receives only too infrequently from our leading
parochial lady. An earth-shaking schism seemed imminent, and
was only prevented by the decision to adopt my casual suggestion of holding two parties weekly, Comforts for Converts on
Monday, and Warmth for Warriors on Thursday. There are not
really enough members to make this worth while, especially
as since our unhappy division no Monday worker will knit on
Thursday, and no Thursday knitter will button-hole pyjamas
on Monday. My hope had been that I could evade both cer-
emonies, as each side had such competent, not to say militant
leaders; but I am recognized as deputy-leader by either party,
and only too often I have to attend both meetings in a week.

"Oh, dear, can't we get the flannelette?" I asked. Here again,
how odd it seems that the War is interfering with the supply of
lurid magenta fabric for a faraway Hindu hospital!

"No, no, Dykes have been most clever and obliging, and
we have got two good bales in now. No, it was only to say that
I can't be there this afternoon, as I've got to go to Leeds. I must
go to visit an old cousin of mine there who's very ill. I've let
Mrs. Weekes know, and I do hope she'll turn up all right, but
she has so many engagements, of course—her life is one long
Whirl, she always tells me! If she can't manage it, could you be
so very kind this week?"

Monday afternoon is, in theory, a parson's holiday, but I
knew Arthur would never find time for a walk or a rest this
afternoon, and as I refuse to admit that my eight-stone figure
indulges in a perpetual whirl like Mrs. Weekes's thirteen, I had
to consent.

"Oh, yes, of course. I'd hoped to get my magazines done
to-day as I have a busy morning of committees to-morrow,
but I can manage."

"You don't mind reading aloud, do you? I call it so much better than the mere gossip Miss Boness allows on Thursdays," said Miss Croft, sniffing.

"I thought she asked people to give talks to her party?"

"Only once a month, and they often fail her. Mind you, I don't say that Mrs. Weekes and I see eye to eye over books always, but I have persuaded her to try George Eliot now, and we all sit entranced over *The Mill on the Floss*, absolutely entranced!"

"How bad for the pyjamas!" I said, laughing, and realized that again I had made the dreadful mistake against which all parsons' wives should be warned at their Ordinations—of jesting on serious subjects. It is such a stupid trick to make an obvious fight comment of that sort, only to find oneself involved in the heavy weather of explanations. I must have told Miss Croft quite ten times that I had not meant what I said in the least, before it emerged, surprisingly, but as a great relief, that what she had really come for was to borrow our time-table if we had one, as the one she keeps in the shop is ten years old and has lost the pages from G. to Q. inclusive, and she hadn't time to get to the station.

I fear that Kate's most excited suspicions must have been aroused by the fact that on this we repaired to the study, just as Arthur was seeing Mr. Elgin to the door. The organist gallantly offered to inquire at the station about the train, and let her know later when he dropped in for a cup of coffee; and as they went off together, he in a very threadbare overcoat and dejected trilby hat, and she in the great red and purple cape which couldn't be warm enough over a home-made art silk jumper, their thin earnest faces turned in excited talk to each other, I indulged in my usual foolish pastime of imagining the death of the Leeds cousin, the discovery of a missing will in favour of Miss Croft, wedding bells, and a presentation by the congregation of a plated teapot and the bound works of John Sebastian Bach to the happy pair.

Unluckily, while indulging in these visions I was caught at the door by Mrs. Jay. However dull and ordinary and wanting in paint a vicarage door may be, it is a door of a thousand histories. For people may abuse and despise the Church as they will and yet those in need or trouble continue to besiege our portals rather than those of the highbrows who assure us so frequently that the Church has had its day. We have indeed had our day, for the most part, as a benevolent institution. We can no longer afford to keep open house in our kitchens for the hungry, hand out chicken-broth and port wine, and temper any moral advice with a half-crown at the close. That was the style of the rectory in the early days of Arthur's mother, but a cup of tea is all that Kate will provide nowadays, and that for the respectable only. Most people imagine that all such private charity is unnecessary, now that the State cares for the worker from the cradle to the grave. So it does, in theory, but there are bad gaps in what Mrs. Weekes growls at as grandmotherly legislation. One of them is the trouble which brought Mrs. Jay here to-day. Jay has been lucky and got taken on at Hall's Works again as a porter, and Mrs. Jay for three months has managed to keep her family of six adequately fed on the dole. But I defy anyone so to manage the unemployment benefit, as to have any margin left for clothes or boots. Jay was out in the bad weather shovelling snow off the streets, and his shoes are worn right to the uppers, and could I oblige with an old pair of the Vicar's or Mr. Dick's to start him fresh? Luckily I could, and disguised my feelings as I handed over a pair which Dick had outgrown (and how are mothers to brace themselves against this terrible sentiment over inanimate things nowadays?) with a suggestion that she might find a pair of mine of some use to herself. Unluckily on investigation it appears that Mrs. Jay takes a whole size smaller than mine, and she deplored so tragically the fact that "the gentry always have such big feet", that I laughed and felt better.

"Could I speak to you or the Vicar a minute, Mrs. Lacely?" Mrs. Bearden caught me before I could go upstairs again. She represented another of a large class of applicants just now. Bearden has joined up, leaving a good job at four pounds a week, and his army pay does little more than cover the rent of their nice superior little Council house. She has been managing with two lodgers but has now by our advice got what we all know as "the pink form" (which has, Dick tells me, a far less polite adjective in the Army) and wants my help to fill it up. These forms are a perpetual worry to anxious lonely wives and mothers, "and not the last of the worry either I expect", said Mrs. Bearden gloomily. The War Office has not a good name for promptness in payment to dependents here. However Mr. Weekes as Secretary of the Benevolent Fund is the stand-by of soldiers' wives in our town, and I sent her on to him for help in arrears in light and gas at once. That must really be enough for "the Door" this morning I decided as I raced upstairs for galoshes and waterproof, without even looking out of the window, because it always rains on Mondays in Stampfield. It had to be quick work for I was sure I saw Mrs. Sime talking to Kate at the basement door and I really could not become involved in her familiar domestic problem about "our Lil". I picked up my bag and shopping-basket and hurried down into the street, leaving the door to Kate's very practical guardianship, and almost fell into the arms of Miss Boness.

"The top of the morning to you!" she cried, for she is always terribly cheery in Lent. ("There's a one for fasting and anointing the face, if you like," said Dick once.) "Coming to Matins, and then on to the Mothers' Guild Committee? Good! Then we can go together."

Miss Boness's age is unknown, but the angle at which her hat perches on the back of her fluffed-up hair suggests a conservative attachment to the beginning of this century. Her face is thin, with a nose and eyebrows and lines round her mouth which suggest a perpetual question mark. She lives with her brother, our nice cheerful and skilful doctor, and devotes herself with unsparing energy to parochial work. She was very fond of our predecessors here, and their time at the vicarage is often referred to regretfully as "the dear old days", and I suspect Arthur feels about her much as I do about Kate. She spoke a good deal in August about being called up, but I expect myself that she found, like me, that our age disqualified us for anything but the membership of some minor order of Saint John of Jerusalem, and had to content herself with tracking down light as an Air Raid Warden, and with more indefatigable zeal in parochial committees than ever. In spite of my polite protests she insisted, on this occasion, on accompanying me to the butcher, grocer and greengrocer on the way to church, in the obvious fear that I meant to shirk my duties.

"Now about this sermon!" she began, as, after Matins, read in a very bellicose and abrupt manner by pallid Mr. Strang, in our chilly church, we paddled across to the parish hall for our committee. "You were at church last night, Mrs. Lacely. I saw you in your prophet's chamber, ah ha! What did you make of it?"

"Mr. Strang is so well meaning," I began, feebly, when we turned to see Mrs. Weekes coming into the room. Mrs. Weekes in the character of our wealthy churchwarden's wife treats me, officially, rather as one of the barbarian emperors must have treated the Papacy, with a show of forbearance to my office, but a come-let-us-have-no-nonsense tone at the slightest sign of resistance. She dresses habitually in elephant grey, a wise choice for her redundant figure, and to-day, shaking off the rain-drops from her skirt and umbrella she looked more like a formidable but kind-hearted cod-fish emerging from the elements than ever.

"Good morning, good morning! What a day! It is the *worst* of this war that we're so short of petrol. Is anyone else expected, Miss Boness? No, I thought not. Miss Grieve rang up that she daren't venture out. Mrs. Gregg and Miss Henly should really resign. They never attend and they'd be no loss. Are we a quorum?"

Unluckily we were, and we sat down to some perfunctory business, for the Mothers' Guild, which consists principally of grandmothers, is rapidly expiring of old age, and we passed on rapidly to the subject of the Sermon. Here, luckily, inspiration seized me, and I sprang up.

"Will you forgive me? I promised my husband not to say one word about this until he has talked the whole subject out with Mr. Strang. It would be very wrong of me to discuss it. I'm sure you'll agree with me."

"In the dear old days", began Miss Boness, "dear old Mr. Brownlee always gave us a *lead* in any difficulty."

"There's no difficulty here," puffed Mrs. Weekes, who always seems to swell visibly when she disapproves of anything. "The church was all forced last night to listen to a sermon which was unpatriotic, irreligious *and* un-English, and my husband says steps must be taken at once or he won't answer for the consequences. I cannot see why you should go off like this, Mrs. Lacely. There are no two words to be said about it."

"Then I may as well go," I pointed out, and got up as gracefully as my mackintosh and goloshes allowed. "And I'm sure you shouldn't come out again with your asthma, Mrs. Weekes. Can't I take the Work Party for you this afternoon?" I felt this a handsome sop to my defection, but it was only a partial success as Mrs. Weekes clearly felt so luke-warm a Christian as myself was hardly to be trusted to read aloud to the Working Party; but I got away with reiterated instructions about the page of *The Mill on the Floss* at which Mrs. Weekes had arrived in the last half-year.

The vicarage was full of the smell of baking when I returned; lunch was late, and Arthur was later, and there was no second post. One of my good resolutions for Lent is always to make cheerful conversation at meals for Arthur; but as I read the papers till he came in, wet through and sneezing, I longed for a foreign phrase-book to help me.

"Ha! I see Mr. Strang has been struck by lightning!" is an opening with which my fancy played, but it was quite unnecessary. Darling Arthur had met by chance a sergeant in the Xth, in the street to-day, who served with him in France, and he told my husband that he can look in and have a talk with his men any time, for they're such a hopeless lot it can't harm them any way; and Arthur looked as elated as if he were a missionary monk just given leave to sail from Iona to the mainland to carry the Gospel. The sergeant even went so far as to say that a bit of a holy sing-song wouldn't hurt them in their blanky billets, and we passed into a candid discussion on the English Hymnaries which would have made the hair of Mr. Elgin and Miss Croft fall out with disapproval.

"Not 'Fight the Good Fight'," I urged. "Remember, Dick says that the national hymn now is 'Abide with me' and nothing else. It brings to a soldier's mind lovely memories of Cup Ties and barrel-organs in the street, and, if they're regulars, intense relief that the Tattoo is over for another something something year."

"Yes," agreed Arthur, "it's another most interesting facet on the English psychology. The thought of thousands of jolly sportsmen requesting that the Cross may be held before their closing eyes as they await the Kick-off is curiously suggestive. I wonder what visual images it actually conveys to their minds."

"I think it expresses emotions you haven't felt but would like to," I suggested, "and that's why it's silly to choose good dull poetry by Blake and Cowper and Addison, and jog them out slowly in church. I don't mean 'Jerusalem', of course. Even my dear old grannies love to shout that they will not cease from mental strife, but that's just a case in point. They can't have bows of burning gold and arrows of desire, but they'd like to."

Arthur exclaimed that at that rate I would hold a brief for all the most sentimental hymns which Mr. Elgin hates, and I went off to my working-party, cheered by unclerical criticisms of popular favourites, promising to ask the assembly to choose a hymn before our Guild Meeting. He had anticipated "Rock of Ages", and I, "Nearer to Thee"; but we were both rebuked by old Mrs. Jones who said that as it was Lent what about "Christian dost thou see them?"—"with a good rumble in the bass if *you* please". I did my best to oblige, and to ignore my memory of Dick's comment that the second verse is the best description of indigestion he's ever seen.

"Oh, not that old 'has-been'!" was the reaction of the working-party, as they settled down to their work —the pink flannelette in its most curious size and shape was all ready. As my feelings about George Eliot are, alas, almost identical, I tried instead bits of *The Diary of a Provincial Lady* and *The Demon in the House* by Angela Thirkell, with unparalleled success. They would hardly allow me to stop; we omitted the last hymn, as Mrs. Jones candidly stated that stop laughing she could not, not even if it was for "Brother thou art gone before us". I could only realize, later, that Mrs. Weekes will think more poorly of me than ever, and the ghost of George Eliot will haunt me eternally.

After tea I sat down to answer Lucy's request, and was disturbed by only three telephone calls and one man in overalls at the back door, and another in a trilby hat and suede shoes at the front door, asking for railway fares to Manchester and London respectively. I am sure that many other clergy-wives must have puzzled as I do over the apparent connection in the popular mind between the Church of England and our main railway lines, but at least my generous confiding husband was out, and I heartlessly refused to oblige.

Private Jenkins, in view of his imminent departure for France, called to ask if Kate might pop round with him to the pictures for half an hour, and of course I was weak-minded

after all, and let her leave the house at 7, and determined not
to hear the back door open on her return at 12. On these occasions I cook a hot supper and eat it with Arthur in the nice
warm kitchen, and we always settle down by the study fire on
Monday evenings with special content. As his head nodded
over a vast theological book, I re-read this, and felt, I fear justly,
that this was hardly a day either of Christian, social or domestic utility, with which to impress Lucy. But let her wait! I have
three committees and a lot of parochial visits to-morrow!

I feel that perhaps at this point I should say something to
Lucy about what I feel when at last I tear myself reluctantly
from the fire and my book, and go to perform the operation
everyone still refers to as "saying their prayers". In the corner
of her front sheet I notice is a PS. in minute writing: "And,
darling, do tell me—are you so old-fashioned that you still
believe in anything at all?" I suppose I should try to answer
that somehow. And yet what sort of apologia can I make to
that outside world which she belongs to, of which, perhaps,
we in the church see and hear of too little, where religion is
still a matter of animated discussion and excited word experiments, but the Church of England is regarded definitely as a
Back Number. All of us, I think, are too much tempted to go
on working up and down at the handle of our parish pump,
without stopping to look up and listen to other people with
their sensational tales of their water supplies and all the newest
gadgets. It's not really enough to dismiss them as flighty, foolish people outside our own sphere of interest, and make prim,
shocked faces when they force their point of view upon us. It
is better to realize from the first that they do include the larger class of both intellectual and empty-headed people, and to
try to explain as best we can, something of the reason for our
comparatively dull and primitive mode of thought.

Many of us in the church feel nearer to them now than
ever we did, I expect, because there is no doubt that any old
routine of religious devotion seems a little inadequate for the

terrible strain on our faith which the War means to us. Let me
confess at once that my old books of devotions and forms of
prayer are all hard to use, not because they lacked sincerity
then, but because they have too many old associations with
happier days to make them endurable, and because we have
to face wholly new conditions of spiritual warfare. If anyone
questions that, he has only to consider the difference between
praying "Thy Will be done" when he really means he wants to
conquer his self-willed clamour for his family's prosperity and
health; and when, as now, he is asking to share something of
the agony of Gethsemane and the death, perhaps, of all his old
life and hopes in the near future; and praying, too, for something of the ultimate faith which will enable him to walk out
fearlessly into the dark olive woods filled with the lanterns and
scowling faces of his enemies.

That is why, since I had influenza, I do not go up to the *prie-
dieu* in my icy bedroom, to take out my books of Devotion
and the portion of the reading for the day. I go to the dining-room, and in adequate warmth by the gas-fire, embark on
what is now the desperate spiritual adventure of trying to pray.

"Phew!" Lucy would exclaim at this point. "That's just why
you should try Rudolf Steiner or Christian Science, or join
the new ethical group or the Church of Rome! Why do you
go on trying to keep to your odd, funny old Church, with its
back-stairs history and out-of-date parsons, and absurd fusses
about tithes and Missions and Special Services and what not?
And why, indeed, try to square life as it is, when were all ants in
ant-hills all over Europe, waiting to be squashed flat by some
heavy foot, with old-world ideas of a Personal God, or a God
of Love, or the Resurrection of the body or Life Everlasting?
How can you fit all that into all the new scientific discoveries
and modern ways of thought?"

This is no attempt at a real apologia. If Arthur were writing
this, he might attempt one, but I shall simply content myself
with my own humble ways of thought.

"You are too prone to visual images and analogies," Arthur would say, shaking his head; but then this is not the apologia of a parson but of that very inferior being, a parson's wife.

I see myself then, in my search for true Faith, as someone groping his way through a huge dark, shuttered house, in this black-out of our lives. At last I see a crack of light, and enter one room where there is an open, undarkened window at last, though the window indeed is small and high up in the wall. That there is a great and glorious view from it, if I could reach up to it, is certain; but that view, the vista of the whole truth of God's scheme for the universe, I must leave to faith. While we must be in the house, our tabernacle of the body, we cannot hope to see the whole.

The room is cluttered up with tiresome partitions and divisions; they have been put up by former inhabitants, and no-one who enters it has the strength and courage to remove them. The division which is mine may be barer and more angular than that of the Mother of the Churches next door, and less airy, if more solid, than those of the fancy religions, as the Army calls them, in other corners. But it is allotted to me by birth and education, and by duty now, and it doesn't seem to me that there is any real difference between the divisions when the sun shines in through our window.

That shaft of sunshine represents to me the Love of God. The room is full of dust in different layers; when the light shines in and the wind blows, every tiny speck of dust is an individual entity, irradiated and transformed. It is only really by that analogy that I can catch a glimpse of God's love for the individual soul. To me, that moment of irradiation comes in the great Sacrament of the Church, which unites my utterly insignificant speck of being with the light of God and His great purpose in the infinite universe outside. It doesn't matter that millions of specks through all eternity have been escaping out of that window, to be transformed into other spheres and shapes and destinies. However many myriad millions, they are, each speck of dust, individual to eternity.

Is it worth sending all this to Lucy? Arthur would say "no", but isn't there always a chance that a vague thought may suggest a far better and more convincing extension of an idea to another? If she went on to ask me what was in my partition in the room, I should tell her that there is a great piece of embroidery, unfinished, on a stand. It is my business to work my little piece in that great pattern, and I cannot possibly understand, beginner as I am, what the whole ultimate design will be. It may be my lot to stitch in a very dark, black bit of background, with no hint of beauty or hope; but when the whole is finished, it will be clear that those stitches were needed for the perfection of the whole. The rest of the furniture Lucy would think dull and old-fashioned; but to me, the chairs and tables and pottery my forefathers used are dear and well-tried friends, and I really prefer them to the modern, shining steel fittings across the way in the new religions, or the Italianate furniture next door. That is just my own personal choice, of course, and I can admire the others. Some day the partitions will be broken down, and then, of course, all of us will have to discard some of our furniture if we are to make a harmonious whole; so I must always remember that what is sacred to me may not be at all sacred to my children, and may not be essential; and I must never grow offensively house-proud or an inveterate hoarder, and those two failings are the temptations of all the occupants of every partition.

I have a little book-case all my own, and everyone, of course, has his own, and would not feel much interest in the others. Mine contains "The Historical Geography of the Holy Land", because in my youthful doubts, the great Scottish author gave me some picture of how that barren passage way between three continents and three civilizations, with its tribe of fierce monotheists, was the fittest meeting-place for the great Revelation of God to the world. There is Illingworth's *Divine*

Personality, because, reading it under Arthur's direction during our engagement, my unphilosophic mind caught some glimpse of God as the revelation of Will, Love and Power to our little human personalities with their own trinity of these which guide our lives.

"I won't say the Bible," said Dick, stubbornly, when he was asked to name his seven favourite books. "I won't, just because I'm expected to."

I am not sure that I would include more than the New Testament now, for if I hear the great prophecies of Isaiah in church, my feeble intellect is only too likely to imagine Hitler thrown to the dogs and Goering's children dashed against stones, and what is the use of hate and revengeful feelings in a world which is dying for want of Christian Love?

I won't bother Lucy with my other choices in Holy Vols., as Dick calls them; they wouldn't be many, but I should certainly have *The Spirit of Man*, so that voices from other worshippers across the way may reach me with their beauty.

So this is the sort of vision I conjure up before I kneel down by the fire, and face the questions which beset us all about the love and omniscience of God in this world of apparent cruelty, and the impossibility that my tiny atom of being can be of any interest or service to an Almighty God. And then—well, I remember Dick saying, when I remonstrated with him on the uselessness of a mere gabble—"Well, look here, I'll pretend I am talking to God down the telephone, shall I, and see if that helps?" I think the analogy was quite a good, if a funny one, because it implied both something urgent to say and listening for an answer. "I'll pretend", said Dick, "that it's a Spiritual Store, and then I wouldn't be asking for sweets or a new bicycle, of course." And that, in a way, has always helped me too. I am afraid Lucy may think all my meditations are on the same low intellectual plane, but what, oh what, is the use of pretending that we can really see out of that high window of my dream? For we must be content to be rather small and humble if we are to try one day to escape from it into the larger love of God.

And I may as well confess that after this I go to bed and read a novel! As I've given up my *Times* subscription for Lent, I am re-reading with infinite pleasure of the clergy ladies of fiction, Mrs. Elton and Mrs. Proudie, Nancy Woodforde and Mrs. John Wesley. As I say, Faith is a desperate spiritual adventure, and one cannot go to sleep with a drawn sword at one's side. I still have a childish vision of four angels round my bed, I know, and I leave my soul to them while I let my mind sink into sleep, fancying what sort of address Mrs. Elton gave to the Mothers' Meeting (if any), and how Bishop Proudie ever found the courage to propose to Mrs. Proudie.

II
TUESDAY MORNING

IT IS HORRIBLE to wake up now.

When we married, after the last War, Arthur was ordained, and we had so little money that we were very grateful to Aunt Selina who offered to present us with a bed. Her Victorian modesty made any hints on the subject impossible, and so we rejoice, or rather don't, in a vast double bedstead with elaborate brass bars, scrolls and knobs at the head and foot, the last of which Dick used to unscrew (in his thriller days) in the hope of finding strange Eastern potions and lethal daggers. It is hateful to dust, and I used to tell Arthur that it was one of my crosses to think that I should be the last woman of my acquaintance to expire on a wire mattress almost wholly surrounded by brass. That was three years ago, and I used to worry about the patch of damp on the ceiling over the fireplace with its miniature (and seldom lit) gas-fire, and the mark where Dick had spilt methylated spirit all over my very nice Chippendale dressing-table. I used to remember, too, how the sun had shone on the old heart-shaped mirror and tallboys, in my old home in Sussex, and wonder how I could afford new matting and how long the old striped green and white chintz curtains would hang together, and, in short, take a morning dose of that self-pity which Stevenson calls the meanest of the emotions. And now, of course, looking back I see I was the happiest wife and mother in the world, though I still owe Aunt Selina a grudge about the brass bedstead, as I usually have to dust it myself!

The first tram always wakes me at half-past six, so it was too early to get up, and my thoughts passed unprofitably, from what Dick calls "holy moments" to the ever-recurring question of finance. Any worry is better than thoughts of Europe.

"If", Arthur always says, "you were a working woman and were told your husband was going to get seven pounds a week, you would cry with joy! Think of the Apostles!"

"If", I retort to him, "you were in a prosperous tent-making business and frequently absent on missionary journeys (see Maps I, II, III, IV, and V), I should probably feel well off!"

"Even the Strangs," Arthur proceeds, "on four pounds a week, with one baby, are better off than half our congregation!"

"But most of them don't pay a maid's wages," I protest.

I am glad to say that even Arthur doesn't any longer ask why I should need a luxury which Saint Paul's wife did without—(or was his wife's extravagance in having a female slave his thorn in the flesh, asks Dick). At my age I cannot manage this house with its basement and ten rooms, with no help at all, and give half my working day to the parish as well. It is no use, as he knows, to protest that a clergyman's wife should not be an unpaid curate, because in a place like this, with a minute leisured class, one has to take up the white woman's burden of committees. Here Arthur always advances his views about self-government in parochial management, but till that ideal is nearer of attainment (which, as the Commination Service says, is greatly to be desired) someone has to put her hands to the plough—(and the fact that I have used two analogies in two sentences proves that I have anyhow not always failed in one duty of a parson's wife, that of listening to sermons).

If I had no other duties and a small modern house, I should certainly manage without a maid, and feel opulent. I am not so sure about poor little Mrs. Strang, for I know well that the diminutive servant who answers the door, looking rather a pathetic little slut in the morning, and emerges with the pram in the afternoon, all cape and streamers as a nurse, is a mark of gentility which Mrs. Strang could not bear to forgo. And it is no use to criticize this point of view. You are born with or without it like a squint, and you must just be thankful if you haven't got it.

Still, my thoughts ran, Kate's wages, insurance and food amount to a third of our income, and it is very hard to see how best to spend the rest of it.

"We eat too much," said Arthur last night, as he finished a fish scallop. "First that excellent soup, and now a savoury to follow, and coffee afterwards. Now a working man and his wife would be eating—"

"Half-a-pound of steak apiece at two-and-four a pound!" I declared. "Or they'd have had that for mid-day dinner—and we have cheese and bread and fruit—and they'd have topped up their cocoa for supper with a tin of salmon, and that's gone up from sevenpence-halfpenny to elevenpence." (In dealing with a philosopher one should always introduce a concrete fact, date or price. It impresses them far more than their own type of generalizations.)

As far as I can see I cannot manage the food, heating, lighting and cleaning of this wasteful house for less than twelve pounds a month, though I am sure Mrs. Weekes would tell me that I could, if only I had more Method. When I consider other expenses I always lose myself in memories of a book my Mother gave me on Keeping House. On our first income—£500 a year, I think—we were supposed to be four maiden ladies living in the country with a pony-cart, and on £600 a year we should have been a smart couple in a flat in town with a boy in the Navy. I can only recall my vivid pictures of these happy beings, living in older, happier days, and the concluding item of each budget, which ran: Newspapers, soda-water and charity—£30 a year. Unluckily, though we only take the *Daily Telegraph* and never buy soda-water, charity doesn't fit into that admirable estimate.

Arthur regulates our donations in theory. His grandmother, he tells me, had fifty pounds given her for that purpose by her husband. She disliked writing cheques—"paper is so dangerous", she would say—and confined herself to church collections. As she was something of a miser at heart, she would dole out threepences for the first half or more of the year, and find herself obliged by the end of Advent to get rid of golden sovereigns, whether the cause was after her own heart or not. "Five pounds to the Additional Curates' Fund, and I do so *dislike* curates," she was heard to complain on the last Sunday of the year, and no consideration in the world would have made her carry on the gift to January, because it belonged to her yearly tithe. I don't know if Arthur inherited the tithe principle, but he certainly gives away more than £30 a year, not in calculated subscriptions, but in that happy open-heartedness and sympathy from which most of us protect ourselves under the aegis of the Charity Organization Society. At best, it always seems, we have something like £70 a year left for insurance, daily expenses, clothes, presents and holidays. We have always recognized that we, too, have been extremely lucky in having relations on my side who practically paid for Dick's education and for one or two critical illnesses. And then, too, we have no rent to pay for this house, inconvenient as it is. So we really have money enough for all our needs, I told myself, as I reached the point of all these meditations, whether I could somehow or other afford a cheap new hat. We are lunching at the Weekes's on Thursday, to meet the Archdeacon, and not even the better days of my tweeds can conceal that worse day when my present felt hat (4s. 11d.) blew into a snow-drift.

"I think the clergy should do a course of bookkeeping in their theological colleges," I said to Arthur, at breakfast. (Still no letter from Dick, still a patter of rain on the window-sills, and Arthur was back from church and I had just "finished" the study and poached the eggs.)

"You've already condemned them at different times to a course of astronomy to make them feel the insignificance of man," said Arthur, "and three months as charwomen so as to understand the feminine point of view. They'd be getting on in life before they were ordained."

"Yes, because you want them to have a year of philosophy, so that they won't mistake analogy for argument and avoid loose-thinking! Well, it would be all the better, darling, because middle-aged clergy are always nicer than young ones!"

"I'm afraid that may be only a middle-aged point of view! Not that I'm feeling very friendly to youth as exemplified by Strang this morning!"

We had been too peaceful to talk about our curate and his sermon last night. Most happily-married couples now, when the days are over and we sit by the fire, safe for one evening more anyhow,

> ... *strive to build a little isle of bliss*
> *Midway the beating of that stormy sea*
> *Where tossed about all hearts of men must be.*

"We'll discuss it in the morning," we say, and then at breakfast we read the paper and don't want to talk, and "it" escapes discussion. But I had to ask about Mr. Strang on this occasion and find out what I had better say to his critics. Yesterday, it appears, Arthur received a letter from Mr. Weekes, who is usually as kind and good-natured a manufacturer as ever talked of the good old days, lamented the crimes of modern youth, and laughed good-humouredly at his wife's superior refinement, to say that unless Mr. Strang's mouth could be stopped somehow he would have to leave the church, and hadn't these modern Bishops, who seem to think they've a right to wear mitres, and peacock about like the Pope, taken to excommunicating people as the Popes did? If so, I gathered, he would present Mr. Strang as a candidate and attend the service personally.

"I got hold of Weekes, and he complains that Strang said England deserves all she can get, and is doomed to the destruction of all capitalist countries. According to Mrs. Weekes, he waved at their pew as he added a brisk little damnation of all capitalists. Later on I met old Chubb, who is quite the best fellow on the town council, and is responsible for the very decent housing movements, and he said that he had heard the Curate had described Stampfield as a warren of foul slums, and what about it? Then I called in at Hantons to ask that very nice foreman about poor Higgs's compensation, and was asked why I allowed my young man to tell his men that they'd no business to work for the Army—they're making rubber tyres for Army lorries, you know. In the bank, old Colonel Greenley roared at me that he heard my Curate was in the pay of the Peace Pledge Union, and that he hoped his sermon was actionable. I can tell you I was glad to get over to Marley in the afternoon to see that nice Mrs. Tonks, and christen the baby and listen to the woes of evacuees, for they don't include Strang's sermons."

At that moment the door-bell rang, and Kate looked in on her way to answer it (a habit of which I cannot cure her) to say it was that Mr. Strang again, and her boy-friend said if he came across the chap who'd spilt the beans over the Army like that he'd give him something to remember. I could only hope that Private Jenkins may get his long-expected summons to France without delay, and I was just going off to the kitchen when Arthur implored me to stay, on the grounds that we must really decide on a unified front in this crisis.

Mr. Strang is rather like a small Irish terrier. He has rather fluffy ginger hair and eyebrows, watchful brown eyes, and the same unfortunate predilection for getting up rows wherever he goes. His father was Irish, so he is unable to see that there is more than one side to any question; his mother belonged to one of those well-known Quaker families whose descendants are ready to fight to the death for Pacifism. He picked up Labour views in his school-days, and adorned them with very advanced ways of thinking at his theological college.

He proceeded to marry a pretty, silly little woman, who is always encouraging him to think they are wronged or slighted by their neighbours; and though he is undoubtedly brave, hard-working and devoted, he is curiously unliveable-with.

He has a very thin and—to-day—very red nose, which twin-kles at the tip when he is agitated, and a way of snapping his mouth tight at the end of a remark which is only less aggra-vating than the remarks when it is open. "What he needs is an orange-box to preach on in the park, and a quiet duck in the Serpentine when he's finished," says Dick. But to-day he looked hardly capable of speaking on anything, as he was ob-viously tired and ill.

I let them begin their conversation while I went off and heated up a good cup of coffee for him. He is reputed to fast very drastically in Lent, "and when he does get down to it," Kate said, "it's nothing but cutlet frills and entrée papers, Ireen says, for Mrs. Strang is such a one for show."

As I stood over the poor, tired, over-wrought little man till he put the cup to his lips, Arthur, I gathered, was able to put in a remark at last. (From the kitchen I had heard distant reverberations of pure Strang.)

"Quite so," said my husband, soothingly. "I am sure any offence you gave was unintentional, but——"

"Mrs. Lacely can bear me witness that I preached nothing but pure Gospel!" cried Mr. Strang. (I wished I had let the milk curdle on the top a little, as that interrupts a man's utter-ances so effectively!) And who, alas, was I to bear witness one way or the other?

"Then, of course, that is all right," said Arthur, looking more affectionately over the top of his glasses than ever. "As Our Lord never criticized the government of his own day, nor interfered with a political system, no-one should criticize you. It was all some odd misunderstanding."

"But there I differ from you!" cried Mr. Strang, bolting down his coffee. My idea was a failure, I fear, for his drink seemed to give him fresh strength for a declamation on those views which we all know so well. We know, and we all feel the hopeless impasse to which they bring our judgement. Is it, I wondered, one facet of man's Free Will that he has to decide for himself between the Christ scourging the money-lenders and the Christ refusing military aid in Gethsemane, between the tribute-money to Caesar and the challenge to Pilate? If it is for us to make our own choice in every given instance between complete pacifism and military intervention, how can Christianity preserve a united front?

"There is so much in all you say," agreed Arthur, with just a shade more weariness than benevolence this time. "But if you wandered from the subject of the imperative duty of Christians to live in peace with their neighbours to the more controversial topic of war as the result of capitalist society, with all its attendant evils, may I say that I think a platform would have been more appropriate than a pulpit."

"When I know that my views are the views of my Master, it is my duty to proclaim them to His flock," returned Mr. Strang, snapping his mouth shut so violently that I almost hoped it might stay shut altogether.

"The longer I live", said Arthur, hunting for his pipe on the mantelpiece, "the more convinced I feel that we cannot dogmatize on the application of Christian doctrine to any particular problem or crisis. We can present its ethic and philosophy, and try so to reveal the divinity and humanity of Our Lord, that He may Himself become the standard of individuals in their daily and national perplexities. But in any generalizations one must distrust human error, so large a factor in many decisions of the Church. The Church, I think, should reflect in humility on the Crusades and the Religious Wars before she can feel positive that she has any right to lay down the laws on public policy."

The argument was so evidently going to proceed on well-worn lines that I slipped away to do the drawing-room and make a steamed-pudding, as the joint showed sad traces of Private Jenkins's perennial leave-takings, and to get ready for a committee at the parish hall at half-past ten. I looked in on my way to the door, with my shopping-basket, to see if Arthur had reached any conclusions. Mr. Strang had gone. He couldn't send Arthur his sermon because he had preached extempore, but he had promised to re-write it to the best of his ability. Arthur was then to judge whether his Curate should try to make his position a little clearer in his mid-day sermon on Wednesday.

"A little more Christian, you mean?" I asked.

"I do, but I don't know that he does. Militant pacifism might be a great force in the world," Arthur added, thoughtfully. "He's a good little man at bottom, you know, and he was most nearly touched when I pointed out how he might have hurt the feelings of those who had relatives serving their country. He'll gladly apologize to any of them, but not, alas, to the Weekes or the Greenleys, and in a way I respect him for it."

"Yes, but you know our Evangelical grandparents would have said that the poor fellow isn't even converted yet!" I answered, impatiently. "What right has he to upset everyone and worry you?"

"Not peace but a sword, he'd reply to that," sighed Arthur. "But I cannot believe such an absurd fuss and disturbance can do anything but die down in a day or two. What thinking man could conceivably give all this another thought at a time like this?"

I left him to this consoling reflection, but I don't feel sure that there are very many thinking men, or any thinking women, in Stampfield.

At the front door I was stopped by Mrs. Tidds wearing a battered man's soft hat and an even more woebegone expression than usual. I knew from experience that one of her children was in disgrace and that it would probably take me ten minutes to disentangle which. And it was a quarter-past ten.

"'E'd never meant to *steal* the bicycle-lamp, my Jimmy," was the point of the story when my visitor reached it at last, "but 'e was always such a one for play." If the Vicar could be so good as to speak a word for him to the Magistrate and the Probationary Officer.

Sometimes I feel that speaking words and writing lines are the last traces of the belief in the infallibility of the Church in our country. I promised to speak to Arthur, inquired after Percy's tonsils and promised to look out a hat for Mrs. Tidds, and leave it when I was next her way, "as the other ladies who char to oblige in the Hospital pass such unpleasant remarks about me grey felt". I can't say how sorry I feel for all the incompetent, woe-ridden Mrs. Tidds of my acquaintance, but there is something depressing in helping oxen and asses out of one pit, so to speak, when you know they will fall into another in a day or two, and you are already late for an appointment—"But you must remember, my dear," Arthur's mother used to say, "that one never meets with any trace of hurry or bustle in the Gospels!"

The annoying part of my three committees this morning was that they were all held in different buildings, though they consist of practically identical members. All clergy people must be suffering now, as we are doing here, from the complete disappearance of the comparatively young and energetic, who went off in their uniforms this summer, leaving the old hacks like myself to carry on, or to close down their activities, without one thought of them again. I used to enjoy the Committee of the Factory Girls' Club in the hall of Stampfield Parish Church, for the Club is well-endowed by an old spinster of the parish, and we have rescued it lately from the ministrations of the old parish deaconess, who was far too tired and elderly to do anything to entertain the few depressed members, and persuaded Ida Weekes, a fine, upstanding girl, full of Roedean public spirit, to help with her friends to pep it up, as they would say. Then I retired from any active work, and heard great stories of cooking and dress-making lessons, amateur theatricals and social evenings for boy-friends. And now Ida and her friends are away in the A.T.S. or W.R.N.S., leaving

Mrs. Weekes, Miss Boness, Miss Grieve, Miss Croft, and such elderly ladies, to try to adapt it to war conditions. It is needed more than ever now in the black-out, which is responsible for as many moral as physical accidents, but the attendance has fallen almost to zero, and none of us has the leisure or youth to reorganize it on new lines. My only hope is Miss Henly, the marvellous headmistress of our high school, who was co-opted at my suggestion, and was speaking as I went in.

"I think we should get permission from the Old Church Vestry," she was saying energetically, "to let us open their hall two nights a week for the militia in Brey Camp, and get the girls themselves to run it as a canteen. That would bring them back in no time, and would make them feel they were serving their country as well."

There is a nice story in a letter of Winifred Holtby's about a French Commandant in the Great War who heard that our W.A.A.C.s were going to France, pure, high-minded, patriotic women who would present no problems. "Mais que feront-elles avec les bébés?" was all he asked with simple cynicism, and I could see the same thought in the minds of the committee at once, though all we heard from Mrs. Weekes was a murmur about licence.

"Oh, nonsense! No drinks, of course! Only tea and cocoa, buns and fags!" Miss Henly is a big, vital, autocratic woman of forty or so, and even her original clothes, high colour and quick, hearty voice suggest her unbounded energy. Everyone but Mrs. Weekes is rather afraid of her, and even Mrs. Weekes has to remember that Ida was at no secondary school, but at Roedean, before she opposes her.

"A very dangerous experiment I should say," she volunteered now, with that curious swelling effect of her bounteous figure in the tight, elephant grey coat. "The place would be a perfect pandemonium."

"One of us would have to be in the background at first, at any rate," said Miss Henly. "But I find that the more responsibility a girl has, the better she behaves."

"I think our brave boys should have every comfort we can possibly give them!" Dear little Miss Grieve's brother was a Territorial Major in the Great War, so she takes a proprietorial interest in the Army, and is our chief source of military gossip (often strongly reminiscent of the tales of 1914-18). As her voice, hair and manner are as prim as her little villa, I should never have expected her as an ally, and spoke up warmly in favour of Miss Henly's scheme, with a sneaking hope that my presence would not often be required in the background. It does, of course, give me a chance of getting to know the younger girls of the place, who don't often frequent our church or any other, and I fully realize that the clergy must do their utmost for the Army just now, but I am often so tired by the evening! But before I could be pinned down, Miss Boness spoke, her face one portentous question-mark.

"Perhaps Mrs. Strang would give us a night a week if we are really going to contemplate the scheme? It would remove a most unfortunate impression!"

Mr. Strang's sermon did this much good, at all events, that the scheme for the canteen was settled rapidly and efficiently by Miss Henly, who will clearly make it a Sphere of Influence, as everyone hoped to catch me afterwards for a little talk, and not so very little either, on the iniquities of the Curate. I could not avoid hearing several comments, as Mrs. Weekes, Miss Boness and Miss Grieve walked with me, a sombre little Lenten procession in goloshes, to the next committee, of the District Nursing Association; but as they all had so much to say themselves, I easily maintained an impression of neutrality under my umbrella.

Here again is a committee on which I have really no business at all, but here again, too, the War has removed our chief props and some of our subscribers. The Treasurer showed, as

most societies do just now, a deficit of £13 19s. 11½d., and
we gloomily debated the necessity of a Whist Drive or a Jumble Sale. "And don't", said Miss Grieve, "forget our Cake and
Candy Sale on Saturday afternoon!" Nurse came in, and made
Miss Grieve blush very much by describing in detail the welcome gift of an indispensable adjunct for invalids, and the Secretary was instructed to write our thanks. Just as I feared that
the Strang Question would come before the house again, Miss
Grieve remembered that a friend had written to her with a
most interesting description of Berlin, from a cousin whose
nephew had been there just before the War. Having hastily
voted in favour of a Jumble Sale, we all listened respectfully
while she read an extract, found with some difficulty, and a
little trouble over the spectacles, from which it appears that
the whole German people were only awaiting the outbreak of
War to rise against the Nazis, that the rebels all recognize each
other by means of a secret number concealed on their per-
sons—(thus surely making recognition very difficult?)—and
that it all fits in exactly with what dear Papa said about the
Pyramids.

With these happy distractions—and luckily Miss Boness has always felt there was *something* in the Pyramids—we
found ourselves re-established as a new committee in the
Saint Simon's Parish Room. This time we were considering
the Women's Branch of the XYZ Missionary Society. Some
twenty years ago the women of Stampfield were persuaded to
undertake the care of a ward in the Szublele Women's Hospital
in Central Africa. Every November some noble, earnest, pallid
Sister comes over to inspire our enthusiasm, and I am filled
with such whole-hearted respect that I have never brought
myself to ask *why* they use square pyjamas. This year, of course,
we had no visit, and though some of their subscribers have
nobly produced their usual donation, many have felt that War,
or the pinch of taxation, oblige them to withdraw or dimin-
ish their contributions. (How naturally, alas, one falls into the

language of reports!) There are practically no donations, and when Miss Boness declared, with her Irish sprightliness still undismayed, that we do seem to be up a gum tree, no-one had any suggestion as to how we were to come unstuck. Even Mrs. Weekes sounded less plumply certain of herself than usual when she suggested a Bazaar, and had no reply to Miss Grieve's obviously true remark that there would be no-one but ourselves either to sell or to buy (and she hoped we would not forget her Cake and Candy Sale), or to amplify Miss Boness's suggestion that "we must enlarge our borders, we must enlarge our borders"!

Miss Cookes, the Secretary of this committee, a drooping, emaciated lady of sixty, shook her head till her beads from Travancore and her bangles from Amritsar joined in a tinkling dirge, and expressed suddenly what most of us realize already:

"Who *is* there to be got? When all of us older ones are in our graves"—(Mrs. Weekes frowned severely)—"all our Missions will have to close down as far as I can see. What young person nowadays has any interest in Missions? Oh, yes, I know we have some societies for children of school age, but what happens when they grow up? Do you ever hear of them again? Every society in Great Britain is appealing for aid, not to enlarge its old work, but to keep its present stations from closing down. Things have been serious enough since the last War, but this War will be fatal!" Everyone looked at me as if I should make some apology, and I could only suggest, what I believe to be the case, that the conscience of young people is more exercised over bad conditions in the slums and the housing question at home. When we were young, I pointed out, missionaries were still pioneers and explorers, and they appealed to the imagination of youth in a way which was not quite so obvious now.

"But what", cried Miss Cookes, "did the Duke of Wellington say to the Curate who objected to Missions? 'Look at your

Gospel, Sir—"Go ye into all the world!" Marching orders, Sir! Marching orders!'"

We all received this chestnut respectfully, because there really did not seem much to say. It is always depressing when elderly people sit together, wondering what has happened to the ideals of their youth, and the tragedy is all the greater, I suppose, because never have there been so many earnest, intellectual and broadminded workers in the Church abroad. Gone are the days when a Missionary was represented as a comic figure with a top-hat and clerical collar, landing on a cannibal island. We can no longer, in these secular times, be accused of conquering the world with a Bible in one hand and a bottle of rum in the other, for we are far too diplomatic, imperially, to produce the Bible. And there are enthusiasts at home, still, of course, as well as a splendid army of Missionaries abroad, but the supplies everywhere are failing, the purse of the public is lean and locked-up.

"Of course", said Miss Grieve, sadly, "it has been people like us with, if I may say so, a tradition behind us—those of us connected with the Church, the Army, and the Professions— who have done so much in the past, and now our class is being taxed out of existence."

"I'm sure business people have not been wanting in their support," said Mrs. Weekes very stiffly. Now and then she grows rather restive about "my brother, the Major".

"Well, but what are we to do?" demanded Miss Cookes, her bangles tinkling again. "How can we raise some money?"

For some minutes we discussed Bazaars (and again we are reminded that Miss Grieve and Miss Croft are holding a Cake and Candy Sale on Saturday), Diminishing Teas, and house-to-house visitations, without much enthusiasm, ignoring the wilder ideas of a Flag Day and Missionary Exhibition advocated by Miss Cookes, and Mrs. Weekes had just said that she would ask Mr. Weekes to see what he could do about it this year (and the capital that good kind man is amassing in Heaven is incredible), when Miss Boness declared ominously:

"If you ask me, it's all this subversive pacifism which is going about which is ruining our Missions. I don't suppose people who preach against our Empire can possibly feel any proper responsibility for it!"

"Did Mr. Strang really preach against the Empire as well?" asked Miss Grieve, in prim disgust. (Either she had not been at church, or had been asleep like myself.)

"He preached against everything!" replied Miss Boness. "I asked myself"—(and her eyebrows disappeared entirely into her hair)—"is *anything* sacred to that young man?"

"I really feel I must ask you, Mrs. Lacely," said Mrs. Weekes, entering upon a direct frontal attack at last, "whether the dear Vicar is *doing* anything about it."

"He has been having a talk with Mr. Strang this morning," I replied, looking at my watch and seeing a way of escape. "If there is no more business, perhaps you'll excuse me? I should like to look in at the Midday Service, and it's nearly one o'clock." That was a lucky escape, for the church is just across the road from the hall, and no-one could criticize my reason for cutting short the conversation. Of course it is impossible to keep up this cowardly technique of rapid withdrawals, but in a small place any remark may be so easily misinterpreted and wrongly repeated.

I like the Mid-day Service in our church in Lent. The building itself is of the most dismal Victorian Gothic, with pitch pine pews and pulpit, and a dismal East window with four lights, one for each of the Evangelists, who differ only in the length of their hair and the colour of their robes. But I always think it has some of the warm, friendly love which Arthur feels for humanity; and in the Early Morning Services, to which Arthur has at length persuaded some of the working people to come in their ordinary clothes, these externals fade away before a real sense of union in worship. And I feel the same at these Mid-day Services, which people are asked to attend just as, and for how long they like, so that there is a casual homely feeling about the place, even though I must admit it is a little draughty and noisy. Arthur seems to mind neither, and refuses to have the door shut for his short sermon. He shocked Mr. Strang once by saying that he believed a sort of ecclesiastical claustrophobia was partly the cause of the falling off of church attendance in England, and that if you could once persuade people to look in and find that they could escape as they pleased, they might come back again. To which Mr. Strang only replied, with a snap of his teeth, that it was disrespect for the authority of the "Chuch" to-day which was at the root of all evils. Certainly the respect for his authority couldn't be lower than it is just now!

There were more people than usual to-day, in spite of the rain, attracted, I fear, by the hope of hearing a violent repudiation of Mr. Strang's doctrines from Arthur. If so, they were disappointed, for my husband gave instead an interesting account of some experiences of early Christian missionaries in the marshes and fens of Northern Europe.

"Or did you", I asked at lunch, "refer to the people of Stampfield when you talked about dangers from wild beasts and men wilder than the beasts? When you quoted that story about the Saxon tribe who waved their right arms above the river they were being baptized in, and said, 'Never will we give up our sword arms to the gentle Christ!' I thought I saw a marked gleam in Miss Grieve's eyes. No, dearest, don't look pained! I know you were hundreds of miles away from Stampfield in time and space."

"I'm afraid it never occurred to me to connect my memories of Bede and Adamnam with this silly little business," said Arthur, in obvious surprise. "In any case, I thought it out on Saturday."

"I know, I know, and really the only reaction it had on me, as Miss Henly would say, was to decide that probably your nice monks were monks because they never had to sit on committees! Coracles in the West Highlands would be more dangerous, of course, but hardly damper than our meetings this morning."

"And I don't think the average mind is so disgustingly ingenious as yours," said Arthur, comforted. "Or do you suppose poor Strang saw himself as one of those heroic figures, plodding by night through the dense forests, where every trunk concealed the form of an enemy, and every crack of a twig was the drawing of an invisible bow? Why shouldn't he, after all? The voices of peacemakers in the world are as faint as the chants of the bearers of the *Vexilla Regis*, but the world heard them in the end."

"That's a lovely little sermon for myself, Arthur," I acknowledged. "But isn't poor little Mr. Strang more like the priest in Anatole France who lost his way, and prayed to the pagan goddess of the well, in his terror, before he slept in the forest? And baptized the well in honour of the Virgin next morning? Because, as you said to him, hasn't he lost his way in his forest of causes a little?"

"I don't think we can describe his zeal for peace as worship of a false goddess," said Arthur, decidedly. "Remember, our generation was brought up on the ideal, 'As God died to make men holy, so we die to make them free', and though we can give a passable idea of our Christian ideal of holiness, no-one yet has ever succeeded in giving a comprehensive definition of what we mean by freedom. Do you mean freedom to murder or steal from each other, the freedom claimed, in fact, by Germany in international policy? Or do you mean, as my friends in Hanton's factory here mean, freedom to get your half-pint, and go to the dog races, and read what news your paper likes to give you, without any crimson Dictator interfering with you?"

"Yes, yes I know," I agreed. All through this argument Arthur had been taking any dish I offered him in the most gratifying way. I can only keep him properly nourished in Lent by starting an argument and thus making him entirely oblivious of the food he's eating, or Lent, or our undue luxury ... Like that poem in 1916, where all the peasants from every country speak, and all end up:

> *I gave my life for freedom, this I know,*
> *For those who bade me do it told me so.*

"But Arthur, though I do see that any generation is a poor judge of its own ideals, I don't see how Mr. Strang can get away from the fact that if we laid down our arms now and let Germany annex us, there'd be very little freedom to worship God (let alone the half-pints and the dogs) for the next few generations!"

"But that's no conclusive argument," demurred Arthur. "Have we, as a nation, worshipped God so honourably in the days of this so-called freedom that we can be sure we should not be nearer Him in captivity? Aren't the truest lovers of Sion those who weep by the waters of Babylon? Mind you, I don't agree with Strang," added Arthur, who rarely fails to dissociate himself from any view to which he has nearly converted you—so passionately anxious is he to see every side of a question. "I am ready to agree with him that our sins and follies have helped to bring Europe into this intolerable position, but I can see no way out but the way we've taken. But I recognize that I seem old and prejudiced to Strang, and I am willing to pay deference to him as a truer Christian and probably a truer philosopher, though I should like him to look up his Aristotle a little before he applies his creed so directly to politics. No, I cannot censure him for his beliefs, as I said, and there is much to be said for his view that he has a right to express his creed as a Christian from the pulpit."

"Except that he's making war in Stampfield! Or doesn't war count to him unless it causes wounds and death? Because that brings you back to what's not so Christian—a belief that a man's life in this World matters more than anything else—

more than his faith and ideals. If by war he means envy, hatred and malice, he's made war here already! So, darling, as you would say, what meaning exactly do you attach to the word pacifism?"

Kate looked in at this point with a request that she might clear up now, as she wanted to pop across for a loaf of bread as we'd run a bit short if Mr. Dick took us all by surprise to-night. That means, I suppose, that Private Jenkins is looking in for yet another farewell, and though I grudge nothing, in theory, to the fighting forces, I do sometimes wish he would bring his ration with him instead of throwing it, as the authorities tell us, into a swill-pail. Meanwhile, Arthur looked at his watch, and rushed off for the door while I made up my mind with much reluctance that I had better go round my district this afternoon with the parish magazine.

III
TUESDAY AFTERNOON

I HAVE THE greatest dislike to this clerical duty of selling magazines, which always makes me feel like an unpopular bagman. The theory is that the production of the magazine is a good introduction to a little conversation, and helps to make acquaintanceship. I believe that men who travel with Hoovers and silk stockings are welcomed warmly by people like Kate, but then, however little Kate means to make any purchase, the travellers are attractive young men with tempting wares. I can never believe that I should warmly welcome any woman who came to my door with a pennyworth of literature, so alien to a film-loving public. The advertisements of the local shops and Saint Simon's Court Circular in the outer pages may, however, have a certain attraction, and our parishioners don't know how my poor Arthur groans over the composition of the Vicar's letter. (There was a terrible occasion once when Dick wrote a skit upon it, and we thought it had gone to the printer by accident. It was a great relief to find it in the wastepaper basket, but Dick always held that no-one would have known it from the original but for the names! "Dear friends," it ran, "yet another sacred season is upon us, though I cannot at the moment recollect which. The funds of all our societies from A to Z are in very low water, and I look to you all to put on your divers' suits and drag them out again. A great loss, as you know, has befallen our parish in the disappearance of Mr. Elgin, our beloved organist, into one of the big pipes of the instrument. It has been found, alas, impossible to rescue him, but his memory will long be fragrant in our midst—" I have forgotten the rest, but, as Arthur sighed, it was horribly true to form.)

The inner leaves of the magazine, which are common for every parish, are united rather too closely, I consider, to the traditions of the Victorian era to appeal to a nation which spends its spare time at the Pictures. "Give me the serial in *Women's*

Wisecracks every time," said Mrs. Bebb, our chief literary crit-ic, as we sat in her icy little room this afternoon. "Gives you something to think about, that do, with the poor gel's husband taking a horsewhip to her, and her kidnapped by the Sultan of Oman's yacht and all! That story of yours is too homely for *my* taste."

Mrs. Dodd, whose husband is "out" for the second time this quarter, looked at my merchandise with lacklustre eyes, and said, listening to the screams of her six children in the yard, that she wasn't much of a one for reading. Her eldest has just reached the statutory age of seven when he must have more sleeping room, and this means that poor Mr. Dodd will have to find another house when he is almost certainly in arrears here. These are the cases which should go to the C.O.S., but our people dislike questionnaires so much that I weakly hesitated to suggest it. Still I know one of the Council houses will be free soon, and I promised to see Mr. Chubb about it at once. (How I hoped Mr. Strang had not outraged him too far!) I put down a magazine vaguely with no request for a penny, and did the same at the Higgses next door. Poor Higgs, who broke his arm just outside the factory, unluckily, so that there is a doubt about his compensation, said he could read pretty nearly everything now they were coming to take the radio away, because his last two instalments were not paid up. It was out of the question to let the poor man lose his only source of entertainment (but for the parish magazine!) for five shillings, after managing half-a-crown for so many weary weeks, so I relinquished the idea of a new hat for the Weekes' party, and handed the sum to him with a sigh; and then immediately felt ten shillings richer, because I had meant to spend 14s. 11d. on a really good plain felt in Stampfield's one passable milliner! Anyhow, in their gratitude, the Higgses insisted on paying for their magazine, and that, I am ashamed to confess, was all the money I took this afternoon. Three houses have been evacuat-ed, two people were out. Mrs. Jones's Doris was ill again, and

I went up to amuse her with cutting out paper figures, while Mrs. Jones slipped out for the bread and marge. The poor lamb had bronchitis six weeks ago, and her temperature still keeps up every night; so I promised to urge her case forward with the committee of the Convalescent Home, remembering sadly that this means Colonel Greenley and Mrs. Weekes again. If Mr. Strang's folly is going to put grit into these parochial wheels, I shall walk him round the parish myself in a white shirt and taper!

I was the less sorry for my long visit because it left less time for Mrs. Sime, and as she comes in to oblige there are often opportunities for seeing her. She is a sad, portentous woman with a large bow-front, which makes her a poor worker; but we do anything we can to help her because we are all so sorry for her troubles. Mr. Sime is a good steady worker in the brewery, and a violent teetotaller, and they are both regular church attendants; but their lives are darkened by their daughter "Lil". It would only be possible, alas, to describe the poor girl in terms of the farm-yard, or with the help of Havelock Ellis, and the use of the word a-moral, which has now reached the provinces, is plentifully employed at the monthly meeting of our Magdalen Home (which does not, fortunately, occur this week). The relation of the church to the new Health Clinic, which was started here two years ago, is one of terribly involved controversy; but, let me state crudely, the subject does not enter into Lil's calculations. "Out of one trouble into another", is Mrs. Sime's gloomy epitome of the situation, which has now become a routine. Each affair begins with the report, through Kate, that Mr. Sime says he'll finish off that girl this time if he swings for it, followed by a hitherto fortunately falsified report that Lil's put her head in the gas-oven this time. On the first occasion, I remember, the Magdalen Home took her in, and there was so fierce and prolonged a committee on the question of making the boy in question, Alf Byng, Right the Wrong, that Mrs. Weekes and Miss Boness would have cut

each other indefinitely had it not transpired that Alf had, perhaps luckily, run off to Manchester, leaving no address. Since
then the Salvation Army and a neighbouring convent have
dealt in turns with Lil, who has the face of a rather grimy El
Greco saint, and the most beautiful little family of offspring
any Dictator could wish to see. Every denomination, however,
now fights shy of her, as her scruples about attributing paterni-
ty grow less and less, and Kate's surmises make me feel that no
Galahad could escape without suspicion in Stampfield.

"Ho, yes, it's the old story," said Mrs. Sime to-day, as she
stood at the open door, ironing the nappies of the last intruder,
"I tells her her father won't half kill her this time!"

"Is she living at home, Mrs. Sime?" I asked helplessly.

"Ho no! My madam has a furnished room with that Sue
Brace, since they both went into munitions. It's all fun and
games for them now, and me to mind the babies all day, and
no-one to look after the little innocents at night. 'I'm through
with you,' I tells her, 'and just you keep out of your father's
sight.' No'm, don't you go trying to see her. You can't even
catch 'old of her now and nothing'll do 'er any good. I don't
know how Sime and I came to 'ave a child like that, I don't, us
as allays kept ourselves respectable."

"Where is she? Perhaps I could catch her sometime?"

"Don't you'm. She's in 7, Hall Road, next to Mrs. Maw
where the Horganist lodges. Making 'erself all the more of a
disgrace in a respectable neighbourhood like that, I tells 'er.
No, madam won't say who it is, and if you ask me I don't suppose she knows. Shutting up, that's what she wants, more than
a poor woman who gets run in for shop-lifting by a long way, I
says. I expect she's accusing anyone who comes into her head,
and you tell all the clergy gentlemen to keep away from her!"

Lil is of course an extreme case of the problem which faces
us all perpetually, and for which we have no satisfactory solution. On the whole question I always feel sadly like Arthur's
mother, who declared once in a rectory crisis, "Really, six is

beyond me", though Arthur was one of a family of seven. As, however, the attention of psycho-analysts and modern novelists is so firmly concentrated on these points, I try to avoid generalizations, and helplessly get tickets for the Infirmary, and bags of baby-clothes as the need arises, and leave it at that. We shall have trouble enough, I know, at the Magdalen Home next Tuesday over the question of unmarried dependents. "And a gentleman in *The Times* saying, 'Why not call them concubines?'" said Matron. "A pretty fool I'd look ordering tea and marge to be sent to the Concubines' Home!"

On the whole I decided to leave the whole problem to more modern minds and to finish my immediate duties.

All these houses, in Bill Bowes Lane are of that low, wizened, cheap-bricked, back-to-back type which are the hateful legacy of Mid-Victorian England. They were on the condemned list of the Town Council for its next programme, but there they must remain now, I suppose. As a matter of fact, Mr. Strang's generalities don't fit in with my district, for all their owners keep their dwellings reasonably clean, and the two new and superior houses which I forced myself to call upon, on my way home, are far greater blemishes on civilization. Number 1, Acacia Villas, is one where the mother drinks, and the children are dirty and verminous. She was cringingly polite to me to-day, because she has lost her ration-book, and needed my reassurance that she could easily get a new one. Next door belongs to a hateful couple who come to church and look respectable, but let out their rooms furnished at exorbitant prices to any unhappy couple who start married life without furniture. ("Fifteen bob a week, and a smell of cats and gas, and put myself on one of her mattresses I would not," says Kate.)

Those two homes weigh terribly on my conscience, while round the corner again is an odd little spot called Dogberry Close, which rejoices me, though it must make Mr. Strang see even redder than usual. Three dilapidated little half-timber cottages hang together behind tiny front gardens, with tinier gardens and lean-to sheds of the most primitive description at the back. They are to be pulled down, of course, as reconditioning is too expensive, but each of their inhabitants will be sorry to leave.'

"This war'll do a good turn to I," said crotchety old Mr. Bimus, spitting with wonderful accuracy into one of the huge cockle shells in his front patch. "They say that there Council won't pull us down now. How'd I get another house and garden like this?"

"The new Council houses have nice little gardens," I suggested, for Mr. Bimus is said to have enough put by to afford a higher rent.

"And what'd I do for manure?" asked Mr. Bimus, with startling outspokenness. "Plugs here, plugs there, says I to that whippersnapper young parson of yours. Plugs don't help my roses!"

Mrs. Leaf, next door, is the sort of woman who would have turned Hercules out of the Augean stable with a sniff, and transformed it into a model dwelling in a few hours. Her son, who has been called up, would have liked to move to something more up-to-date, but, like so many spotlessly clean women, Mrs. Leaf distrusts and dislikes any new neighbours. She and Mr. Bimus have reached some sort of tacit truce after years of enmity, "and a man don't go nosing out how many times a year you washes your blankets", she says, though I feel sure no-one in Stampfield washes them as often as she does. She welcomed me very warmly to-day, as she wished to make out some War Office papers about her position as a Dependent (a word which annoyed her), and I am sure did not mean me to see her wiping my footprint carefully off her immaculate hearthstone, as I knocked at her neighbour's door. She does not quarrel with dear little Mrs. Smith because nobody could. Mrs. Smith is too small and white and gentle, and so wholly preoccupied with her anxious little efforts at dress-making. The cheap guinea frocks, which all the factory girls purchase now, threatened her trade sadly a few years ago. She belonged to the old school which liked fancy buttons and bits of black lace over white satin, and a nice bit of jet somewhere on the corsage, and the only subject on which she grows a little bitter is the rise of the ready-made. But as stout figures inevitably strain cheap frocks, she has her niche now in letting-out, mending and taking-up gowns, and just makes a living for herself and her daughter, May. May is a charming, clever child who has recently won a scholarship at the High School, and Mrs. Smith was pathetically anxious to ask me to inquire privately if she might make May's uniform at home instead of getting it at our big draper's. "Such a save, and I'd reproduce the effect exactly, Mrs. Lacely," she assured me in her tired, refined little voice; so, adding that to my list of messages, I turned to go home. "And if her new teacher could put in a word about not encouraging May to take a prejudice against our little home," added the anxious mother, "I'd be ever so glad. Of course, this is a poor little place, but if they're not to be pulled down, I'd be thankful to stay. I should never get such a retired little house at such a moderate rental anywhere in Stampfield—and such a central position too, and nice neighbours."

I promised to make Miss Henly suggest to May that it was interesting to live in such an old-world historic little home, and walked back, with the old question at the back of my mind, the question which worries all parsons' wives, I am sure: "What use am I to any of these people? What do we really do to help them or make them happier?"

We clergy have, as I said before, a certain use as go-be-tweens, between official England and its alarming circulars, and the uneducated who view their efforts with a mixture of bewilderment and distrust. Like the wholly admirable em-ployees in the Post Office, we can translate and explain and we can also grease the wheels of those charitable efforts, like Convalescent Hospitals where a little influence goes a long way. We can, in short, aid in the great social effort of the last thirty years or so, to make their lives more certain and more comfortable. Do we do any more? None of those who, in the flush of youthful philanthropy, did a little mild slumming in our second or third Seasons can possibly under-value that work. Everyone must believe in the progress of the social conscience who remembers what it was like in those days to visit families where accident or illness meant a grim prospect of starvation or the House, where medical advice was shirked, or only gained by presuming on the kindness of the surgery doctor, where Clinics and free milk and nursery schools were unknown, and sweated labour in the home evaded all Government restrictions. In those days the houses in Bill Bowes Lane would have seemed nice, respectable little homes, and it shows an advance that Mr. Strang, however tiresome he may be, really views them as a warren of slums. All of us rejoice that the standard of living has improved, and mourn over the check to progress which is one of the hideous side-lines of the War.

But the difficult side of the question is this: does one make people happier necessarily by making them more comfortable? Because it is our business, presumably, as servants of Heaven, to inspire not only comfort but serenity and hope in the lives around us. A century ago our forefathers had no doubts on this point. They had no measuring-tape for themselves or "the Poor" but spiritual values. I just remember great-aunt Louisa who, even though she gave up dances, theatres, cards and wine in her youth, lived in a vast comfortable house in Stanhope Gate, whence she descended on the slums of North Kensington. On the other side of the family was' a brisk, fiery, military great-uncle, retired from the Guards who, besides hunting two days a week, put in innumerable hours at Saint Alban's, Holborn, commanding and dragooning men and boys to services and processions. Neither of these two predecessors of mine worried about the differences in their circumstances from those among whom they worked. They were infinitely charitable, I am sure, but their hearts were set on souls to be saved rather than on bodies to be comforted. Confident in their faith of another world, where inequalities would be forgotten, they spoke of and saw only the immortal spirit of God and man in their labours. They saw happiness as a possession quite independent of external circumstances, whereas we see happiness as dependent upon comfort. I don't mean that this entirely represents Arthur's real point of view or mine. Certainly he views the things of the spirit as on a higher plane than anything else, and yet, in my efforts to help people, the thought that I, with my comparative comfort, have no right to preach to them in their poverty and anxiety makes me shamed and tongue-tied.

I had meant to discuss all this with Arthur, because he always sees some side of any given question which I have ignored; but as I entered the cold, darkened hall I heard voices in the study, and, I feared, angry and protesting voices. While I stood hesitating, Kate's head popped up at the basement stairs, her cap well on the back of an agitated perm, and her voice came in a dramatic stage-whisper.

"They're at it in there, all of them, over the Strang business. That shufflé you meant to make of the rabbit won't do. I'll stew it up and keep the pudding hot, though if you ask me I'd say those apples were more fit for a pig-tub than for apple-charlotte."

So a meal of some sort anyhow was ready, and over-ready, when I at last heard the sound of people rising and chairs scraping back in the study, and voices exchanging curt and chilly farewells. Two calls at the door had filled in the time, as one man was drunk and wouldn't go, and the other in search of a job which asked apparently no skill and no credentials.

Arthur came in looking so exhausted that I went to the book-shelf and took out *Mr. Mulliner Speaks*. I propped this against the water-jug for him, and *Wild Strawberries* by Angela Thirkell, which I have read thirty times already and will probably read thirty more, against the loaf for myself. There is nothing so good for worried people as to read at their meals, and funny books if possible; for laughter grows so rusty in war time. It wasn't till we were settled by the study fire over coffee that he looked up at me and laughed a little. "We are to be martyrs for our opinions, Camilla dear! Mr. Weekes brought a message from Mrs. Weekes that, all things considered, we had better not go to lunch with them on Thursday. They want to consult with the Archdeacon alone!"

"What a good thing I didn't get myself a hat!" was all I let myself say, though I could have said much, much more. "Tell me what happened at your meeting."

"Nothing, or nothing that brings us any nearer a decision," said Arthur, rumpling his hair. "Do you know, I sometimes think this drama, or something like it, must be going on all over Europe. Personally I believe we have all reached one of those points where political and religious thinking can't be separated. When the Emperor Julian said, 'Thou hast conquered, O Galilean!' when the Middle Ages saw the twin keys of Saint Peter in the care of the Empire and the Papacy; when the French mob cast down the Cross and raised the goddess of reason, you get such moments. The soul and the political instinct of man are for the moment identified; though, of course," added my cautious husband, "I use those terms very loosely."

"But surely people do always put their religion into politics," I said. "When I was small I know I always imagined from my father's breakfast-table talk that Gladstone was a sort of devil. My nurse used to leave me in the dining-room while he and grannie had breakfast, and one day grandfather threw the paper down and cried, 'My God, he's in again!' and I thought he meant the devil was inside the house, probably, I imagined, in the grandfather clock!"

"Yes, yes," said Arthur, sighing a little. I knew he wished Dick were back so that they could laugh at me together for always bringing the general down to the particular.

"Politicians have always differed; the Churches have fought their un-Christian battles; but it is only at certain moments, it seems to me, that every thinking man is dragged into their disputes, and has to see himself on one side or another of an impassable gulf. Can a man call himself a Christian and a Bolshevik to-day? How long can the Papacy tolerate totalitarianism? Can we turn the left cheek to Germany, and let it smite us and our Colonies, as Strang holds Christ would bid us, and trust that, not only the Church but Christianity and the Christian ethic, will survive? It's that which is really at the bottom of this Strang business," he added, turning to me affectionately. "Like you, dearest, I must leave the general principles to consider the particular case in point."

"What does Mr. Weekes want you to do?" I asked, encouraged thus to descend to the details I wanted to know. "He wants me to report Strang to the Bishop through the Archdeacon, and to repudiate his views very strongly to the whole congregation on Sunday morning. And when I went round to see Strang, to have yet another talk with him before I see Pratt, I was told he was very far from well and could see no one."

"Did you see Mrs. Strang?"

"No, I sent in a message, but she sent an answer that she could not leave her husband."

"I must run in to-morrow morning to see if I can be of any use, I suppose," I said, with some depression.

"No, no, I met Boness on the way home, and he says he'll probably send in a nurse and it would be wrong for you to run any risk of infection after the fright you gave me last year." (Arthur always refers to my fairly sharp attack of 'flu as if it had been a critical illness.) "I wish I could have seen him and persuaded him that, though he was perfectly right to urge peace upon us all, if he felt it his duty, he really had not thought out his political position seriously enough. Is that the telephone?"

It was the telephone, and though Arthur loves me, provides for me adequately, and would certainly die for me, it is an unwritten law that I answer the telephone for him. He is, says Dick, like most men of his age, really afraid of the beastly thing. I don't mind the convention in the least now, as I am always convinced that it is a telegram from the War Office, saying that something is wrong with Dick. It always rings with diabolical cunning just about ten o'clock when I am warm and happy at last. However, this evening it was only a wrong number, so, by some wholly inconsistent mental process of my own, I felt absolutely reassured of Dick's safety, and in spite of all the worries of the day, went off relieved to bed.

IV
WEDNESDAY MORNING

THERE WAS A letter from Dick waiting for us when we got back from Early Service in a cold, grey mist, and Kate was waiting with it, beaming all over, in a way which makes it impossible for me to mind that she obviously hadn't done the stairs, or means to wash the front doorstep. The delay is explained by the fact that he has had mild 'flu ("and ha! ha! who never guessed it?"), and is now "only suffering from what the medical profession call"—(I flung open the middle page in horror)—"that bloody awful feeling!" Arthur laughed at my face, but predicted that the regimental doctor will never, probably, become a leading ladies' specialist.

Dick's next item of news was even more startling. "I took Ida Weekes to our local cinema last night. You know she's cook in a camp near here? We were discussing leave, as we'd like to be at home together at the same time about Easter, and she's pretty sure she can get hold of some petrol and motor me up."

The Weekes' only daughter is just about nineteen, as I said, and having finished with Roedean, Domestic Economy and Paris, had just come home to have a good time and civilize her parents in September 1939. Then she had, I knew, gone off on volunteer jobs, but I hadn't realized exactly what. She is a tall, golden-haired athletic girl, and I have always thought her charming and delightful; but Dick's letter is startling because for the six years of our life in Stampfield he has consistently referred to Ida as a pie-face, and wriggled out of every invitation of the Weekes if he could possibly manage it. It is at these moments that one does long for a female friend to whom one can repeat one's ejaculations and surmises ten times in slightly different words, and with whom one can discuss whether Brussels lace veils are still worn—for I have kept my wedding one so carefully—with whom one can go upstairs and have a good look at the drawers of baby-clothes. As it is, I was making the best of Arthur for these confidences, in spite of his placid remark that Dick and Ida showed no signs of anything but ordinary neighbourliness, and that he didn't see old Weekes allowing his only daughter to have anything to do with a penniless subaltern, not just now at any rate.

"But don't", he added, as he saw my face fall, "begin to weep at the prospect of a Montague and Capulet feud here, or imagine that poor Strang has wrecked two young lives. They can dispense with balconies and friars and vaults quite well, you know, and get married without any old Nurse in Colchester, if indeed, as I refuse to believe, they have the faintest idea of doing so."

The telephone bell rang and when, after an interval, Arthur returned, I was just deciding that Kate could be asked to do the nursery if Ida's nurse wouldn't mind carrying up meals for herself and the baby.

So I certainly deserved to be recalled to ordinary life again.

"That was Strang asking if he might preach instead of me at the Mid-day Service to-day," Arthur said, rumpling up his nice thick hair. "He says he will undertake to explain his position and put an end to what he calls 'the certain tension one feels about one'. I really didn't know what to say! I can't manage to see him, for I've got my class in the schools and my hospital visits later."

"What did you say?"

"That I'd let him have a line later. May Heaven forgive me for a want of charity, but I can't bear to have him spluttering on the telephone again so soon. And anyhow he has to go to a call-box you see. I wonder—"

"Whether I could leave a note?" I suggested, gloomily.

"Well, I must confess that was rather my idea," admitted Arthur.

"But what are you going to say?"

"Well, what? I should be quite glad not to preach because I gather Weekes and Co. are all going to look in in the hope of hearing me stand up and deliver a smashing attack on the enemy. I wasn't going to, of course, but it would enable me to stand back and let Strang make peace on his own account!"

"If he will!" I protested, hopelessly.

"I had only meant myself to speak about tolerance, and respect for the point of view of one's opponents, in such a way that both sides might take it to heart. It wouldn't do any good, I know, and it might conceivably be better to let Strang try again. I wonder if by any chance you could just see him for a moment and try to hint—it wouldn't seem too official, you know!"

"He might think it officious!" I protested, though I knew, of course, that I would do anything to help Arthur. "Perhaps if I saw Mrs. Strang—"

"I don't suppose she bullies him as you bully me," said Arthur most unjustly, with a beaming smile. "But if you don't mind delivering an ultimatum! I was so taken aback by the suggestion on the telephone."

"Telephones weren't meant for philosophers who always say 'yes *and* no'," I agreed. "It would save a lot of time if people didn't ring you up. Write your epistle to Strang and I'll deliver it with my truncheon, only agree I don't bully you!"

"Only for my good, Mrs. Proudie dear," replied Arthur, meekly, picking up Dick's letter again.

I had to leave him, for loud thumps were coming from upstairs, and I ran up to discover, to my surprise, that Kate was turning out the drawing-room. It is one of my very minor regrets that we don't use the room more, as it is the largest and pleasantest in the house. From the side bow-window you can catch a glimpse of a little orchard behind a nursery garden at the end of the street, and its white walls and (rather torn) matting on the floor give one a feeling of a country home. But the big windows and small fire-place make it almost un-inhabitable in cold weather, even if Kate and I could spare time for the work which a third sitting-room on the first-floor entails. Kate, of course, approves of the idea of having a "best room" which is seldom used. I don't know that she cares for the rather nice marquetry desk and chairs I inherited from my old home, and she thinks the three Indian rugs and old frail damask curtains might well be replaced by "one of them nice Ax. squares and something light in cretong" which she had in her last place; but as she loves an Occasion she invests it, I think, with a sort of respect, and was once heard to refer to my rather cracked old Coalport china as "airlooms" in a rebuke to Dick. She was busy balanced on a table with the feather brush when I looked in, and was evidently enjoying herself.

"Is it worth doing the drawing-room to-day, Kate?" I asked. "I'm in rather a hurry, and we must do the beds now—and I hadn't meant to use it this afternoon."

"Best be ready," said Kate, leaping down with a heavy thud and preparing to follow me. "I thought I'd put a fire on in case Mrs. Weekes dropped in this afternoon. You're in at tea-time, aren't you?"

"Mrs. Weekes?" I murmured feebly.

"Yes. I slipped into Weekes's last night for a minute or two to borrow a jumper-pattern. Of course, I'm not one to gossip, but I couldn't help hearing the remarks passed. Well, in my opinion, I said, Mr. Dick could do better for himself, not but what I've always thought Miss Ida seemed pleasant-spoken enough, and the girls there always have a good word for her."

I resisted the temptation to inquire into the perfection of the espionage system in the Weekes' household; it could hardly have been in ours, as I don't believe Kate either could or would have steamed open Dick's letter this morning; I merely said that anyone who married Miss Weekes would, I was sure, be a very lucky man.

"Yes, she's a nice girl and handy about the house, they say," agreed Kate, pleasantly. "But I said we'd look very high for Mr. Dick!"

"What nonsense, Kate!" I protested, indignantly. "Sometimes I think that all that matters to a man is to marry someone who's good-natured and knows how to cook."

"Better than the flashy kind or one of them typists," agreed Kate. "When people go on clucking about these mothers of evacuees I always say it stands to reason that a girl out of a factory or shop or office isn't likely to make much of a job of her house or her kids."

"No," I agreed, glad to reach this safer topic. "They can't have much experience of house-keeping."

"Not a wink, and worse than that if you know what I mean," said Kate, tucking in the blankets ferociously. "With them at their jobs it's all clock in and clock out, and then off to paint themselves up and go to the pictures or a dance. Very nice too, but stands to reason you can't treat your husband or kids that way. There's no clocking-off about a house, I says only yesterday to Private Jenkins. It's work day in and day out for me here."

"But you do get some time off, Kate," I said, with a sinking heart at this gloomy picture. "After lunch, for instance, and in the evenings, because we don't take long over supper, and I always say you can wash up next morning."

"Oh, yes, I'm not complaining. I'm not a Lil Sime, thank Heaven! I takes my time off as I finds it. And I often thinks when I'm having a good sit-down with the *Herald* after lunch with my feet on a chair, that I wouldn't like to be in Dykes', saying 'Change please!' and 'This yellow's just the shade, Moddam' with the Irish stew barely down my throat; the food they give those girls who live in is something chronic. I don't make a song about only popping in and popping out as suits all parties, but it comes hard on these girls as have only worked by the clock, and that's why their kids aren't house-trained and get the itch and worse. It's what Private Jenkins says to me; these business girls have never had to think of anyone but Number One, and a man would rather have a well-cooked bit of steak than see his girl working an hour to make her nails look as if she'd dipped them in blood. I tell him he's proper old-fashioned, but there's something in it if you know what I mean. That's what's wrong at Strangs'," concluded Kate, collecting the hot-water bottles and shoes and turning to the door. "She doesn't half make that poor little Doris of hers slave away, and if Doris asks as much as to pop out for a penny stamp she'll say it's not her time 'Off Duty' as is printed up on the kitchen wall above the boiler. Don't give me time-tables in a house, says I! Give me plenty of give and take!"

It was quite true, I thought, as I hurried off to the Curate's, after a review of the kitchen, which showed that Private Jenkins and Kate together had certainly taken a good deal of my bread and margarine and cake last night. Business life is not the best preparation for a home-maker, though better, probably, than the busy pursuit of having a good time which was just as much a preoccupation of girls of my period as the much abused modern young. I am quite sure that in the impoverished world of the future every wise young man will look for a wife who can manage a home cheerfully and competently. Old incompetents like myself, with nothing to recommend us but a vague tradition of being ladies, must certainly vanish off the face of the earth very soon. Any girl of any class, with energy and a taste for bettering herself, has nowadays all the standards of personal cleanliness and toilet-care, of accent and good manners which were once the prerogative of one class only. And all that survives of birth and breeding as distinguishing marks are, on the essential side, courage, self-control, honesty and unselfishness (and plenty of "real ladies" are wanting in these) and in non-essentials, a whole set of taboos in manner and speech which vary from one generation to another. The other day I saw one of the tough, tweed-coated County girls who condescend to come into Stampfield for imperative shopping, run round a corner almost into the arms of Alice, Miss Grieve's pretty, demure, fair little cook. Miss de Freyne only glared and whistled for her spaniel while Alice stopped and murmured, "Pardon me!" And yet, so ingrained are our silly prejudices that I myself, I suppose, and most of my friends would prefer the former to the latter as a wife for our sons; we should put down the stony glare to absent-mindedness, and we would hate to welcome someone who said, "Pardon me", or "granted". Let us hope any coming social revolution will end our follies, for there really can be nothing more fatuous than the tiny almost invisible caste divisions of old-fashioned England. Surely in the dark times of the future only the very best of the old ideals of ladyhood will survive, I told myself as I turned into Byng Butts. But I wish I hadn't remembered, even before I reached Number 24, a story of a French aristocrat who climbed the guillotine-steps in a fury because a lawyer's wife had had the *pas*, and lost her head before he did. (That was a story from a great-grandmother of ours who was only just rescued from the tumbril by an American friend and protector, but I hope it wasn't really true!)

The Strangs have a convenient but very tiny bungalow in this new little street. It must have been Doris's time "On Duty" for though Mrs. Strang must have seen me from the window on one side, and Mr. Strang on the other, I had to stand shivering in the cold raw mist for five minutes before the poor breathless little maid appeared, very grubby except for the clean cap which Mrs. Strang had sent her to fetch, in a whisper which was quite audible to me outside the door. I was ushered into the dining-room, where Mr. Strang sat, trying to write, at a table still covered with breakfast things. The poor little man looked dreadfully cold and ill, I thought, and I feel miserably sure that Mrs. Strang does not give him enough to eat. As with so many girls who have lived in shops and offices, her values are all wrong. She looks on so many things for show as necessities which seem to me merely luxuries. In them I include permanent waves, a weekly visit to the pictures, cosmetics and cigarettes. She is so young and pretty that it is quite easy to understand, but I met her once at the hairdresser's bewailing that she couldn't afford a nice steak for Herbert on their income, and she had obviously spent the price of it on a set. But I rebuked myself severely for a critical, grizzled old lady when she came in now, delightfully fresh and trim, with her quite adorable baby, Pamela, of five months old. Needless to say, Pamela is being brought up on a modern system, infinitely superior to anything I ever knew, and has never given any trouble, by night or day, all her little life. Every mother should be glad to know that I repressed my vehement longing to say, "Wait till she begins teething", and sat looking as old-world and incompetent as young mothers like.

Pamela grinned and gurgled, and I should have enjoyed her if Mr. Strang hadn't grown more and more like an Irish terrier (though a sick one) as he read Arthur's letter, and anyone who grows pugnacious over my husband must be a confirmed case of militancy. Nothing would have induced me to offer him my opinion unasked, but Mrs. Strang was only too anxious evidently to gain an opportunity to present her own.

"I do think it's so wrong of people here, Mrs. Lacely, don't you, to dare to criticize Herbert like they do? As if a priest hadn't the right to tell his people of their duty!"

"One often fails to find sympathy," said Herbert, looking at me under his eyebrows pugnaciously. "I gather from this letter, Mrs. Lacely, that one is not to preach unless one is to consider oneself positively muzzled!"

"I think my husband is very anxious to avoid any further strife in the parish," I said, trying not to let myself dwell on the exquisite appropriateness of a muzzle for Mr. Strang. "You must see his point of view, as he's nothing but a pacifist over all this."

"A pacifist is not one who makes peace with evil," snapped Mr. Strang.

"No, but peace can only be maintained by compromise, everywhere, I'm sure you'll agree," I said. "And I know it must pain you to realize that you hurt the feelings of those whose relations are serving their country."

"We are all serving our country," said Mr. Strang, austerely.

The worst of the Strangs of this world is that when they air their views the listener suddenly discovers, welling up from his subconscious self, the Saint Crispin speech of good King Harry and the poems of Newbolt and Kipling set to the music of a Guards' band and the waving of banners. However, instead of squaring my shoulders and saying, "'Pon my soul!" I replied mildly that in that case Mr. Strang must surely make allowance for capitalists and town councillors, and try not to spread the war all over the home front.

"I don't see why," broke in Mrs. Strang. "I'm sure everyone here has a spite against my husband!"

"Hush, dear one," said Herbert, looking a little ashamed of his wife. "If it were true, I should only wish to return evil with good. One would never stoop to criticize others for their personal feelings. It is my cause alone for which I speak."

"Then you don't feel you can preach to-day?" I asked, anxious to come to any conclusion.

"I cannot accept your husband's offer. No, I cannot. To tell you the truth, it surprises me that he should make it."

"You don't look as if you should preach, anyhow," I said, with a pang of pity for the little man as he collapsed into a chair. "You look to me as if you'd got the 'flu, Mr. Strang."

"Herbert never spares himself," said his wife, aggressively. "He was out till I don't know when last night at the Boys' Club."

"I thought everything shut early in the black-out," I said, looking at the curate really apprehensively. He had gone terribly white and was shivering uncontrollably.

"One was delayed getting home," he said, his teeth chattering audibly, and I really felt rather alarmed.

"Do put him to bed and take his temperature, Mrs. Strang,"
I urged. "It was so wet last night, he should have got home
quickly."

"There was a good deal of horse-play, and I mislaid the
key," said Mr. Strang between his shivers, and I made haste to
say good-bye and get away, promising to ring up the doctor
for Mrs. Strang at once, as she escorted me to the door.

"He looks so ill," she said, with frightened eyes, "and I really know nothing about nursing, Mrs. Lacely."

By great good luck I met Dr. Boness on my way home, as
one may often seek for him in vain in these busy days, and he
agreed with me that it might be a good plan to ask the District
Nurse to look in.

"You know what happened, of course?" he asked. "Tell it
not in Gath, but two of the big lads who are waiting to be
called up got hold of some story that he'd preached against
the Army in church. There was a rowdy gathering, and the
little brutes locked poor Strang into the hall at the end of the
evening and went off with the key. I got all this from my gardener this morning. He heard his boy and another laughing
over it when they got home, and he walked them back to let
Strang out. He says he's going to report 'em to your husband,
though he doesn't hold with that Strang all the same. Well,
well, I'll have every opportunity to give the poor fellow cool-
ing draughts now, anyway. How's my friend Dick?"

"Very well, thanks. But you know," I couldn't help adding,
"what seems to me so pathetic about the whole business is
that I can't help feeling this is the first sermon which ever
attracted any attention in Stampfield!"

"True, O King!" said Dr. Boness, who combines his sister's
love for *clichés* with her indefatigable devotion to duty, and
drove off at once to the curate's little house. I rushed off to
the shops with my string bag, gave Arthur the news about Mr.
Strang, rang up Colonel Greenley and got a grumpy promise
about the Convalescent Home, did the other odd jobs I'd un-

dertaken yesterday with the Food Control and the Post Office, and arrived, a little out of breath, at the one meeting before me this morning, that of the Parochial Guild Committee in the church hall at 11.30.

The Parochial Guild was instituted in the dear old days by our predecessor, with the object of bringing the congregation together socially in friendly meetings, and encouraging the laity to work in the; parish. It is, I think, an excellent institution for drawing lonely strangers into a circle of friends, and awakening a sense of responsibility for the Church among the laity. Arthur and John Hay did their best to encourage it and make it a self-governing body, and though the difficulties of the black-out, and the dispersal of many of our members, have curtailed its activities, we are hoping that it will do something in the summer. As a result of the Guild meetings, Mr. Elgin and Miss Croft started a Musical Club; there is a Hiking Club for young people; members with cars undertake to drive the elderly or invalids to church services, and it is extraordinary how popular this form of vicarious churchgoing proves to be. The members used to organize all the various choir and club outings, and took a lot of work off the shoulders of the clergy and their wives. Sometimes it seems almost as strange to think that distant continental crimes and aspirations should crush out such little institutions, as that youth should march away from us in uniforms. The Guild seems so remote from, so innocent of, the whole world tragedy, yet already the loss of John Hay and his many young friends in this town has meant that this committee, too, has fallen into the hands of old hacks, like Miss Boness and myself. As energy and enthusiasm will probably be wanting, the Guild itself will lose its old character. I have persuaded Miss Henly to take an interest in it, but of course she cannot get off on morning committees. Miss Croft and Mr. Elgin will struggle to preserve the Musical Society. For the rest, there in the parish hall sat Miss Boness, Miss Cookes and Miss Grieve. Not Mrs. Weekes, I was relieved to see, as I feared she might wish to probe me about Dick's friendship with Ida. Mr. Strang naturally could not attend, and dear Miss Croft, who has enthusiasm and energy enough to make anything a success if only she were a little less eccentric and muddle-headed, was of course away at the cousin's funeral.

I was glad to realize, from the expressions on the faces of the committee, that the Strang affair had already been discussed pretty thoroughly before my appearance. "And I say it serves him right," Miss Grieve was saying with the ferocity which sits so strangely on her gentle pussy face, while Miss Cookes, in a blue dress with a slightly soiled Armenian lace collar, was shaking her head.

"But, as Livingstone said," she was beginning, when Miss Boness interrupted her.

"Youth will be served," she enunciated drastically, as they all turned to me. "Ah, welcome wanderer at last! We hoped you would come soon, as we were all saying we must look in at the Mid-day Service to-day. Now that clouds hang so heavy about the parish, all of us are ready to rally round the dear Vicar with a cheer!"

"But not in church," I protested evasively. "I'm so sorry if I'm late, but we haven't much to arrange this month, have we? There's the Guild Service in Holy Week, of course, but the first Guild Meeting isn't till Easter week, is it? As everything is so unsettled, my husband feels we can hardly suggest any definite spring programme before then."

"I do *not* see", broke in Miss Cookes, "why Mr. Strang's views should interfere with our activities!" Miss Cookes has always suspected Mr. Strang of having no interest in missionary work as compared with British social questions, and her long-simmering hostility was on the surface to-day.

"No, no, I meant the War," I hastened to explain.

"Or Hitler," persisted Miss Grieve.

Miss Boness, as chairman, rapped the table violently, and we all became a committee at once. I was asked to say a prayer, with the usual disastrous result that I began on one Collect and ended with another, well as I know them all, in a discreet mumble, and we hastened through the minutes of the last meeting, and signed the accounts, with the importance and severity of a Cabinet meeting at least. It is only when we study the agenda on these occasions that femininity intervenes again.

The Easter Meeting is a gala occasion, followed by tea, and in a minute we were all discussing the attitudes of our grocers to the sugar question, listening respectfully to and, in Miss Boness's case, writing down, a receipt for apricot and pineapple jam made with glucose. The question of Ceylon tea involved an interesting account of the adventures of Miss Grieve's nephew's wife's friend on her voyage to India, and it was a quarter to one before we had done with the best way of spreading marge for sandwiches. At this moment, Miss Grieve remembered that Miss Henly had written to suggest that the Guild should make use of her new canteen for that one evening, a labour-saving device which we all hailed so warmly that no-one was rude enough to comment on the time we had wasted in planning a tea-party. "Now about our spring programme," said Miss Boness. "I wonder if Mrs. Strang would perhaps help us to organize a little Study Circle? You've heard, I suppose, Mrs. Lacely, all about this unfortunate affair at the Boys' Club?"

"Yes, indeed," I said, as repressively as I dared. "I think if we have any Study Circle, Miss Henly should organize it, though, don't you? She has such knowledge and experience."

"I suppose he won't preach as his leg is broken," was Miss Croft's only reply.

"But it's not!" I said. "Why, I saw him just before I came here."

There was a little chorus of "And is he?"—"And will he?" which made me feel rather desperate, so I asked Miss Grieve what she thought of the news from Finland. As Miss Grieve has a brother who intended once to go to Helsinki, though an

attack of influenza unluckily detained him in Oslo, the minutes passed quickly, until Miss Boness seized the opportunity
of a sneeze from Miss Grieve to ask eagerly, "Then will he
preach to-day?"

"Oh, no. He has a very bad chill, I fear. I left your brother
on his way to the house."

"Dear, dear," said Miss Boness. "Under-feeding, you may
be sure. My Helen tells me that their butcher's bill …"

"Well, we'll all have small butcher's bills when rationing
comes in," I said, flinging down this red herring, if you can call
meat a red herring, hopefully.

"Do you approve of Pacifism, Mrs. Lacely?" demanded
Miss Grieve, scattering that hope to the winds. All the rest of
the committee bent forward earnestly in their chairs, and I realized that the thing which was exciting the parish even more
than Mr. Strang's gauntlet was the way in which my husband
intended to handle that tiresome, mischievous glove.

"There are so many sides to every question, aren't there?"
was the best I could do, in a truly Arthurian manner. "I read",
I added with a sudden inspiration, "such an interesting book
called *Europe Must Unite*. The motto of the New League is
to be, *In necessariis unitas, in dubiis, libertas, in omnibus caritas*. I
suppose that charity is the most important of all." (Long, long
ago I discovered the value of any quotation in any foreign
language in a stormy debate. While people are translating, or
not translating it, to themselves, one can change the subject,
and I tried to do so rapidly in the little pause.) "We can't really
settle any more without Mrs. Weekes, can we? She is so good
and helpful."

"I suppose you know they are inquiring about sittings in
the parish church?" Miss Boness's voice implied that she might
not understand Latin, or might not get anything out of me
about my husband's views, but could deal me a good straight
blow if she felt I needed it.

"That would be very sad," I answered, politely. Really, of course, it would be almost the end of every parochial charity and institution, for Mr. Weekes is one of the very few and the only generous wealthy member of our congregation. "But I think we should wait till it really happens, and now I am going to run across to church."

I always tell Arthur that I suffer far more for him than he does for himself. When I saw how full the church was, and felt to my finger-tips the attitude of expectancy and criticism my heart ached for my husband, and I longed to rise up suddenly and tell them all how I hated them for mistrusting and criticizing him, as well as his firebrand of a curate, over the burning question of the day. Could they not understand how Arthur must preserve his loyalty to a colleague in public, even if he reproved his curate in private? I hid desperately behind my pillar, only looking out again and again to mark the back views of Mr. Weekes, Colonel Greenley, Mr. Chubb and all our lady workers. Oh yes, they were all there! And they had all come hoping to hear Arthur disown Mr. Strang and pacifism and labour views in no measured terms, and well I knew they would hear nothing of the kind.

They did not. My dearest Arthur, with the most lively sympathy told us that he knew how worried we had always been by the translation in the vulgate of the Graeco-Aramaic phrase *Καɩ γαρ ουν*, (or words to that effect). It would be his task this morning to try to make things a little clearer for us all.

On such occasions I always feel that the Church has not lost all its influence over the laity. Almost everyone in the congregation must have wanted to get up and go away, as Arthur traced the source of worry back to Q., and urged us to consider the apocalyptic literature of the close of the first century. Did those who knew my husband perhaps realize, I wondered, as I did, that this was no evasion of Arthur's, no cowardly way of escape from controversy? Arthur, I could be sure, had looked over his address with the idea of exchanging it for some remarks on the epic of the day, and then had become so much interested in his theological point that he had forgotten all about Mr. Strang. Or hadn't he? For he was now saying, "But that brings me to another point which must be occupying all your thoughts this morning—"

Everyone sat up, and I felt hot and cold shivers running up and down my spine, and then I was conscious, for a moment, of a great and absurd relief. It was the gallant struggle of Finland against Russia that Arthur was speaking of, with all his heart in his voice. And once more I felt hot and cold with shame to think how our petty parochial difficulties had absorbed me this morning, and so many of us. Nero at least, I told myself, made music while Rome was burning, while we are out making discords at our pump while Vipori is in flames. How right of Arthur to ignore it all—or was he not perhaps ignoring it all in his conclusion. … "The literature of the childhood of our nation circled round the story of the little hero, Jack, in his struggle against the giants of this world. To-day we watch that conflict in Europe, and our hearts are all on the side of the little hero against the giant cowardly bully. But let us remember that any majority is likely to unite in any of its opinions as an unwieldy, stupid giant, and that we may not always recognize the small hero, the common man, who ventures to tilt against our giant prejudices and ignorance. The moral of Jack's tale is not only to admire the hero who stands up against overwhelming odds. It is also for us to have a care that we do not present ourselves as giants of self-sufficiency against those who raise their voices to decry what they consider to be abuses. Every stump orator on an orange-box is, in some sense, a follower of the great little national hero, and if we are still to value chivalry and freedom of speech, we must let him have his say instead of feeling for the dub at our belt."

My thoughts wandered as Arthur finished up with a return to his original theme, and we all stood up to sing for God's forgiveness on foes who are backward driven (so much easier to achieve than for those who are still advancing), and we all knelt down to pray. It was ominous, I felt, that he and I made our way back to the Vicarage so easily, when as a rule so many people stop us for a chat. Miss Harris, our District Nurse, alone pursued me and caught my arm.

"Do go into Number 3, Queen's Court, this afternoon if you can," she said. "We've had to arrange to have poor old Granny Hodge moved away to the Infirmary to-morrow. Yes, she's taken a turn for the worse, as this sclerosis often does, and she can't move herself any more, and the others aren't up to looking after her and moving her."

Nurse Harris is a fairy-tale Jack, pushing about briskly on her bicycle in her campaign against the giants of Dirt and Disease. It would be impossible to tell what our little homes owe to women like her, and their ceaseless, cheery efficiency. She is kindheartedness itself, and I knew she would never have Granny Hodge moved from her little room in our Almshouses unless it were absolutely necessary. For if the ten old women who live in its precincts enjoy harmless quarrels among themselves when all is well, they are solid as an army against any intruder like Death or the hated summons to the Infirmary.

"Is she minding dreadfully?" I asked.

"Yes, and she wanted to see you. She said, 'Her's one as'll understand. Her's another as likes to be left alone.'"

"Oh dear! Poor Mrs. Hodge and Finland and shepherd's pie!" I said when at last we sat down to lunch at two o'clock.

"Small troubles are a great help in war-time," suggested Arthur. "They fill the foreground of one's mind, and enable one to keep a sense of perspective. Let us grumble cheerfully over Kate's failure and forget the rest!"

"But I read somewhere that Napoleon lost the battle of Leipzig because he ate greasy sole the day before," I protested, trying to be as sensible as Arthur. Living in war-time is rather like skirting the edge of a bottomless pit. The least slip over some tiny obstacle may make one lose one's footing and sink into the black gulf of despair awaiting you. "Suppose this pie makes you unable to cope with the Strang affair?"

"I've no coping to do till I go to the Hardy Committee after tea. I suppose I may hear some more complaints there, but the whole thing must die down very soon," said Arthur, so convincedly that I forbore to repeat the gossip at the meeting. Anyhow, the telephone bell rang, and I found Mrs. Pratt asking, in her rich full contralto, if she might come in to tea this afternoon. As Kate will be overjoyed to find that there is a reason for using her best room this afternoon, and as I really like Mrs. Pratt, I was very glad to consent, though I must confess I should have enjoyed a peaceful solitary tea over a new library book better still. Sometimes I feel that Trappist monasteries weren't really founded in any excess of asceticism, but just to fulfil a felt need, a place where the naturally silent might escape from the born talkers. The Church of England is no home for the former class. Scattered through the length and breadth of our unhappy country are those who are quite convinced that the world can be saved by lectures and meetings, discussions and re-unions. To satisfy their lust for speech there must always be an army of patient, silent listeners, seated perpetually in hard rows of chairs enduring the incessant hose-pipe of earnest addresses and talks and sermons. Mrs. Pratt means well, but she is a talker, "and didn't the Greeks", I asked Arthur, as I returned with really good, strong, hot coffee to the dining-room, "say that their best women shouldn't talk?"

"Not to be talked about," amended Arthur. "But Saint Paul suggested we should be silent and mind our own business, you remember."

"Then I'll go and do mine," I said, as I finished my coffee and felt better.

QUEEN'S COURT is one of the few surviving beauty-spots in Stampfield. The little almshouses were built in the reign of Queen Anne by a Sir Humphrey Queyne, whose name and family disappeared when the industrial revolution blackened and ruined the countryside. Stampfield spread its tentacles out over the green fields to the village of Queyne and engulfed the Old Ladies' Home and the park of its benefactor. Sir Humphrey's house was pulled down half a century ago, so only his generous benefaction has kept his name alive.

> *"Only the actions of the just*
> *Smell sweet and blossom in the dust,"*

said Miss Croft to me once, sentimentally, but as a matter of fact Queen's Court is so badly in need of a new sanitary system that one can only take this in a metaphorical sense.

I don't think that the want of modern conveniences troubles the ten old ladies who live in their demure little red brick houses round a pleasant court-yard. After all, as they are mostly round about eighty years of age, they are no worse off than they were in their youth for what Miss Grieve primly calls, "toilet luxuries". Their comfort is far more dependent on the warden, who occupies the gate-house, rent free, and receives a salary of two pounds a week for looking after the inmates. The post is one which is eagerly sought after when it falls vacant. All the families in England, one might imagine, says Arthur, look on it as a heaven-sent opening for their decrepit and disagreeable relatives. But the Cousin Janes and Aunt Evelyns who competed so vigorously for the post seldom stayed very long. Either the quarrels and sicknesses of the old women, or the rather invidious position of being half in, yet half in charge of, the almshouse was too much for them, and they always aroused the most bitter opposition by petty rules and interference. Arthur was largely instrumental, I think, in getting

quite a different type of woman at the last vacancy. Mrs. Hill
is a good, kind, honest widow of their own sort, and instead
of brooding over the little jealousies and troubles which must
arise, laughs heartily and tells them it will be all the same a
hundred years hence. I don't know why this is so soothing in
the case of those who haven't more than a tenth of that time
to live at the most, but I have seen her administer this form
of spiritual consolation with the best result. Should Arthur, I
wondered, as I turned in at the little wicket-gate, have used
that as the text of his sermon this morning? Would it be my
best panacea for the War, I wonder, and murmur:

> "There is a great deal to be said
> For being dead."

as Mrs. Hill rattles with her old bolt and handle of lovely Sussex iron-work.

"Well, it's lucky you've come!" she declared, cheerfully.
"Poor old Mrs. Hodge was asking for you this morning, and
I doubt if she'll last the night. She was taken awfully bad an
hour ago, and Doctor and Nurse have both been out. It's gone
to her heart muscles, the paralysis, they say, and she's pretty
near unconscious already."

"Poor old thing," I ventured, hardly knowing how to treat
Mrs. Hill's loud cheerful diagnosis.

"Well, it's all for the best, and she knows it," said Mrs. Hill,
wiping her hands on a rough towel, her smile as cheerful as
ever. "I couldn't bring myself to think of her being taken away
in the van! She doesn't really care for anything but her bits of
things and her little home, and she's enough put by for quite a
nice funeral. I asked her if she'd like me to send for the minister—she's a Methodist, you know—but he's not one to hurry
himself! She's always had a fancy for you, Mrs. Lacely."

It was quite true that Mrs. Hodge and I always had a bond
in common. A committee takes it in turn to visit the almshouse monthly, and our friendship began when I took Mrs.

Hodge half a pound of peppermints instead of the packet of tea which is the usual gift. Crunching away with her few remaining teeth, she told me that she did like the smell because it reminded her of church in the country when she was a little girl. And then she told me all about the lovely, lost little Sussex village of her childhood, and we both discovered that we liked solitary places and lonely walks, and sitting alone and cosy by a fire-side. She was quite friendly with the other old dames, and they have been very good to her during her long months of helplessness, "but you can have too much dropping in, and that's a fact," she confided to me, and I heartily agreed with her. I had rather a choke in my throat as Mrs. Hill and I walked along the little paved path, round the beautiful turfed courtyard, with its erect boastful stone statue of Sir Humphrey in wig and top-boots, in the centre; for Mrs. Hodge and I had a bond here I have with no-one else, and some of my happiest hours have been spent in her little room, while I've read her country poems or books, and she has sat gloating over the little mixed posies I brought her. I had managed to beg some scillas and crocuses and snowdrops and aconites from kind Miss Grieve on my way this afternoon, and I was sad to think she might be past caring for them.

But fortunately she was not. She could hardly move her poor hands as she lay in the funny little wooden bedstead in the low-panelled room, but she put a shaking finger on the petals and smiled a little. The room seemed very full, not only with all her queer effects, the cloak and bonnet she hasn't worn for two years, on a peg, the china dogs and faded photographs, the old velvet chair-cushions and shrunk antimacassars. Nurse was there as well, and two old cronies had dropped in, sitting with a touch of interest in the apathetic eyes in their shrunk, shrivelled old faces, as if they were waiting to have a view of the end of a race or the tail of a procession. Nurse and Mrs. Hill turned them out on my arrival, for my sake I expect, but I was very glad to see the relief in Mrs. Hodge's eyes.

"I'm just going to give her a dose," whispered Nurse, "and it's odds if she'll come round again, the doctor says, so I'm glad you've come to say good-bye to her." It wasn't easy to say anything as I looked at the poor, tiny, wizened face, looking so oddly old and so oddly young, as people often do in the presence of death. I had to bend very low to catch the words she could hardly utter.

"They won't take me away?"

"Oh, no, no!" I said. "You're to stay here. That's all settled. Don't worry about that."

Nurse was waiting with a professional air, which showed me that she felt some form of prayer was indicated in case the Methodist minister (a dear, kind, but sadly over-worked man) didn't arrive; so I knelt down and picked up my little bouquet for her to see. But the only words that came to my lips must have seemed terribly inappropriate to Nurse.

> *"The tall trees in the greenwood,*
> *the meadows where we play*
> *The rushes by the water,*
> *we gather every day."*

Mrs. Hodge smiled faintly again, and I knew that she was far away, back again among the primroses and cuckoo flowers of a stream beneath the Downs, on her way to a little grey Sussex church, with wooden beams crossing and recrossing into the darkness of the roof. And then I found my voice a little more securely, and murmured Newman's words: "Oh, God, support us all the day long till the shadows lengthen and the evening comes, and the busy world is hushed and our work is done. Then, God, in Thy mercy give us a safe lodging and a holy rest, and peace at the last."

Nurse gave a loud Amen, and advanced to the bedside. It was nice to see that Mrs. Hodge did not shrink at all (and some efficient women are rough with old people) and only smiled again.

"The river running by," she murmured very low, and drifted away among the rushes and meadow-strife, I felt, on her last journey of all.

"I expect she'll go off in her sleep before morning," said Nurse, packing her bag. "No good for you to stay. It was very nice of you to come, Mrs. Lacely. I'll look in this evening again."

"Nurse," I said, a little desperately, "do you find that anyone is much use to people when they're very ill, or very old, and going to die?"

"Death-beds are clean gone out," replied Nurse, with her usual brisk efficiency, looking round for her thermometer. "That's what medical science has done, and a good thing too. Romans make a point of it still, of course," (Nurse is a confirmed Evangelical) "and very fidgety they are at times; but it's not often a patient knows just when it's coming, as they did in the old story-books. And I've never found myself that illness makes people specially interested in religion. It's how you live not how you die that counts in my experience, Mrs. Lacely. Still," added Nurse; tolerantly, "if her minister does come and pray later on, it won't disturb her, and it'll please the other old ladies."

As I was at Queen's Court I made the rounds of my friends there, reflecting, as I always do, on the sad truth that bores don't like bores, the sick don't like the sick, and the old don't always like the old. It's perfectly natural because we all do like our opposites in everyday life, and would be hideously bored to be segregated with nine other people exactly like ourselves in age, sex and circumstances. And then I don't think that either the sick or the old ever do live quite on a level with other people. They want to be important because of their infirmities; they need someone (unlucky as that someone may be) to tell their friends either how wonderful they are, or how infirm they are, and how can Mrs. Jones impress Mrs. Smith with "my rheumatics" when Mrs. Smith has as much to tell in return about "my bilious trouble"? But, as I say, when one of them is near death or, far worse, the Infirmary, the dear old things are full of interest and sympathy, even if it is of rather a ghoulish kind. Only Mrs. Murphy was cantankerous and rude to-day, and she, I felt, had right on her side.

"I am sure," she said, blinking very rapidly again and again, her claw-like little hands clutching her frayed skirt, "I'm sure I hopes they'll be in time to get My Priest in for me when my time comes. It's well enough for the likes of Mrs. Hodge to pass on with no-one but you beside her, Mrs. Lacely, but it wouldn't suit me."

"Indeed, Mrs. Hill would never fail to send for Father Merrion," I protested. "She has asked Mrs. Hodge's minister to come in, I know. I just came in as a friend to see Mrs. Hodge."

"Mrs. Gilpin says she saw you kneeling alongside of the bed," said Mrs. Murphy, so suspiciously that I found myself assuring her that I would never do the same for her!

"Your last Sacraments are so beautiful and impressive," I added, anxiously. "And indeed, indeed, dear Mrs. Murphy, I was praying, as you do, that all the wonderful roll of Saints and Martyrs would intercede for her soul!"

Mrs. Murphy sniffed, obviously feeling that this would be unlikely in the case of a heretic, and that I had obviously, so to speak, been gate-crashing at the portals of Heaven. But she unbent as far as to say that she was sure I meant well, "though when my time comes", she began, and again and again I reiterated my assurances. It was no business of mine to point out that all the priests in the world could not have called back Mrs. Hodge's mind from those Sussex meadows, or the great yews in the churchyard with the snow- drops below. Or to suggest that our Lady and the Archangels are not perhaps as obsessed by the unhappy division of the Church on earth as Catholics of Mrs. Murphy's persuasion. At the back of my mind was a story of Dorothy Whipple, as a Protestant child at a Convent school, demanding, "Sister, is *God* a Catholic?" and Nurse's tolerant phrase, "fidgety". Meanwhile, I diverted Mrs. Murphy's interest to her pain in her windpipe, a friend of old-standing, which does not, I fear, receive all the attention it deserves from Mrs. Hill. "For she's the worst grumbler of the lot," said Mrs. Hill, briskly, as I said good-bye, "and when she goes on and on about sending for the priest for her, it's all I can do not to say, 'Well, I wish he would come and be done with you!'"

The worst of a busy life is that you have so seldom time to think things out. I walked home with thoughts of new model almshouses, including young people who would, however, have their freedom; on death, and whether our church doesn't insist enough on intercession for a perfect death just because, at the Reformation, a boisterous young England rejected the monkish insistence on it; and on beauties of the Church of Rome, degenerating into the problem of whose son Dick would have been if Arthur had been a Catholic priest and I had married someone else; of the wonderful kindness of the poor to the poor in trouble, and their equally surprising gossip and spite in everyday affairs. All these problems, however, faded before the market clock which showed me I was late for tea, and reminded me that I had still to see about the man for the kitchen washer.

Mrs. Pratt was in the drawing-room when I arrived, and I was glad to see that Kate's work this morning had not been wasted. In the firelight, and that strange dim radiance which often lights up the end of our dull northern days, the white drawing-room, with its rose-coloured curtains and big chairs and shimmering marquetry, really looked, like my tweeds, as if my home had seen better days and was still, to me, best of all.

"But don't you find all this white paint dirties very quickly in a town?" asked Mrs. Pratt, after assuring me, with what I felt unnecessary accuracy, that she had only been waiting thirteen and a half minutes.

"We don't use this room much," I said, trying not to notice, as Kate came in with the tea-pot, that her feet, straight from the coal-house no doubt, were making marks on my matting.

"Of course I think that's such a mistake," said Mrs. Pratt. "I do think it's our duty to our country, especially just now, to keep up our standards of living."

As I couldn't be bothered to ask how the use or disuse of my drawing-room would affect our Forces, I let that pass. My eyes had fallen unfortunately on a sheaf of paper obviously containing flowers, and unluckily Mrs. Pratt caught my glance.

"Those are just a few cyclamens and snowdrops for poor Adela Weekes," she said. "She has had such an anxious time lately. And I know, my dear, that you must be far too busy to have time to arrange flowers." Mrs. Weekes may have had an anxious time (over Dick or Mr. Strang? I asked myself) but she has also plenty of money, a gardener and a hot-house. And I am never, never too busy to do flowers, as Mrs. Pratt knows quite well. So I averted my gaze, and as I rebuked myself for envy, asked with unnecessary sympathy what was wrong with Mrs. Weekes. It was an opening for Mrs. Pratt, of course, but she would find an opening in a steel wall anyhow.

"Poor dear, she says Mr. Weekes can hardly sleep at night for worry. My dear Mrs. Lacely, what is your husband going to do about this dreadful young man?"

"Which?" I asked, very busy with the tea-things. "Do have some sugar—we really have plenty."

"Never in Lent, or at any other time," said Mrs. Pratt severely, if a little inconsistently. "You know quite well, I expect, that I mean this Mr. Strang. You remember, my dear, I always told you that married curates are a mistake!"

"But no-one is objecting to his marriage, surely!" I said, playing for time. "My dear, a curate who marries is one who is going against the advice of the bishops and diocesan clergy, and that makes it certain he will be one of those tiresome people who have views of their own."

As I looked at Mrs. Pratt's firm, brisk long face I felt that the Dillney curates probably have their own views about Mrs. Pratt, if about nothing else.

"Arthur is meeting Mr. Weekes and a few friends after his Confirmation Class to-night," I temporized. "I'm sure he feels that all this unlucky excitement will soon die down."

"He is *not* helping it to die down, I fear," rejoined Mrs. Pratt, looking suspiciously at Kate's sturdy slices of bread-and-butter. "Nor can he be supposed to be doing so when he refers to poor John Weekes as Giant Blunderbore in the parish pulpit."

"But he didn't!" I had to pretend to choke over a crumb at this majestic accusation. "I don't know who's been talking to you about the sermon to-day, but he or she got it all wrong. Arthur was only referring to prejudice and bigotry as giants in Europe to-day. He really didn't mention giant—giant Weekes."

"I always thank Heaven that I have a sense of humour, but it should *not* be applied on the wrong occasions." Mrs. Pratt looked at me severely. "We all know you are flippant, dear Mrs. Lacely, but how can you laugh over an affair which is, I gather, causing serious anxiety in your parish? You know the Archdeacon is lunching with the Weekes's to-morrow, and he is very much afraid that there may be some real trouble over all this if your husband is not very careful."

"I know Arthur is hoping to talk things over with the Archdeacon before lunch to-morrow," I said, notwithstanding that terrible inclination to giggling which besets you when you are tired and have once let yourself go. "Of course he's worried, dear Mrs. Pratt, and of course all he wants is to see his duty clearly on this occasion. But it's not all so simple, is it? I mean, in the abstract, you'd never approve of the laity dictating to the clergy, would you?"

That was, perhaps, a little rash, but it brought Mrs. Pratt up short for a minute.

"Not in an ordinary way, of course, but in this case Mr. Strang was not speaking as a priest, I consider. Not one of our clergy is a pacifist!"

"My dear!" I cried. "What about the Bishop of X? What about dear Dick Sheppard, and …"

Mrs. Pratt raised her hand to stop me. "None of the clergy in this Archdeaconry!" she said, firmly. "Or at least they ought not to be. Why the Archdeacon most beautifully referred to our fighting forces as Crusaders some time ago, you may remember, and said we too were Crusaders when we followed them in prayer."

I do remember, because Dick was at home and said at lunch that he'd give anything to see the dear Old Arch, in armour on a palfry, and Mrs. Pratt as a camp-follower behind, and that they'd quite enough equipment to lug about without being issued with a Government Red Cross apiece. ("And that's right, Master Dick," chimed in Kate most unsuitably. "Jenkins passed the remark 'No bl—, I beg your pardon—Cross for him,' he says.") Arthur always says that the few months he passed in the ranks, before he would consent to a commission, gave him a view of the average lay mind which no parson should be without, and my mind wandered now to the happy possibilities of an interview between Mrs. Pratt and Private Jenkins, while she went on:

"It's not as if Mr. Strang preached peace as a duty of all Christians, I gather. He obtruded all his dreadful Radical views." (Mrs. Pratt still refers to the Labour Party in this way.) "And spoke in praise of Russia too, I gather! Russia! If he had been the Archdeacon's curate—"

What a Sunday supper there would have been at the Rectory! The picture of Mrs. Pratt's oratory over the cold blancmange dazzled me again, but still I tried to throw oil on the waters.

"He's very young, you know, and very earnest, and if his views are mistaken, it's all the more important not to let him feel like a martyr if he's taken the wrong way."

"Taken the wrong way! As Adela Weekes says, I wonder you did not rise and walk out of the church!" protested Mrs. Pratt.

"Do you know, you've had nothing to eat," I said, as I could not possibly explain that I would have had to walk in my sleep.

"I think I must leave the whole question to my husband, Mrs. Pratt. I have been very careful to say nothing about it so far, for indeed I don't think it's any business of mine. I suppose the objection to married curates is partly that their wives may make trouble in a parish, and it's the same with vicar's wives, isn't it?"

"I don't agree in the least," said Mrs. Pratt. "It is our duty to stand as rocks behind our husbands" (I hoped this simile was not suggested by one of Kate's stony buns) "and to present a united front. You know as well as I do that the trouble about a curate's marriage is that he's so often led astray by a pretty face in his youth, and makes a quite unsuitable match. I gather that this little Mrs. Strang is *not* what one would really call—"

How one's snobberies get up and stare one in the face! I had been thinking on much the same lines, and yet I felt hot all over now. So I restrained myself from saying, "I expect if we'd lived in Nazareth we wouldn't have called on Joseph's wife," as my grandmother remarked once in rebuke to such a criticism. Also I remembered Dick, as a schoolboy, after one of Mrs. Pratt's visits, asking tolerantly, "And who is the great Lord Pratt?" and felt better.

"I'm quite sure she doesn't influence his views, anyhow," I said, politely. "I think he is very young and very earnest, and is trying to translate the Gospels into modern political life. So he does need our patience and tolerance. I wish," I added, with sudden inspiration, "that you could see him and talk to him yourself, you know. Someone in your position—"

I have never fancied myself as a diplomat, but this remark was an undoubted success. Mrs. Pratt began doing up her fur collar at once, and if I hadn't remembered in time that Mr. Strang was beginning influenza, she would have started on her campaign at once; and serve him right, thought my unregenerate self.

"I'll make that suggestion to Adela myself, and tell her it comes through you, my dear," said Mrs. Pratt. "I know the

Archdeacon thought of visiting him, but he disliked anything that seemed like going behind your husband's authority. But, of course, a woman can often do so much unofficially, and I often think that a woman's, especially a mother's, influence can do so much for a young man. Will you let me know when he is well enough for a little talk? I must be going on now, and I shall be very glad to tell Adela of our little chat. What news have you of Dick?" (Everyone asks this, and no-one ever waits for an answer, I notice. Soldiers aren't news in this war.) "Do you know, I think I must leave you some flowers—I see you haven't any! It was only that I promised to show Adela our new cyclamens, but I'll just take one in my buttonhole."

Do diplomats feel ashamed when they get Foreign Orders they don't deserve? I don't know, but I was more charmed than ashamed to be so well and truly forgiven and I accepted my nosegay shamelessly.

"Still running about as hard as ever?" asked Mrs. Pratt, now in high good humour, because she really loves to do a kindness, and had, I am sure, only meant to discipline me for my good. "Well, I shall see you on Friday, and we shall all have a nice restful day then."

"Friday?" My face and brain registered a blank.

"My dear girl, you can't have forgotten it's the Quiet Day in the old Parish Rectory! You had! But my dear, surely, surely you keep an engagement book. Let's see if you haven't got it down."

Not for worlds would I let Mrs. Pratt see my engagement book. I have never really kept a Diary, but I do put down in the big engagement book which "the Fish" sends every Christmas any date or notice I remember whenever I come across the volume—(it seems to travel by itself all over the house!)—and also, I regret to say, any odd remark which amuses me, or joke or quotation I come across in a book, or any stray event which seems of importance to me. I knew that I had had one of my unexpected re-unions with it on Sunday, and had copied out in it a poem from a review in the *Observer*, and notes like: "Call Mrs. Jones with beads for D.; Remind A. of Higgs; Try catch Lil Sime." Now, too, for the first time I understood what had puzzled me over my entry for Friday: "Whoopee at R." I must have written it under the momentary inspiration of some memory of Dick's usual terminology for such clerical events, and as it had conveyed nothing to me since, and my memory offered no solution, I had been hoping for Friday as a real quiet day at home, with some mending and making up a parcel of cakes and socks for Dick, and an orgy of reading. But it would clearly be as much as my place is worth, clerically, to fail to appear at the Rectory now, so I only told Mrs. Pratt that of course I would be there, and that I remembered now that I had noticed it in my engagement book on Sunday.

"Adela and I sometimes fear you are a little wanting in *method*, you know," said Mrs. Pratt. "I don't think you would look so tired and thin if you planned your days better. I have every hour accounted for in my book from ten in the morning to seven in the evening, so I have no rush or confusion."

I didn't like to make her feel uncomfortable by suggesting that my day usually starts at seven o'clock, but I did protest that engagements don't always last as short a time as one hopes. Punctuality, said Mrs. Pratt, is the politeness of princes, and left me, after prolonged good-byes, on the doorstep, with just five minutes to race to our parish hall for the Quarterly Meeting of the Mothers' Union.

Luckily Miss Boness had been entertaining Mrs. Leny, the speaker, an old school friend, at tea, and a hymn was still in progress, so I hoped my unprincely behaviour would go unnoticed; and when once Mrs. Leny was well under way, I could sit back and feel most of my responsibilities for the day over. My thoughts wandered, and, I fear, I had settled on the vases suitable for Mrs. Pratt's flowers (if only Kate didn't take them and wedge them into something unsuitable), and reflected that the onion soup was ready and that Kate fries fish passably when I have left it ready, before I jerked myself to attention. It would never do if Mrs. Leny were to preach heresies and again I was unable to give any account of them!

She did not preach heresies, but I found myself wishing, as I so often do, that I had provided our quarterly speaker with a more youthful audience. I am sure that it must be my fault that young married women here show so little interest in this admirable society, and I have sometimes a sneaking fear that it is because the grandmothers have dug themselves in so securely that the young naturally feel it a "has been". I inherited from "the dear old days" a Sunday Class of elderly ladies, and they one and all retain their membership in the Mothers' Union, though some of them boast of great-grandchildren. And though I call on the young married women and urge them to join, I am met usually with the reply that they prefer the W.R.I. When I point out that these two admirable societies are not in the least mutually exclusive, they say they'll wait and think it over, but they don't see themselves on a bench alongside of old Mrs. Debb. The few young people who have joined all herd themselves together at the back of the room, so that poor Mrs. Leny, a sweet, earnest, eloquent little woman, was left to urge the sanctity of home life on what seemed to my heated imagination, rows of elderly widows with Old Age Pensions. She omitted, I noticed, a page of notes which contained, probably, advice or prayers for what she had already, I was sorry to note, referred to as "toddlers", and dealt faithfully with the urgency of keeping a note of purity and sanctity in our homes for the sake of our growing daughters. Tell them, she urged, that though men play with fast girls and flirt with giddy girls, yet they *marry* good girls. ("That's an old maid's story," I heard from Mrs. Higgs in a stentorian whisper.)

Mrs. Leny, with supreme tact, passed on to the evensong of our lives, and the influence we may have on our grandchildren. My thoughts at this point reverted sadly, I fear, to the question of a possible nursery in Stampfield Vicarage for

Dick's and Ida's babies, and I only returned when Mrs. Leny, on whom by now the age of the audience was beginning to tell, was picturing the happy moments when, our life's work done, we sat back with our knitting to reflect on the blessings which motherhood had brought into our lives, and how best we could hand them on to the coming generations.

The happy picture of myself in an arm-chair, knitting, to the murmur of:

> *"By still waters they would rest*
> *In the shadow of the tree;*
> *After battle, sleep is best,*
> *After noise, tranquillity,"*

was only disturbed by her sudden appeal to us all to be up and doing, which reminded me of the fish, and I looked anxiously at the clock. Arthur does like fish in batter, and our war-time fish is all the better for this disguise, but I feared this was an unworthy translation of the summons when I found Mrs. Leny had suddenly turned to the subject of Family Prayers. As I was the only person who could possibly hold them, and we don't, because Kate announced that church now and again she could do with, but "set her on her knees in the dining-room and she'd think of nothing but the back door and the bacon", I felt embarrassed and shame-faced. I was losing my feeling of unworthiness as Mrs. Leny made rather a beautiful little peroration about our prayers for our sons and all the sons of mothers all the world over, in war-time, when Mrs. Leaf exclaimed audibly, "S'more shame to Hitler!" and my helpless inclination to giggle overcame me again. Fortunately we soon stood up for a hymn, and though the choice which led Mrs. More to shout cheerily and vociferously that her "life's brief day was sinking down to its appointed end", did perhaps emphasize the advanced age of the gathering, it ended at least with a show of enthusiasm. And, to my infinite relief, Miss Boness and Mrs. Leny refused my wavering invitation to look in for a few moments, and I could hurry back to the kitchen.

Arthur was very late and very tired, with a tendency again to feel our food unduly luxurious, and a strong reluctance to come up afterwards to the drawing-room. But his study fire was out and his books awaited him, I told him, and by the time I had finished helping Kate to clear up, he was comfortably asleep over a vast new volume of Saint John. I was just following his example when the telephone bell went.

Again, to my relief, it was not the War Office. Still, the dining-room was so cold that my teeth were literally chattering, and I felt very angry when I had to wait, after answering the call, to be put through by some maid to a mistress. I peeped through the edge of the black-out blind, and saw the soft mazy drift of snowflakes in the pitch darkness; snow in these unlighted nights is curiously uncanny, and I was sighing at the winter which would never pass away, in the world or in our hearts, when a little rustle told me that someone was at the other end of the instrument at last.

"*Good* evening," said Mrs. Weekes. "What a cold evening, is it not—it almost seems like snow." She paused, and I said good evening and left it at that. "I've been seeing Mrs. Pratt this evening," she began again, and again I refused to help her out. "You are there, Mrs. Lacely? Hullo, are you there? … Oh, I quite thought we had been cut off. … Well, as I was saying, I have been seeing Mrs. Pratt, and she told me that the Archdeacon was hoping to see your husband at two o'clock. Well, of course, as I said to Mrs. Pratt, that would quite break up our little lunch party, so I have been thinking …"

"Think away," was my unregenerate comment to myself, and I regret to say I made a face at the telephone.

"I have been thinking that perhaps, after all, it would be more satisfactory if you were both to give us the pleasure of your company at luncheon," said Mrs. Weekes, and as I heard the poor old dear literally swallowing her pride at the other end, my heart melted.

"It's so good of you," I said, "but don't bother, because I expect Arthur really does want an interview alone with the Archdeacon."

"Yes, yes, I know, but they can have my husband's den to themselves, or the lounge if they prefer it; we shall be in the drawing-room, we ladies, you see! Mrs. Pratt is so sure that you are ready to help us all in this difficulty, and if I was too hasty at first in thinking you didn't understand our point of view ... well, of course. ..."

"I think I'd better go and ask Arthur about his appointments to-morrow," I said, because I simply had to retreat upstairs for a minute to laugh, and ask Arthur what on earth we shall do.

"Do? Why go, of course," said Arthur.

"Christian forgiveness or sheer greed?"

"Both, but principally the latter," replied Arthur, serenely. He would live on air if I neglected him; he calls onion soup and fried haddock undue luxury at home, and yet, like every normal man he enjoys a really good meal out of his own home with quite simple hearty pleasure now and again. If he felt like that, it was silly for me to rage inwardly at Mrs. Weekes' insufferable impertinence, and better to remember that at all costs we must be friends for Dick's sake. And if I was sacrificing my proper pride, poor old Adela had been obliged to sacrifice a lot more! I longed to know whether the invitation was due to anything but the intransigeance of the Archdeacon, but I had no desire to stay and chatter—as my teeth did at once.

"Good," said Mrs. Weekes, "good, very good. At one o'clock then. It is most unlucky that Mrs. Pratt herself cannot come, but there it is. I have got another guest, a surprise for you. Tell me, is it true that Mr. Strang is so very ill?"

"He's a bad go of 'flu," I said, knowing that to Mrs. Weekes, who adores illness, his political views would seem less obnoxious at once.

"Dear me, I hope his silly little wife knows how to look after him! One has to guard against chills so carefully at this time of year."

"Yes," I said, doing an audible shiver down the telephone, "And it's so cold in here I must now run away. Good night, and thank you."

Once long ago when I was taking Dick for a walk, someone who met us annoyed me by just such a display of bad manners, and ignorance of what you can and can't do, as Mrs. Weekes had shown just now. I was younger and even more indiscreet then, and burst out suddenly with—"Oh, the insufferable manners of these provincial big-wigs," and Dick, who was always Arthur's son, insisted painstakingly on an exact definition of the meaning of each word. By the time we'd finished with it, the sentence was rubbed into my mind as a typical fall from grace, and I repeat it to myself at moments when I am very cross inside as a suitable reminder and penance. At the top of the first flight of seven stairs I felt better, and by the time I had reached the place at the next corner which has worn so thin that it soon won't be carpet any more, I was quite composed, and able to rejoice that to-morrow I needn't cook lunch or know what I'll have, and that as it was Kate's afternoon out I should have to come straight home to answer the door and the telephone, and have time to arrange a nice dinner. This prospect gave me strength to refrain from awaking Arthur to hear the latest news of the great Strang controversy. "Men dislike talking things over as much as women like it", was one of my mother-in-law's dicta, and I do remember to let a sleeping husband lie.

I was just going upstairs to bed when the front doorbell rang. As Kate is officially in bed by eleven o'clock, though actually I could hear a manly laugh in the kitchen, I went down to answer our door, hoping that it was not an urgent sick call for Arthur. Obviously, I decided, it was not, as I found myself face to face with a very stout woman in a draggled fur coat, who faced me with the glassy stare of the happily fuddled.

"Ser sorry I'm ser late," said my visitor in a conspiratorial whisper, "Fac' is I come to see the Vicar here about some banns! I want some."

"To-morrow morning," I replied firmly. "It's too late for banns to-night."

"Coo—she says it's too late," reported my visitor to some invisible companion in the darkness. "And me coming out in the snow for them too. Must report this! I wonder—" she paused on the steps and turned to me with an entire change of manner, "now there is one thing I wonder if you could oblige me with and that's a fried egg!"

"I'm sorry, I haven't one in the house," I replied stoutly. "Have you anyone to see you home?"

"Not a soul, no Christian charity!" wailed my visitor, showing a distinct inclination to camp out on the door-step. I had a dreadful fear that Arthur would appear, refusing to turn the poor away, but luckily the unseen friend pulled her up and out of the gate remorselessly, and I could lock our door—our ubiquitous door—and go to bed at last.

VI
THURSDAY

THE HAT PROBLEM became really acute this morning.

As I returned from Early Service, I most unfortunately caught sight of myself in the side glass of the little shop at the corner of our street which sells "haberdash", baby linen and ladies' corsets. It is not a prosperous business, and the glass is far from clean, so that, in pausing, I did gather a general impression that at our next jumble sale my present head-gear would hardly go off, even at the "All on this counter—1d. Stall," and that no woman could be expected to show tact on the subject of pacifism, the charm of a prospective relation-in-law, and the dignity of the Church of England to the Weekes's under a battered relic of black felt. Kate, who was washing the step as I came in, strengthened this impression by remarking that now the spring seemed coming along at last, and Dykes was having a throw-out sale, it did seem as if we'd all have to think about a bit of shopping.

My thoughts, however, were diverted from Dykes when the telephone bell went, just as we were sitting down to breakfast. Miss Boness, at the other end, told me in tones of such despair that she was up the spout and down the drain, that I really thought for a moment that she was mistaking me for the plumber. "Only you can help me, dear Mrs. Lacely," she went on, however, "and I know we never appeal to you in vain! Miss Jedd has scratched! Simply scratched!"

"Miss Jedd?" (Where, as Mrs. Pratt would say, was my method or engagement book?)

"Yes, Miss Jedd! She was to speak to my Comforts Club this afternoon—surely you remember. Surely you meant to attend the meeting at three!"

"No, no!" I could reply with infinite relief. "You know it's my maid's afternoon out, so I have to be in the Vicarage from three o'clock onwards. We can't leave the house empty because of telephone calls."

"I know, I remember. But I'm in such a pickle, really at my wits' ends. Now let me see! Yes, Eureka! I could send my Louisa to sit in your kitchen and answer the bells for you, just till four-thirty, and your Kate is such a good pal that they won't mind, either of them."

"But why should …"

"Because then, don't you see, you can come to the meeting and give us a little address instead of Miss Jedd! It's not a big affair, as of course you know. I don't suppose more than twenty or thirty will attend, if that. It's so unlucky it's such a fine day, or we might have expected more. You will help me, won't you? You're my last hope!"

Nothing was further from my plans for a peaceful afternoon. I detest having to make a speech of any kind; my heart sinks into my shoes, and my voice rises to a high trembling squeak. And, after all, I had given Monday afternoon to the rival Work Party and would infinitely prefer, when I can find time, to go direct to the Red Cross, and work at the right job in a businesslike way. Nor do I see why I should be victimized to take the place of one of the many (alas, too many!) idle women who love to talk to others and have lost their audiences in a busier world. I don't know if this audience is restive or not, except that Kate, who looked in once "to oblige" said darkly that it was enough to be shut up with a pack of women anyway, without having to listen to a back number chatting on China!

"What was Miss Jedd speaking about?" I temporized.

"Her travels in Finland—so interesting! It is really too annoying of her to go and get 'flu just now. It never rains but it pours!"

"Well, I really can't speak about Finland," I protested, "so why not just work without an address?"

"Too late! Too late! Ye cannot enter now!" quoted Miss Boness, evidently even more upset than before. "We must have someone to address us. Even if you don't know Finland, perhaps you would describe the course of the war there?"

"No," I said, firmly. I couldn't explain to Miss Boness that to read these heroic stories of hopeless tragic endurance every day is, to me, to read of someone whom you love being slowly stoned to death. Already I recognize the symptoms of the last War, when it grew daily more impossible to pick up the newspaper, so that I often discover that Dick learnt more about the years 1914-18 at school than I did by living through them. "Couldn't Miss Cookes tell them about travels in India?"

"She has, twice," replied Miss Boness. "At least, it was Ceylon last time, but it came to much the same thing. Besides, it needn't be travel at all. Better not, perhaps; I always say change is the Breath of Life!"

"Wouldn't it be the breath of life to them to have no speech at all?"

"Ah ha! Dear Mrs. Lacely, you're always so sarcastic! As a matter of fact, even that wouldn't be a change, as the speaker failed at my last monthly meeting!"

"Then why not just talk as you do the other times, or read aloud to them?"

I could almost hear Miss Boness's head shaking at the other end of the telephone.

"My dear! They only talk, nothing but talk, and get no work done. You know how it is! And this week the Red Cross has issued me with hundreds of bags for sphagnum moss for Finland. I want to nail every hand to the mast!"

"But why not make them with machines?" I asked, remembering not to enhance my reputation for sarcasm by pointing out that this position would be seriously unsuitable for needlework.

"Do you think", demanded Miss Boness, so shrilly that I winced, "that we should grudge our eyes and needles in the good cause? No man putting his hand to the plough …"

"But they *do* put their hands to the sewing-machine at the Red Cross, for I've been there," I said. And I should have liked to have added how pleasant it was to work there in that sane, businesslike atmosphere, instead of in the fussy heat of Miss Boness's drawing-room. Unluckily their quarters are so comparatively small that the Society have to encourage these subsidiary gatherings, and Miss Boness never needs encouragement from anyone at all. "Why not have your machine in to help the people who are sewing by hand, and then they couldn't be spoken to at all? There would be too much noise!"

"I might have the machine in to help, of course," said Miss Boness, obviously weakening a little. "Still we should all enjoy it much more if we had a little speech to begin with. Our people live such *narrow* lives, you know, dear Mrs. Lacely. How about a little address on Classical Literature? We all know how well-read you and your husband are."

"Couldn't Miss Croft talk to them about Browning or pottery?" I suggested, ignoring this preposterous suggestion.

"She only gets back this evening. She was too late to see her poor cousin, you know. So tragic, though as a matter of fact, I believe he'd been senile for some years. The funeral's to-day, and she has to return at once because she can't well leave the shop longer. In the midst of life, as I always say, we are in death. One's hope is that he's left her a *little* something, just to bring grist to the mill."

"Couldn't Miss Grieve give them a talk about the Western Front? Surely they'd like to know about the War?" I asked, unable to cope with this flood of news and original comments.

"She's gone to Manchester for the day—I've just rung up," said Miss Boness, thus proving, in a not wholly flattering way, that I was indeed her last hope.

"I was wondering if you didn't feel up to a real address at such short notice, whether you wouldn't give them a few extracts from dear Dick's letters, with a little running commentary?"

Miss Boness would certainly be the first to run if I gave unexpurgated extracts from my son's letters, which deal far more in caustic comments on my parochial gossip than on what he terms "my gory jobs".

"But surely we're asked to repeat *no* news about the Forces," I replied with dignity, and then the apologies and splutterings at the other end grew so interminable that I found myself pledged, when I rang off, to give a few words at three o'clock on any subject I liked to choose.

"And not even a real form of War Service!" I told Arthur indignantly. "I could machine those bags up myself in an hour all alone!"

"Then why did you consent?" asked Arthur, reasonably.

"Because I couldn't help it," I admitted, truthfully, reflecting that that is really the main excuse for my life at all times. "And anyhow, it was the first time since Monday that anyone has talked to me without mentioning Mr. Strang, and I suppose that weakened me. I must run round this morning and find out how he is."

"No better," said Kate, looking in from the hall where she had been dusting, as she does all too frequently when I am telephoning with the dining-room door open. "He'd a very bad night, the Milk told me, and the doctor may be sending in another nurse. And, if you please'm, I'd be glad if you'd tell that Louisa I don't want her poking her nose in my kitchen. I won't be starting out till four o'clock anyway, as Private Jenkins is dropping in then, on the way to choose my new costume for Easter."

Of course I ought to scold Kate for eavesdropping, but when I looked at the weekly books, which arrive on Thursday here, I felt that she was so good to be contented with all my economy and cheeseparing that I would leave abstract manners and morals alone. I always think we should remind ourselves that our Kates belong to a class which look upon open-handed wastefulness as a sign of gentility, and that they have a shrewd suspicion that our war economies are really being made at their expense. I aim at keeping the books down to £2 a week, and this week they only reached thirty-three shillings and ten-pence-halfpenny. Even though I must deduct another shilling for some grapes for Mr. Strang, with my kind inquiries, I may yet manage a throw-out hat from Messrs. John Dykes!

Poor little Mrs. Strang looked very pale and nervous when I called, but she was preoccupied with the arrival of the Nurse—who was bullying poor little Doris at the end of the passage for an arm-chair, a syphon of soda-water, some cotton-wool and safety-pins. What the expense will be for the poor Strangs I can't bear to think, and if the feud with the Weekes's continues unabated, the dear old fellow won't come to their aid, as he did to our Vicarage after my illness last year, saying apologetically that we must forgive him if he was ob-truding, but he knew what illness meant, and if there was one weakness he had it was for putting his hand in his pocket to help his friends. Arthur was unnecessarily proud, I felt, in passing his offer on to other sick cases in the parish, but the Strangs would have had every right to accept such an offer. It was depressing to think there seemed little hope of it now, es-pecially as Nurse came forward to assure me the gentleman'd pick up in no time in *her* charge. Only a really dangerous illness could make a reconciliation now, I fear.

I couldn't help running on to Queen's Court, but there was no news there save merciful, prolonged unconsciousness; and then I rounded up my bills briskly. All the same, it was twelve o'clock before I reached the millinery department at Dykes', rather breathless because it is upstairs, and the lift, as usual, was Out of Order. No doubt it shares with me a lack of method.

The worst of shopping in a provincial town is that you cannot do it anonymously. In London you can give yourself up to the job whole-heartedly, though even there I must confess my favourite little woman, just off Knightsbridge, became a personal friend, and I had to watch my face growing ever sadder and sadder under each creation as she gave me the last report of her poor delicate husband in Switzerland. But in the old days, if I were in a hurry, and wanted something cheap, I could go and hide myself behind a barrage of hats in front of a mirror in some big shop and get down to the job. Here, in Stampfield, the head of the department sent for the buyer, Madame Burt, at once, as she is a great admirer of Arthur's, and I had to chat to two assistants from our parish before I could begin about a hat at all. And then I saw Miss Henly, to my surprise, seated at the central mirror, tossing hats aside rapidly with caustic comments on provincial millinery. There was in Cranford, I think, an excellent tradition that neighbours did not watch each other shopping, and the same unwritten law holds with the *habitués* of Stampfield. But Miss Henly is new to us and our ways, and I don't feel that there would ever be anything private about any activity of hers.

"Are you looking for a hat, too?" she called out, cheerfully. "I can only hope you'll find one, for it's not easy. What do you think of this?"

How are princes both punctual and polite? Clearly I hadn't time to choose a hat myself and dissuade Miss Henly from equipping herself with a pork-pie of leopard-skin. I think it is the inimitable Miss Delafield who says that every woman sees her face as it was twenty-five years ago when she looks in a mirror; and indeed, one needs it with any sort of modern hat. I gather that Miss Henly has always let herself be turned out complete, without question, by a friend in Hanover Square, and a very good job she has made of it; but the result is that a long-stifled desire to be daring, modern and conspicuous is now assailing Miss Henly's breast in Stampfield, with disastrous results.

"Don't you like something with a brim better?" This was my feeble expression of my certainty that I would not trust a child of mine, even at half-fees, with a headmistress who wore a hat like that. "I want something with a brim myself, please, Miss Mathers—to match this tweed as nearly as possible—and not more than ten-and-eleven."

"I know you married women!" cried Miss Henly, gaily. "You want the facsimile of the dear old mushroom you got engaged in before the last war, because that's what your husband always likes!"

True as this remark is, I might at least retort vulgarly that I *did* get engaged anyhow, and Miss Henly hasn't!

"Would Moddom like a contrast?" asked Miss Mathers, dauntingly, appearing with a yellow beret and a rust-coloured tam-o'-shanter which, I feel convinced, I noted with loathing quite three years ago in Dykes' shop window.

"I *like* that! It's original!" said Miss Henly, approvingly, and tried on the yellow beret at a dashing angle, while I insisted that I wanted something in the tone of my darkish blue-grey tweed, and if I couldn't match it (as I knew I shouldn't) probably black would be best, and size seven at least.

While Miss Henly returned to the leopard pork-pie I discarded a matron's hat, with a high ruche of black velvet (15s. 6d.), a turquoise blue saucer, and a grey soup-plate, and saw to my horror that the time was already twenty to one, and that my hairpins were rapidly losing the battle with my last grey curls. It was with infinite relief that I saw Madame Burt appear, with the look of a conspirator, and announcing aloud that she had *loved* Mr. Lacely's sermon on Tuesday, and how ever did he find *time* to read up all about those old monks, produced, out of Miss Henly's range of vision, a charming, sedate, little stitched corduroy velvet hat. It was almost exactly the colour of my tweed, though not, as Madame Burt flatteringly insisted, the colour of my eyes; it was big enough; it looked as if it was still seeing better days; and it was certainly becoming.

"Not your colour and too trying. May I try it on?" asked Miss Henly, rapidly. "How much is this?"

"That was a three-guinea hat, Moddom," said Madame Burt, disapprovingly.

"Oh, then it's far too much for me!" I said, picking up the matron's curse again.

"And it is too old for Moddom," said Madame Burt, picking it neatly off Miss Henly's head. "Moddom needs something a little harder to wear, if you know what I mean! Miss Mathers, go and fetch that Paris model we put away yesterday—with the ermine crown. …"

Miss Henly was happily distracted at once, and Madame Burt became conspiratorial again. "Half a guinea for you, Mrs. Lacely," she hissed, in the best stage villain manner, "it was marked down to twenty-one, but I'll halve it for you, only you must never, never give me away!"

I accepted the offer with becoming gratitude, and no sense of shame, as I saw that the ticket had already been re-marked to 15s., and if Madame Burt likes to testify to Arthur's value in the only way she can, why shouldn't she? But I realized sadly that either I must betray Madame's secret or live for ever in Miss Henly's eyes as a monster of clerical extravagance when I came up to bid her good-bye, complete in the new hat. "Very nice, but more your style than mine," said Miss Henly, appraisingly. She was now equipped with a black hat, and the ermine crown and aigrette suggested a prize-giving with the Bishop in the Chair at least. "I do hope she reduced it for you. It's quite nice in a quiet way, but *not* worth what she asked—"

"Oh no, no, it's been much reduced," I said with relief. "And you look quite charming in that hat!"

"Moddom is definitely marvellous, isn't she?" said Miss Mathers, who has not quite acquired the sliding scale of adjectives for each customer yet.

"My good girl—why 'definitely', and why should you describe me as a 'marvel'?" Miss Henly began, and then, as I turned to go, she waved me back with a gesture that made me feel, far more certainly than my hat, that I looked years younger.

"I do want you to look in at our canteen," she said. "We open experimentally on Saturday evening. Yes, it's a great rush, but I believe in putting things through at once. Do you think Mr. Lacely would look in and say a few words?"

"Oh, not on Saturday," I pleaded. "And I'll only come if I need say nothing but please and thank you; but it's wonderful to have got it started so soon—definitely marvellous!" I added, defiantly with a laugh and a glance of sympathy to Miss Mathers.

"By the way," called Miss Henly, negligently, as I walked away to the stairs, "what is all this fuss about Mr. Strang?"

It was only as I realized the pang of shocked horror I felt at this casual, loud inquiry over our local scandal, that I knew how absorbed I am in the storms of our Stampfield tea-cup. But tea-cups are important when you live in them, and I answered, "Oh, nothing to speak of," in my most repressive manner. It wasn't needed, however, as Miss Henly was already hunting up a sort of carmagnole in tricolour, which I feel she may well be persuaded to adventure in at the canteen on Saturday afternoon.

"Do you like it, Arthur?" I whispered feverishly as we met, both in good time I was relieved to find, on the Weekes' step.

"Your pretty new gown?" asked Arthur, affectionately. "It's charming, my dear, and makes you look quite different. Now you must let me buy you a new hat!" I don't know if women really dress for men or not, but they certainly should not bother about their husbands.

The Withers always interests me so much as a home, that I am often, I fear, a little absent-minded when Mrs. Weekes welcomes me, as it is, like country railway stations and waiting-rooms, more completely part of old-world England than any historic building now. (For all old houses have been petted and cosseted and repaired till they are self-conscious and museum-like.) The Weekes's have not, like so many people with their wealth, remodelled their home altogether. I don't mean that progress and Ida's taste have passed them by altogether. The big entrance hall is now called the lounge, and is fitted up after the model of a first-class provincial hotel, with big, low leather arm-chairs, little tables, a huge radio, and every convenience for smoking except, indeed, spittoons. But the exterior is complete Victorian, well-appointed and cared-for in every detail. The big front which faces the road shines with large plate-glass windows. A huge conservatory flanks it on one side, and immaculate stables on the other. They are used for a garage now, of course, but they still look as if a neat brougham and horse and liveried coachman might emerge. There is a vague turret rising from the back, and a stucco porch and pillars in front.

The drawing-room is a real period piece. One side has doors which open into the conservatory, and I must say that I always have thought there is something very fragrant and pleasant about the moist smell of maidenhair and primulas and tea-roses in a room. But apart from that, no horror is wanting. There is a huge walnut overmantel, rising in a hundred fretted-wood little compartments, each with its own china cat, dog, or souvenir from foreign travel. There is a Turkey carpet whose reds and blues dazzle your eye till you are glad to rest it on any piece of the walnut drawing-room suite with its fawn silk padding. There are Venetian blinds and lace curtains, and great inner curtains of fawn and yellow brocade; there are little tables with silver, and a huge grand piano entirely covered with silver-framed photographs.

"Isn't this an awful room!" Ida says with a tolerant laugh. "But Mother won't have a thing altered, not even those frightful Marcus Stone and Alma Tadema prints, or those awful vases of prehistoric bulrushes in the corners. I do hope I'll never be

sentimental about my junk, Mrs. Lacely!" I don't suppose she
will, and I have a sneaking fear that my old things will also
seem junk to her. Anyhow, she could never conceivably unite
our two drawing-rooms.

Mrs. Weekes was looking stouter than ever but quite benevolent, in an elephant-grey crêpe dress, very bountiful above
the waist and very tight behind. She was wearing a small high
hat on the top of her white coiffure, because in her early married life you always did wear a hat for lunch; but her short skirt
and high heels gave her a faintly coquettish air from the waist
downwards. Someone rose from a chair beside the conservatory and advanced towards me, and Mrs. Weekes said, in a voice
which was an odd mingling of suspicion and respect, "I believe
this is an old friend of yours, Lady Cyrus."

Who is it who says that forty years make a great difference in a woman? It was most embarrassing to find my hands
seized, and a kiss implanted somewhere on the side of my
nose by a tall, lanky stranger, who seemed endearingly shabby
but for very red lips, two rows of real pearls, and marvellous
brogues, and I had to say, "Why, is it really you?" more than
once while I was trying in vain for any connection. And then
when the unknown put a monocle to her eye, I suddenly remembered imitation spectacles from a cracker at a Christmas
party long ago, and a little girl with drab hair, a long nose and
long thin legs, and I finished up triumphantly with, "Is it really
you, Serena?" Which of us, I wonder, was the greater liar as we
insisted in turns that neither of us had changed in the least, and
would have known each other anywhere? As a matter of fact
our mutual reminiscences chiefly centred round a tool-shed,
a lion-skin rug, ginger-snaps and crackers in her home, and a
swing, a musical box and a brown retriever called Jerks, in mine.
Since those days Serena (I can't remember what) has married
a soldier, been half round the world, reared six children, and
is now only staying two nights in Stampfield as her husband,
retired, is inspecting the swill-tubs of our camps, while she

casts a gracious eye on our Red Cross activities. We are never likely to meet again, and the only importance Serena can ever have in my life is the fact that she heard of me from some mutual friend of long ago, and when Mrs. Weekes, as President of our Red Cross, was emboldened to ask her to lunch, dangling Archdeacon Pratt before her eyes as a bait, Serena Cyrus replied that she would have loved to, if she hadn't quite determined to drop in on her old friend, Camilla Lacely. That, I see now, was the reason of the olive-branch thrust down the telephone last night, and Mrs. Weekes hadn't even the social sense to offer it when she renewed her invitation. Well, well, blessed be snobbery, I thought, as I enjoyed the delicious salmon savoury and racked my brains for one more memory of Serena's home (or former name). Blessed be "the pestilential snobbery of these provincial bigwigs", I repeated to myself. Mr. Weekes, dear, sturdy old fellow was still looking suspiciously under his thick white eyebrows at Arthur, and obviously got no snobbish pleasure out of his guest; but I could not help knowing that, as far as Mrs. Weekes was concerned, Serena Cyrus was going to be a greater bond of union for Dick and Ida's future than any years of parochial activity on my part or Arthur's. It was on the tip of my tongue to remark what odd people we English are, when Serena went on with the good work by asking (another great effort of memory) after that cousin of mine who succeeded to some property, and though honesty compelled me to admit that Harry was only a second cousin, and that it was a very small place in Perthshire, the effect on Mrs. Weekes made me begin to imagine Ida's wedding reception at once.

Mr. Weekes would not have given twopence for this remote connection with the "Birth" which his wife esteems so highly. He was not, indeed, in the least interested in Serena, as he was intent on the conversations of the two parsons. He had hoped, I think, that the Archdeacon would treat Arthur as a schoolboy, and begin on the subject of our Stampfield scandal at once; but our Archdeacon is far too competent an organizer to start on any given subject at the inappropriate moment. Lunch and Diocese come under separate headings in his card-index mind, and he would never deal with the two headings simultaneously. I always wish we knew him a little better, for I believe when once one is under the entries of Pain or Trouble he is most kind and helpful, and one sees the spiritual side which is rather obscured by his passion for Commissions, Committees and Boards in everyday life. He is small, immaculately neat and precise, and his big head contains an absolute mine of information on every conceivable subject, so that many people think him pompous and priggish. Even Arthur said once, in a fit of exasperation, that the Archdeacon would never get into Heaven, as Saint Peter would find his passport in such suspiciously good order, but he is, I believe, invaluable in Convocation, and brisk efficiency is, after all, a very rare virtue.

When the Archdeacon made it clear, therefore, that he would not deal simultaneously with salmi of chicken and Strang, Mr. Weekes turned his attention to me.

"Well, well, I'm glad to see your good man can use a knife in Lent, Mrs. Lacely. I've no patience with these chaps who starve themselves into a decline just because the Papists do. Your husband isn't any too stout, you know. Do you ever give him tripe? I always tell you ladies that there's no need to spend money on luxuries while you can get tripe. Many's the dish Adela and I had for supper in the old days—you should ask her for the recipe."

"I will some time," I said, earnestly. "I do it with tomato and mushroom sometimes, and we like it."

"Splendid, splendid, Mrs. Lacely. I'd no idea you were such a chef. Well, you take my advice and give it to your husband often. Feed the brute, you know. I expect I've told you that one. Have you heard the one about Hitler and the Jew?"

Already this war is beginning the moral deterioration of the last. How well I remember then wishing, when, for once, one was sitting down to a luxurious meal, that one could just eat it and enjoy it without the interruption of conversation! That was how I enjoyed the *pêche melba* now, with the lady-like laugh always ready, as Dick would say. I was ashamed to think how I was enjoying food in Lent till I remembered how exiguous the Quiet Day meals would be to-morrow! ("It's little but watercress goes into the old Rectory in Lent," said Kate, when I told her of my engagement next day, "and not fresh at that.")

"How's Strang?" was the next thing I heard from Mr. Weekes, as I had been listening, askance, to some wholly apocryphal reminiscences of my childhood given by Lady Cyrus to my poor Arthur. (Whatever she says, I never climbed a monkey-puzzler or watched a pig being killed in my life.)

"A little better, Mrs. Strang said at eleven; but the doctor has sent in another nurse, poor dears."

"I call it a judgement," said Mr. Weekes, explosively. "Look here, gentlemen, shall we have some port and liqueurs in my room? We've got something important to talk over, your Ladyship, I fear."

Serena must have had too much of the sherry or moselle, for she exclaimed quite coquettishly that it seemed *too* hard when she had got two such delightful clergymen to amuse her! The three men escaped with such obvious unanimity of relief that I felt their common emotion might soften the whole interview. Really, Stampfield, or the Lacelys at least, were indebted to Serena, and to reward her I asked for the names and ages of her children in detail. Mrs. Weekes and I had only to sit back and listen after that, and when it transpired that her second girl had been to Roedean, and I had exclaimed that you had only to look at Ida Weekes to see what a splendid place it must be, Mrs. Weekes patted my arm just as if we were joint mothers-in-law.

Altogether I had enjoyed myself, and when I am tempted by improper pride again I shall remind myself how dreadful it would have been if I had haughtily refused Mrs. Weekes's invitation, and Serena had carried out her threat of dropping in, to find me eating cheese and bread and marge while Kate finished the last bit of rabbit in the kitchen! But from the moment I had finished coffee I was assailed by certain symptoms which always recur when I have to raise my voice in public, a shaking at the knees, shivers down my spine, and a strong temptation to tears. For the hundredth time I was telling myself how silly it was—as Serena described her third child's unfortunate habit of stammering—and tried to discover at what point the trouble began. None of us mind making a remark before two, three, four people. Is five the danger-point, or is it just that one doesn't make only one remark but a lot in a speech? And if so, how many remarks produce these interesting symptoms I was asking myself, dazedly, when we heard Mr. Weekes' voice, raised evidently in anger, in the lounge hall. A door was banged, and Mr. Weekes and the Archdeacon re-entered the drawing-room, looking so heated that I made my farewells very hurriedly, feeling that in the crisis which might be upon us, if Mr. Weekes were really estranged, not even Serena's embrace and earnest invitation to me to drop in whenever I happened to be in Forfarshire, would assuage the parochial feud. It might count with Mrs. Weekes, but not, alas, with her sturdy husband.

Still, I evidently must put that out of my mind as I walked to Miss Boness's house still utterly at a loss whether to talk about Munich (which I visited thirty years ago) or War-cookery, or Lenten readings. The sight of the coats in the little hall, and the buzz of voices from the dining-room brought on my symptoms so acutely that luckily I couldn't run away.

Anyhow, I was grateful for two things; that the meeting was jumbled anyhow about the room, on the chairs and on the floor; and secondly that Miss Boness mercifully did not intend to make any opening remarks. It is really better to plunge into the heart of one's embarrassment, and the only delay was caused by my own cowardice in pretending to take an overwhelming interest in sphagnum moss and the bags and their uses.

"And now, ladies, we are all going to have a little treat," said Miss Boness. "Mrs. Lacely has come to give us a little talk about—about …"

I looked at the rather heterogeneous groups of women assembled, in despair. Some were pale, plain, lonely souls who probably preferred Miss Boness's warm rooms to the pathos of days out from shops or service without a boy friend; some had the tired, anxious appearance of those who wait on invalids or elderly mothers; there were some dear, earnest, busy little creatures who were patriotically giving their one free afternoon to war work of any kind; and there was a sprinkling of those socially superior girls who had not managed, or wanted, to get into uniform. They were, I guessed, the wreckage of a diocesan society, the object of which is to encourage gay young things to bring culture and amusement, and some mild religious interest, into the lives of their poorer sisters, by way of study circles, concerts, and mystery plays. Our branch doesn't flourish very well here, partly, as Miss Henly says cynically, because the smart set of her High School girls are afraid of meeting their less prosperous and ignored relations if they visit the slums; and really, I think, because in these sturdy northern midland towns, the less socially select detest and suspect any form of patronage. These two or three wealthier girls —for wealth is our only standard here—were sitting aloof, very much made-up, and wearing trousers and gipsy scarves, a costume for which I could see no reason at a working-party. Balzac would see in these red-lipped Pamelas and Dianas an infinite variety of *Vie de Province*. Only those who have lived in a Stampfield can begin to understand the smallness of these petty princesses, and how little the circles of modern thought and culture and artistic activity in London mean to them. But obviously I could not talk on Dull Lives or Balzac or the Provinces, so I shut my eyes metaphorically and with memories of the dreadful proportions which the Strang affair has assumed this week, I plunged into a short (very short) address on Gossip.

It was candidly a very poor address. A malign imp seizes me always, just when I am trying to represent a Real Middle-aged Parson's Wife, and puts Dick's slang and Dick's phrases into my mind. And really, as I laboured on—my ideas disturbed by a fear that my hair wasn't too tidy and my face flushed with my un-usually good lunch—about words in season and out of season, and how truth should always be spoken but all truth should not be spoken; and how on a seat at Saint Andrew's is the old motto: "They say; What say they; Let them say." I heard Dick say, "Atta-girl! Let them have it!" and found words like "lousy" and worse hovering on my lips, though mercifully they got no further. In about five minutes I seemed to have exhausted every single aspect of the subject, when I had the inspiration of describing the game of Russian Scandal we used to play in my youth. (Why was it called "Russian" I wondered? In the Russia of my youth surely a fear of Siberia checked the mildest whispers?) They laughed a little over my illustrations, and I sug-gested rashly that we should try a round for fun. But it was no fun at all when the last in the chain of whisperers announced proudly: "Mr. Elgin tried to run away with Miss Croft, but Mr. Strang ran after them and gave them both influenza!"

I said, with all the impressiveness I could muster, that this exemplified all I had been saying. "I expect," I added, "that the story began with some innocent remark from one of you and that someone else"—here I looked distinctly at Pamela and Diana—"gave it a malicious twist. Nothing could prove to you more clearly than that what a detestable thing gossip is. I don't suppose you know, of course, that poor Mr. Strang is very ill indeed, and I don't suppose you can realize that the views of a few people in a small place like this don't contain all the truth of the world. But at least I do hope you will remember all this when you are next tempted to speak idly or unkindly."

After that I retreated in not very good order, avoiding Miss Boness's baleful eye. It was an infinite relief to enter my quiet, empty, echoing house, and to make tea by the study fire. I had expected to sit in self-abasement and contrition—for of what conceivable use is a parson's wife if she can't "say a few words" without rousing mischief, when the afternoon post brought a letter from Dick, and I forgot all about it—and what better can one do with one's failures?

Dick's letters used to break my heart at first by his gallant determination to make the best of everything, but there was nothing save his old high spirits in this one. "Leave might come any minute now instead of later, so just you be prepared with Kate's three-ton explosive puddings! I can't really tell you till I'm coming, but Ida's promised to make it with me whenever I get off. By the way, better not say anything to Ma Weekes about it yet, as we gather that things in the old home haven't been cordial latterly in the Church line. But who could resist a gallant hero who hasn't had a proper bath for months?" The fact that "it" was already referred to as "it" stunned me so completely with joy and surprise, together with those reflections on the lightning passage of years between a baby in his bath and a bridegroom at the altar, which no mother can quite avoid, that I rushed to the doorstep headlong when the front-door bell rang, and had to try very hard not to look disappointed when I saw, not Arthur, but Miss Croft.

"Oh, do come in, I'm just having tea," I said, hurriedly adjusting myself.

Certainly Miss Croft didn't notice. I thought at first it was because a mourning dress gives few openings for arts and crafts that she looked vaguely different, but as we sat down by the fire I realized that there was more in it. She pulled off her gloves quite portentously—it was a relief to see a relic of old times in a large moonstone surrounded by pewter twists on her middle finger—and spoke in a tremulous voice.

"This is very good of you, Mrs. Lacely. I wanted to come straight to you, or the dear Vicar, to tell you that something has happened which has made—will make—the greatest difference in my life. I never guessed," she went on, becoming suddenly tearful and incoherent, "I never dreamt … I mean he was only my mother's first cousin, but no children … after all these years, and he was always supposed to be so hard and quite poor … and all in trust securities, my lawyer tells me … and even with the Income Tax … it's all like some wonderful dream."

It was quite easy to gather the main plot, and no doubt, though I was the first to hear that Miss Croft had inherited her cousin's money, both Kate and Miss Boness will be able to tell me to-morrow just how much a year she will get and what her plans about the future may be. At the moment I only sympathized and exulted, and listened to a confused account of the cousin's death-bed and the liabilities of "Ye Olde Teapot" all mixed together, till Miss Croft had been persuaded to eat something and grew more tranquil.

"And now you are asking yourself", she said, in her old dramatic manner, "why I came first to you? Well, the reason is that now at last I can do something for our dear church—what rapture there will be in *giving* instead of merely *taking*, Mrs. Lacely. I want at once to do something for the music in dear Saint Simon's, and I think the best, the very best way I could do it, would be by adding something to the stipend of our organist. No man can give his soul to music when he is so poor, so grindingly poor as Mr. Elgin, I feel, and if his worst anxieties were removed, he could give his whole heart to the services!"

Terrible visions of two anthems at every service and the parochial disturbance if Mr. Elgin clamoured for a sung Mass, flitted across my mind, but I only thanked the dear little lady for her kind thoughts.

"It is so like you to want to help others at once," I said, warmly. "And if I may say so, you look quite ten years younger already!"

"I was thirty-nine last birthday," said Miss Croft, simply. "But I can assure you I feel more like nineteen to-day. Though, oh dear, it does seem so unkind when I think of Cousin Benjamin; but it's ten years since I even spoke to him and he was quite odd then! I assure you I have been walking through the streets feeling like Pippa Passes, absurd as it seems, even in spite of the War! I keep thinking of such odd little luxuries … for years I have lost *Diana of the Crossways* from my set of Meredith and have never quite seen the way to purchasing another copy … and I always felt a *Cambridge* sausage a little beyond my means, though they are so far from the best make. And it will be so odd to *choose* one's shoes instead of looking through any of my size in sale reductions. … However, I mustn't go on like this."

I suppose it was these confidences which led her further still, for as she got up to go, she said, bending down to smooth the new black kid glove over her moonstone, "I have often read with such interest of those cases where a woman feels that some man whom she—in whom she takes an interest, feels himself removed from her by any difference in age, or station, or fortune. It always seems such a sad position, doesn't it?"

"Like a Queen having to propose to a Prince Consort," I said, sympathetically. "But don't you think in real life that if two people are feeling the same—affection—at the same moment they discover the truth without words? I don't suppose that many proposals get really *said* in real life." I smiled as I spoke, remembering how Arthur and I were alone on the river, and we both retrieved a paddle which had dropped from our canoe at the same moment, and looked up at each other as our hands clasped on it accidentally—and the next thing I remember is telling him how odd it was when I'd always vowed I would never marry a parson!

"'One moment long—or only a little longer'," quoted Miss Croft, softly. "I fear you may be only thinking of youth and passion, my dear. Well, I must be going. You have been so sweet and sympathetic."

"But not practical!" I said. "You must come and see Arthur about your most generous proposal, and you must be here, too, when he tells Mr. Elgin of this delightful surprise. Write your exact proposal to Arthur, will you, and then come in to tea on Saturday, and I'll ask Mr. Elgin, too? I'm sure you'd like to see him when he hears the news, and we needn't say at once who the benefactor is, if you'd rather not. Of course, he must know very soon."

Miss Croft had only just left when Arthur arrived home. He was on his way to his Confirmation Class at the Girls' High School, but I could not quite restrain myself from my matrimonial agency reflections till the evening. And by that time the news about Mr. Strang's illness on one hand, and the interview he had had with Archdeacon Pratt about our poor curate on the other, made him very tired and depressed.

"I wonder", he said, "why, with the world as it is, and life as it is, you women are so eternally interested in the propagation of the human race?"

When a husband says "you women" to his wife it is always best to leave the subject, and, after all, Arthur had indulged me in speculation about the Weekes' affair only two nights before! He was soon nodding peacefully over his Saint John, and I got down *Pillars of the House* by Charlotte M. Yonge, and found comfort in the reflection that at least I have not thirteen children, and that my husband is not just about to die of consumption, leaving me to support them on £150 a year!

As Kate was "in" for once I had fewer interruptions than usual. She has, we fear, rather a rough and ready manner of dealing with applicants at the door, but it is probably just as efficacious as my wavering suggestions. "Be off with you for a bit of no good", was one loud cheerful remark I overheard, and in the three other cases acquaintances of hers were urged, after long draughty chats, to "go straight off and see what you could get out of old Weekes", which is her invariable form of suggesting recourse to the Secretary of the Benevolent Fund. I was only called out to help to fill up a form for a dependant's allowance and, later on, to hear Mrs. Jones's difficulties about sending Doris off properly clad to the Convalescent Home, and luckily I have a store of old children's clothes, the gifts of my relatives, which enabled us to settle that problem very satisfactorily. It was less satisfactory to hear from Kate that two sick people had sent their relatives to ask Arthur to visit them to-night, and all I could do was to see that he had a tolerable supper before he went out again. "And you might just as well worry about me for a change, instead of Dick or Finland", were his parting words when he set out again at half-past eight. He did not get home again till nearly twelve o'clock, an interval during which, I must confess, I thought very favourably of the celibacy of the clergy.

IT WAS, I regret to say, eleven o'clock on Friday morning before I began my Quiet Day.

Mrs. Pratt looked at me with a long equine glance of re-
proach as I slipped into a seat as near the door as I could find
in the old Rectory drawing-room. (Why is it that in clerical
and other meetings these seats are always full and those in the
front row empty?) Is it due to modesty or, as I was tempted to
feel this morning, a malicious if subconscious desire to show
up the latecomer? Most of the ladies assembled had been, as
Dick would say profanely, hard at it being quiet since eight
o'clock, so of course I felt a spiritual black-leg. And as the ban
of silence was laid on our lips for the whole day, I could not
present my quite adequate excuses. I could only hope that
Mrs. Pratt and the others were laying to heart the charming
address on charity and the sin of misjudging others of whose
lives we know so little.

"I always get my household orders done the day before,"
Mrs. Eardley-Gage, our hostess, said to me the other day, when
she invited me. "Every one of my servants knows exactly what
their work will be, and that it is their business to help me by
keeping any worldly cares from me." She is a charming, wil-
lowy, ethereal looking woman, quite ten years younger than
myself, with no children, and with money of her own. That,
and the comparatively large stipend of the Stampfield Parish
Church, make it possible for her to keep four servants in her
nice roomy Georgian rectory, so that they have each other to
confide in, tied as Mrs. Gage's lips are all day, if anything goes
wrong. Whereas if I hadn't begun the day badly by finding
Kate in tears, and having to lay aside all plans to console her, all
alone as she is, I should surely have been wanting in Christian
charity. I did not really believe that Private Jenkins was going
to France next week—this climax has been foretold, as I said,

ever since the first week in September. I am not even sure if
Kate was not using it principally as an argument for going
home to his people with him for Saturday night; but if it were
true, and I had refused Kate leave, how could I ever forgive
myself? So, of course, we agreed that she must go, and I had to
plan the meals for this new emergency.

"It's not", said Kate, comfortingly, "as if you and the Master
ever did more than peck at your food. Why not a good roast
for the two of you to-night, and then you can take cuts off it
cold all the week-end?"

"But, Kate, it's Friday!" I said, my heart sinking lower than
ever, as I realized this meant that Kate hoped to be off before
lunch-time on Saturday. "And a Friday in Lent!"

"Oh, go along with your Lent! I've no patience with it,"
said Kate. "Why, Maggie Murphy, whose grannie at the Court
is ever so pi, tells me that the Pope says he's no objection to a
good joint any day now there's a war on!"

That is all very well, but the Pope quite certainly wouldn't
meet Miss Grieve or one of the parish ladies at the butcher's when he was ordering a roast for Friday night. After a
strange but inevitable diversion of our conversation to the discussion of Kate's new costume, and its suitability for a visit to
the Jenkinses in their remote country village; the sad medical
history of Mrs. Jenkins, who, if she's been tapped once has
been tapped a dozen times; Kate's views on Hitler, and the
report that five aeroplanes flew over Stampfield last night, in
hot search, apparently, for our Vicarage, we suddenly arrived
at a happy compromise. Kate promised to hustle up with her
work to-morrow and have lunch for us all (and Jenkins too, no
doubt) at a quarter-to-one, so that she can clean up (this refers,
I fear, to Kate's person rather than to the lunch things) and
"make the 1.42 Blue". Again I readjusted the meals, and was
just starting for the little shops round the corner when Arthur
looked out of the study.

"This is very lucky," he said. He had been worried about the Sunday services, and so had I, ever since Mr. Strang fell ill. It is too much for Arthur to have two Early Celebrations (usually well attended), Sung Matins and another Celebration, Catechism and Evensong, with no assistance. We had already tapped the sources of those clergy in the diocese who used to be called guinea-pigs, and only this morning our last hope had failed. "The Archdeacon has just rung up to say that he'll be glad to help me with the Early Services if we can put him up on Saturday night. He hasn't got petrol enough to get home on Saturday evening and out again next morning, when he's preaching here. It's really very kind of him, so I hope you'll forgive me for accepting off-hand and saying we would be delighted."

There was an appalling blow to fall on me after my promise to Kate! I think Arthur must have felt a little doubtful about that "delighted", as he retreated hastily and shut the study door with a sort of "now for my sermon" note. I went down to Kate once more, trying to remind myself that Bishops should be given to hospitality, but as Arthur isn't one, and Bishops presumably have adequate staffs, it didn't seem to help. Kate's sympathy was profound, though naturally it did not go as far as to make her offer to change her weekend. I just refrained from telling her that if Jenkins is not sent abroad this month, and I have a complete breakdown, I shall expect her to put flowers on my grave; again I readjusted my shopping-list with special reference to toilet-soap, new bed-lamp burner, call about man for window sash, and flowers for dinner-table. Kate also promised to try to get in Mrs. Sime to oblige on Saturday night, if it's not true that old Sime has been at Lil with a chopper and is in gaol!

Besides all these jobs I had to call at the Strangs, and as ill-luck would have it, Mrs. Strang answered the door herself. Poor little thing! Anxiety makes some people hard and defiant and others weak and helpless; but in her case I had to go through both phases. Standing in the minute chilly hall, she told me that her husband had been hounded to death by the malice of the parish, and she considered my husband responsible.

"He's ever, ever so ill, the night nurse says. She says she's never seen such a case of pneumonia."

"Come, come, Mrs. Strang!" The competent-looking day nurse emerged from the bedroom, shutting the door very softly behind her. "You'll wake your good husband if you talk so loud. And I don't think you quite understood Nurse Wethers. All she said was that she had never seen one or two symptoms in such a case as this before, and they are not at all necessarily bad ones. But I'd be very glad if you'd send a message to the chemist to hurry up with the oxygen."

At that Mrs. Strang began to weep hysterically, and drew me into the drawing-room to tell me that the day nurse was a harsh brute, that no-one but myself had ever tried to be kind to her in the whole of Stampfield, and that if anything happened to Herbert she would die, go into a Roman convent, and write to the papers about it, all apparently simultaneously. Luckily, as the baby began to cry and the oxygen was needed, I couldn't stop to try to soothe her much, and indeed the only words which really came to my mind with any force were, "Consider what a great girl you are!" But I promised that Arthur would pray for her husband at the Mid-day Service (which I fear she seemed to feel more of the nature of a revenge than anything else), and took care to let Mrs. Weekes know, when I met her in the grocer's, that poor Mr. Strang was very ill indeed and his wife absolutely beside herself. I saw in Mrs. Weekes' eye a gleam which foretold that she would soon be on her way in the car with grapes, champagne, chicken-broth, one frock at least for the baby, and flowers and cooked meats for Mrs. Strang; so my shopping hadn't been wasted. Then I looked in at the Vicarage with my message, got caught at the door by Mrs. Higgs, asking if I could spare linen for bandages, found two telephone calls which had to be answered at once (both engaged to begin with) and so arrived at the Old Rectory at last, longing to break the rule of silence at once, and tell Mrs. Pratt and everyone else that I'd like them to have treated my morning methodically.

I regret to say that as I was reviewing my activities, I discovered that the Words on Charity had changed to an Address on Meditation. It was in fact only borne in on me because all the others had stopped scribbling notes (in which I couldn't join as I had no paper but the dairy receipt and an old bus ticket), and were listening with the rapt repressive looks which every good parson's wife but myself, I feel, can adopt naturally at will.

Mrs. Eardley-Gage had it, of course, to perfection. In her youth she was, we all know, the childhood's pet of all the leading Anglican divines of her day. Her father was a prominent man on every Church Committee in Westminster, and her curls (now, I noticed, distinctly flattened) were stroked by a great Archbishop, her infant *mots* quoted by a great Canon of Saint Paul's, and she bore proudly the nickname of Bobo, given to her by an even more famous Bishop because she confided to him that Bishops were more alarming than geese. When one of that great clan of noble Anglican families who rose into prominence in Gladstone's later days, stayed at the Rectory, he was distinctly heard to call her Bobo twice in the presence of the Pratts, and when she is sitting, as she did now, with her fair, saintly face upturned, her frail figure gracefully erect, her thin fingers clasping her loose diamond rings, and her mind so clearly remote from all mundane affairs, I have a mad longing to get up and address her as Bobo and see what happens. As this is clearly due to nothing but the deadly sin of envy, I rebuked myself now severely, and reminded myself how charming and unusual a witness she is to that gracious wealthy set in society which adorns so many biographies of the last generation. As my forebears were for the most part hard-headed Evangelical colonels, who would have regarded their little holy jokes as profane, and described their little services in Bishops' chapels (black mantillas for the ladies at Compline) as hotbeds of Papacy, her old world doesn't touch mine; and sometimes I wonder if there can be any real friendship between those whose households run on four greased wheels, and those like myself who have to trundle along with a one-wheeled barrow, and spend all their time keeping it straight. Perhaps what is really at the root of the trouble is that she hasn't approved of Dick, and Dick has described her as an Anglican pussy-face, ever since we left the house together, after a croquet party with two of her gay yet serious Anglican nieces, and Dick declared outside the open windows, with an emphasis which must have been overheard, that he believed even the balls and hoops had been baptized by an Archbishop.

The Address ended, and we all moved across the hall to the Rector's study, now fitted as a temporary chapel, with a great deal of polite drawings-back and waving of hands over our precedence. All the bedroom chairs had been collected, and I made a mental note to avoid if possible, on our next progress here, the very exiguous and sharp-backed cane seat in front of me, which cut my arms and slid away from me if I leant on it. (Mrs. Pratt had manoeuvred herself far more wisely opposite a good solid sofa which could sustain her weight.)

Father Merrion, who was in charge of our retreat, urged us at this point, in the quiet hushed whisper which suited his ascetic face and figure so well, to remember that it is a danger in meditation to become too wholly detached from the conscious, thinking self. Great care, he emphasized, must be taken, in emptying the intellect, to listen only to the Interior Voice until we are sure of our spiritual armour. With this warning to my conscious mind I was indeed horrified to discover that I had spent the first few minutes in trying to discover the Rector as a chubby schoolboy in a Radley group, in remembering with horror that I hadn't ordered enough fish to do for kedgeree on Sunday morning as well as supper to-night, and, lastly,

that if we went on much longer I should relapse into what An-
glo-Catholics call, I believe, the Protestant Squat, or collapse
on the floor altogether. It is very strange and shame-making to
possess, in my profession, a mind that will not turn to order to
holy things. When I am put for a walk, or visiting some of the
poor people I love, or alone in my bedroom, I do sometimes
feel conscious of all that spiritual world in the fourth dimen-
sion just beyond our vision or conscious apprehension. And I
don't think I ever see a sudden view of hills beyond our street,
or a tree in blossom, or tulips in massed colours on a barrow
without remembering Francis Thompson's words: "Sworn to
poverty he forswore not beauty but worshipped through the
lamp beauty the Light, God." And in my visits to the Hospital
and my friends in my district, how often I recall words of a
war poet, which, said Arthur, came to him like a vision on the
way to Damascus:

> *"We that have seen man broken*
> *We know man is divine."*

But I fear I quite understood what Kate meant when she
withdrew herself from an admirable girls' society, saying, "Shut
me up with a pack of women in a small room, and I go all
goosey, Ma'am."

It is a sin, this resistance to communal emotion, I know,
and I try to correct it; but I suppose a wandering mind is
the inevitable revenge of time on a housekeeper, whose duty
it is to think of a dozen things at once; and my tendency to
flippancy and criticism have been sadly rejuvenated by a really amusing son, and never damped by a husband who values
sincerity rather than conventional expressions of thought. But
what I really wonder always is how many of the congregation
are feeling just as I do, and wandering just as I do. Because as
you grow older, you do recognize that there is nothing unusual about yourself, and that they may be thinking much the

same thoughts as mine, even while they look at Mrs. Lacely and wish they were as attentive as she is.

Again I pulled myself up and tried to meditate, but by this time the text on which we were to concentrate had wholly eluded me, and by fumbling in a prayer-book I only hit the Psalm which, as a clerical correspondent in *The Times* so wittily pointed out, would just coincide with meat-rationing: "They run hither and thither for meat and are not satisfied." No other woman present, I am quite sure, could have sunk to such a low level of inward debate between the respective merits of point steak and neck of mutton for a household of three, when we all rose and trouped back to the drawing-room.

This next hour raised my spiritual tone considerably. I should not like to give a precis of the Address, but I had secured a seat near the bow window, and enjoyed I my view of the garden more than I can say. The Rectory stands back from the market square, red-brick, with plaster facings, and at the back an old walled garden slopes gently downhill to a row of poplars before the town obtrudes itself again. Mrs. Eardley-Gage is, of course, a keen and successful gardener, and is a little liable to say that flowers grow for those who love them, whereas "we all know that she doesn't mind what she spends on manure", says Mrs. Weekes with a sniff. I found it much easier to attend mildly to the Address of Prayer in Wartime as I looked out at the groups of snowdrops and crocuses, and still more at the fat pink shoots of peonies and the gay green growth round the dead stalks of the herbaceous plants. For they do show that winter and seeming death have a purpose at least, and that the efforts of the poor little strugglers underground are rewarded, however helpless they may be. The sun was on my back and I was feeling warm, mentally and physically, when I was distracted by Father Merrion's pronouncements on Prayers for Victory.

He is a delightful man, I feel sure, with a heart of gold beneath his cassock, and a most acute mind behind his gold-rimmed spectacles. But is he not, I asked myself, one of the old arguments which crop up in everyday life against a celibate clergy in spite of my reflections last night? I am quite sure that in the monastery of his Order there is no thought but for the things of the Spirit. I quite see that the bewildering cares of a clergyman with a family on an inadequate income must distract the mind at times from God. But when even the noblest of celibate priests grow older they do tend, I think, to take a very academic view of parenthood. Very few men have enough imagination to realize anything they have not experienced, and in this question of prayer, one of the important sides, it seems to me, is the conception of a child praying to his Father for what he really needs. I was so full of the thought that when Father Merrion stopped, and urged us to discuss the point with him, I found my tongue for once (or was it the demoralizing result of my speechmaking yesterday?) and broke out.

"But shouldn't we feel our own children very affected and insincere if they came to us and asked for everything except the thing they really wished?" As usual my voice rose and my eyes grew moist, but Mrs. Gage cast me a glance of approval. Nothing, as we all know, is so daunting as the moment when an audience is pressed to ask questions and sits dumb in embarrassed silence.

"But is victory what we all want *most*?" asked Father Merrion kindly but disapprovingly.

"Surely," said Mrs. Pratt, briskly and rather officially. "What we desire most is the coming of God's Kingdom upon earth."

"Well, as far as we can see, that's what we are fighting for— freedom of speech and freedom to worship God," put in Mrs. Stead, who has, I remembered, a son in the Air Force.

"I pray for victory, and peace on that condition," announced old Mrs. Cummings, majestically.

"I pray so much for our enemies," said Mrs. Gage, leaning forward more intently than ever, and crossing her thin beauti-

ful ankles. "I pray daily for Thy child Hitler, Thy son von Rib-
bentrop and Thy child Stalin. You don't know how it *helps*."

It is a beautiful thought but the condescension of it rather
took away my breath. I could see that Mrs. Stead felt too that
it would take one of the famous Littleways to presume as far
as that.

"There I differ from you," said Mrs. Cummings, still more
pontifically. "To my mind these people are Apollyon and the
power of darkness. I would no more pray for them than for
the Devil."

"Oh, but I often do!" Little stout bubbling Mrs. Jay has a
local reputation for being so clever and original, but everyone
clearly felt she had gone too far this time.

"Do you qualify your prayers by that clause, 'If it be Thy
Will'?" said Father Merrion, turning to me, rather unfairly, I
thought, as quite four people had spoken since I had.

"Yes, I do, and I ask to be helped to mean it!" (Now that all
our tongues were loosed my voice was under control at last.)
"But if your child came to you and saw a box of chocolates on
the table, and asked for a kiss or a new lesson-book, and didn't
ask for a chocolate, you would think him rather affected and
insincere, wouldn't you?"

"My children are never allowed sweets or chocolates of
any kind," put in Mrs. Holm, suddenly. She is always described
as such an excellent mother, and has developed the face and
figure of a broody hen on her reputation; but Father Merrion
was not the man to let the conversation glide into a discussion
of nursery regime, as it showed some tendency to do from the
confidential murmurs in the corners of the room.

"Could you not assume that your child did not ask for
one because, knowing they were indulgences rather than necessities, he preferred to wait for you to exercise your own
judgement?"

"You can see he's no children of his own," murmured Mrs. Stead under her breath to me, thus reaching the identical point of my meditation on the celibacy of the clergy.

"I shouldn't think he was behaving naturally to me," I said, "and shouldn't prayer be natural?"

"I wish", said Mrs. Jay, undaunted by the failure off her previous effort, "that someone could explain to me why prayers sometimes seem such a bore."

"Perhaps we might return to that point later," said Father Merrion, as the clergy always do when they feel a little nonplussed. "The question is, how far are we justified in praying for victory? I suppose the real difficulty we all admit is, to continue the analogy, that there is only one chocolate in the box and several children are asking for it. The Germans and Russians are doubtless praying as earnestly as we. ..."

"Not the Russians," said Mrs. Cummings, shocked at Father Merrion's laxity. "They are heathen now, and you must remember we have the Jews on our side. My dear father always used to say that God's blessing would certainly rest on any nation which was kind to the Jews."

"Let us only admit the Germans, then. Your theory would", he said, turning to me again, "make a mere duel of prayer."

Of course I know that argument and I know none against it, but I am still convinced that it is hopeless to try to pray in love and trust if you leave your chief desire out of your petitions.

"Well, if our armies were defeated," said Mrs. Stead, whom I hardly knew before as she lives at some distance in the country, but is becoming rapidly my greatest friend in the audience, "there'll be nothing left worth living for!"

"May it not be", said Father Merrion, "that there comes a point in the lives of certain nations as of Our Lord Himself, when they must be sacrificed on the Cross for the ultimate good of humanity? It is a hard saying, and needs a mystic's submission, but must we not school our minds even to that?"

His eyes grew very beautiful and far-away, as he withdrew himself to the last outpost which the true saints are taking refuge in now, I know, and Mrs. Stead only whispered to me, instead of voicing her opinion aloud: "Well, I can only hope it'll be the Germans who have to be sacrificed."

"That is a wonderful thought," said Mrs. Gage. "That is something to help us in all the privations and anxieties we have to undergo." (And what these are at the moment, compared with ours, Mrs. Stead and I would very much like to know!)

"But we are told to pray 'deliver us from evil'," I ventured. "And surely we can all assume that German victory would be an evil."

"Personally," put in Mrs. Pratt, "I think that politics should never be mixed with religion at all. It is just that which has caused so much trouble in your parish, Mrs. Lacely."

Two or three of the audience who had remained remote and uninterested in the discussion brightened up perceptibly at this.

"In fact, I don't think we could do better than pray that Mr. Strang should be made to see the error of his ways," continued Mrs. Pratt, to the evident discomfiture of Mrs. Gage and our spiritual adviser. In the circles in which Mrs. Gage moved normally I am sure such discursive and reasonless discussion would have been unthinkable. Some cultured lady would have quoted Dante, another produced a *pensée* of Pascal, and a third have remembered what the dear Archbishop had said to her the other day at Lambeth. I do humbly agree that it is very good for us to meet the superior spiritual culture of our hostess and our pastor, only I can't help thinking it rather funny when the two parties clash as they did to-day.

"I think we should indeed pray for him," I murmured to Mrs. Pratt as the bell sounded again. "He is very ill indeed to-day, I fear."

Mrs. Pratt could say no more, as the bell was the signal for a relapse into the silence. We left the Arundel prints, Morris wall-papers and chintzes once more, and I regret to say, to my acute disappointment, did not file into the dining-room, the door of which stood invitingly open, but once more to the chapel for the Litany. It is true, as I told Arthur, that the Litany alone seems to me a perfect war-time prayer, but not after the morning I had spent, and not, I concluded then, for clergy wives. So many of us are so much in the habit of finding ourselves one out of two or three gathered together for extra services, that we tend, as a class, to develop a resonant style in responses. I am always ashamed that this is no gift of mine, for I cannot bear to order Heaven in a loud voice, but most of the gathering were adepts, and when we were all united the fervour evidently surprised Father Merrion. I even had an unworthy suspicion that Mrs. Cummings had determined from the first that she would have no nonsense about playing second fiddle, and beseeched God in a loud, positively minatory voice. Mrs. Gage, on the other hand, murmured quite softly, but so very swiftly and efficiently that she had got her whole phrase in before Mrs. Cummings was even under way. Mrs. Holm lisped very clearly, as if leading a choir of children; Mrs. Jay's voice was audible with resigned hunger and despair. One little lady near me with a tight, sallow, repressive face, showed by her voice quite clearly what she thought of us all. Altogether a very undevotional ceremony, and my knees were so stiff that I could hardly stand when at last we were safely among the Raphael cartoons and heavy oak of the dining-room.

The lunch was beautifully laid and served for the twenty-odd of our party. The only breakdown in the arrangement was that we seemed to sit avoiding each other's eyes for some time before the first course appeared, and that I felt a weak inclination to smile over our polite bowings to each other as we offered or accepted water, our delicate curtseyings for the salt, and ostentatious shakes of the head to the servants who offered us second helpings. I rather regretted the last, as the fillets of fish offered to us were tiny thought delightful, and the portion of stewed rhubarb almost infinitesimal, especially as Father Merrion accepted second helpings on each occasion without losing one jot of his ascetic preoccupation. But after merely toying with her fish, Mrs. Gage stood up and read aloud to us a very fragrant story about some little Italian saint who ate, apparently, nothing but a few chestnuts from the day of her birth to that of her rather repellent death, so that no clergy-wife could have imperilled her position by showing any carnal greed. My one water biscuit at the close seemed positively large and satisfying, and Mrs. Gage did break off her story and her silence very kindly to press us to take butter, "as Cook says the grocer gives us as much as we want".

This confession of perfidiousness, and a slight sense of emptiness made the next address rather torpid, I fear. I was still preoccupied about the fish and the window blind, and was prone to wonder whether the Archdeacon would bring his own hot-water bottle and whether the old stone one leaked if he didn't. And whether I should run in to Mrs. Strang again this evening, and what effect his illness was having on the militant laity of our parish. By this time I had acquired a pencil and paper from Mrs. Stead, but all I found on the paper afterwards, I regret to say, was:

(1) A drawing of snowdrops under a cedar tree—quite good;

(2) *The Problem of Pain*. Incomplete: cf. Saint Paul and parable of sheep and goats—Vic; Redempt.;

(3) A sketch of Mrs. Gage's gown—she always calls them gowns and says her maid makes them for her. This I can well believe, as whatever their material they are of a design which always suggests the fashions of 1910 modified by a study of last year's *Vogue* and a subtle hint of ecclesiastical vestments;

(4) A very poor Clerihew—automatic writing, I trust:

When Dr. Angus MacTain
Was asked to speak on the Problem of Pain,
All he said was, "Ye needn't fash
As long as it's not below your sash."

(5) Mem. Find bathroom key if poss.

We did not discuss the problem of pain, but went back to the study-chapel. There I tried to summon my concentration and conquer my disconnected thoughts with greater success, till my chair—the type called *prie dieu*—on rather excitable wheels, took a little run into Mrs. Cummings's back. This accident and the look which the old lady turned upon me shattered me so much that I did not recover till we were back in the drawing-room with our note-books, taking abstracts on an imaginary debate on free-will. If Father Merrion imagines that any of us willingly embark on such a subject with our Sunday Schools or classes he is almost certainly mistaken, and when he proposed that we should continue the debate ourselves, and Mrs. Gage looked encouragingly at me, there was a complete silence. Mrs. Jay remarked that she knew there was a very amusing and helpful Limerick on the subject, but as she could get no further than that it began, "There once was a man who said," and ended in something about a tram, Mrs. Gage hastened to say it was all so difficult, and she herself felt *faith* was the only solution. Mrs. Holm, after a shattering pause, said that after all, nature always did bring its own punishments, didn't it, and if you let a child grow up self-willed it would meet with troubles all its life, wouldn't it? She had found in her own nursery—but what she had found we never knew, for Mrs. Gage tinkled a little bell, and it was time for Vespers. These I should have appreciated more if the floor had not by now become so hard, and my back so tired, that I might have taken to my seat, as Mrs. Cummings did (I hoped not as a result of my little accident) but for the merciful sound of tea-cups in the distance. I don't know if we were really supposed to be out of the Silence, but with teacups in our hands we all began to break it with one accord, and I had time to tell Mrs. Pratt, now all sympathy and anxiety, about the poor Strangs before Mrs. Gage rang her bell and, discarding her tea-cup, began to read aloud to us. At an ordinary time I am sure we should have enjoyed the rather cryptic little parable about a sunny little Anglican stream and a very talkative kingfisher, but we were all, I fancy, too sadly disappointed by the failure to exchange views with each other to do it justice. At this point I own I disgraced myself. One of the French windows of the dining-room was open, and I escaped through it into the garden, where the late afternoon sunlight was falling across the grass on a daphne bush, and a winter jasmine was flowering against a wall. But I do not think anyone saw me, and I did at last feel myself nearer to God in the garden (much as I dislike that sentimental poem on the subject). When I saw the drawing-room filling up again, I crept back, and the last address was really very peaceful and beautiful; but I began to grow anxious about the time, as Arthur had to have dinner punctually, as he has to look in at the choir practice to-night. This made my farewells very inferior, I fear, to those of Mrs. Pratt, who was assuring Mrs. Eardley-Gage that the day had been an inspiration and would help her through the War *whatever* happened. As I felt that nothing I had heard would make any real difference if even Dick's little finger were hurt, I felt it best just to mumble, with the hope that the radiance of Mrs. Gage's smile (was it partly due to relief and the prospect of a quiet *tête-à-tête* with Father Merrion?) might spread its reflection on to my face. Like all parties of this kind we all declared that we must hurry away (but I saw to my relief the drawing-room clock was, perhaps intentionally, fast), and then stopped and chatted to each other in the drive.

"I must say," said the sallow, severe little lady, "that if I had been warned how very very ritualistic the whole affair would be, nothing would have persuaded me to come."

"Well, my dear, you knew, as he was a Father, that was the kind of thing you must expect," said Mrs. Pratt very sensibly.

"There are fathers *and* fathers," retorted the little lady no less severely, and I took care not to catch Mrs. Jay's eye.

"I thought it was all beautiful, quite beautiful," murmured a tall, vague, wispy woman near me. "If only one could carry it all back into one's daily life!"

"That's just it," agreed Mrs. Holm. "I'm sure personally it would be a help to meditate every day, if only one had the time, and to have a little oratory of one's own; but it's so difficult, isn't it? We haven't even got a second bathroom now that the children use it for developing photographs."

"My bedside, where my dear mother taught me my prayers, is good enough for me," said Mrs. Cummings, moving off our slow, straggly procession towards the gate.

"I", said Mrs. Stead, anxiously, "have a drawer bursting with extra Collects I've been asked to say at one time or another, but you know if I really used them all, I should never get down in time for breakfast."

"Let alone massage and nail-polish," said a woman whose red beret, shoes and gloves had distracted my attention through almost the whole of the Address on Free-Will. Her tweed suit was the only clerical thing about her, and even that was brightened by a red button-hole and a red scarf. As this was the only remark she made from first to last and no-one seemed to know what part of the neighbourhood she had come from, she will only live in my mind as the one parson's wife I ever knew who came to a Quiet Day wearing mild but quite obvious make-up. She reminded me of the boy who said that the only person braver than a boy who said his prayers in a dormitory when no-one else did, would be a bishop who didn't say his in a dormitory of bishops. Oddly enough, she departed in the custody of the severe little Evangelical, and they both remain an enigma to this day.

Mrs. Stead and I parted with warm promises to see something of each other this summer, and I hope we shall. But our lives are very much like those of travellers on a cruise; when we get back to our homes and parishes, we forget to make plans for our own amusement, and we don't meet people with such identical interests often enough. She had to hurry away to her bus, and Mrs. Pratt was paying a call in the other direction; so I found myself walking off with Mrs. Jay, whom I never met before, talking as if we had known each other all our lives.

"I do hope I didn't say anything dreadful," she said, anxiously. "You know our parish is such a remote, lonely one that I get into the habit of saying my thoughts aloud, I really do! And my husband is so strict and reserved in his own wonderful way that I often feel afraid of just uttering my own silly thoughts to him!"

I remembered Mr. Jay then, a big, stern pompous man, Rector of Cudbury, Kate's home village, and reported by Kate to be a tartar and no mistake. She had never spoken of Mrs. Jay, and I had vaguely imagined that the Rector was unmarried. I expect he does his best to suppress poor irrepressible little Mrs. Jay.

"It was funny, wasn't it?" she giggled now. "I mean, of course, it was wonderful, and all the things the rest say, but it was screamingly funny too. You missed one of the queerest parts by skipping out into the garden like that."

"Oh, you didn't see me!" I protested, horrified.

"Only once—your blue hat behind a cedar bough. It's such a pretty colour, if you don't mind my saying so." (I didn't!) "Well, you see, it said on the board that in that interval anyone with any private anxiety about their faith could consult Father Merrion. My dear, there were *two* queues in the passage, if you know what I mean, and won't think me too coarse. Well, of course, being me, I got into the wrong one and suddenly found myself in Mrs. Gage's little sitting-room upstairs, with

Father Merrion standing among quite a dozen little holy statues and photographs of bishops, asking me so kindly how he could help me and what was it that troubled me."

"Oh, my dear, how awful!" I exclaimed with most unsuitable emphasis. For there might well be moments in life when one wanted such help and comfort as that saintly man could give. Only it would take me weeks of screwing up my mind to it, and I should have to go alone, quite alone, and in secret, and never as a member of a rival queue. I am quite sure that as a nation we are far too reserved and alarmed of speaking of spiritual things, and that the methods of the Oxford Group, which Dick calls "jollying up", are a reaction in the right direction; but it is very, very difficult for elderly leopards to change their spots.

"Well, it wasn't too bad. I was so sorry for him, because that little woman like a lemon stuck on a poker, you know, was just bouncing out of the door (I'm sure *she'd* got into the wrong queue) saying, 'Confession is contrary to the laws of the Protestant Church of England, and if ever I wanted direction I would speak to my husband!' (Oh, dear, I'm sorry for him, too!) 'Well,' Father Merrion said to me, with a very nice twinkle, 'I do hope you don't misunderstand me as completely as she has done!' I nearly told him about the queues to comfort him," Mrs. Jay continued (and I was very much surprised personally that she hadn't), "and do you know, apart from that, I could only think of our kitchen range which is so extravagant, and that the bother we had in all the snow with a shortage of fuel nearly drove me out of my mind, but I couldn't very well, could I?"

"No," I agreed, "but do, do tell me, if it's not inquisitive what you did ask him about."

"Oh, about the Immaculate Conception," said Mrs. Jay, blithely. "Do you know, I've never had the least idea what it meant, so I thought it would do quite well. But I must say," she went on dejectedly, "he only told me that it wasn't an Article of Faith in our Church and I needn't let it bother me again. Well, it certainly won't. He can be sure of that! Mrs. Lacely, don't you think days when we could talk would be nicer?"

I nearly replied in Miss Dunstable's words to Mrs. Proudie: "Very true, but it wouldn't be very like a ball if you had no dancing, Mrs. Proudie," but I only assented sympathetically. What Mrs. Jay evidently needs so badly is someone to talk to, and someone who isn't in her parish, and with whom she needn't remember to be tactful, reticent and discreet, "which", Mrs. Pratt said to me once, "is the duty I always try to impress on the wives of the clergy."

"We're a funny set, you know," continued Mrs. Jay. "I can't help thinking how my two daughters who are working in London in a beauty-parlour—they can't stand the country unluckily—would have laughed at us all as a set of has-beens."

"Oh, we're not all so old," I laughed. "You must have married very young, and Mrs. Holm and Mrs. Stead are youngish, too, and there was such a pretty girl in brown in a corner."

"Yes, and she looked scared stiff from first to last," put in Mrs. Jay.

"I'll tell you what I really thought as I looked round," I said, more seriously; "that there we all were, busy, rather overworked people, not very smart or amusing, and with funny little fads of our own, no doubt; and yet you could be sure, couldn't you, that not one of us would let our husbands down, or our children or friends or servants. We haven't time for accomplishments or graces, spiritual as well as physical, I mean, but we are all trying as hard as we can with our hopeless limitations, to bring God's Kingdom to earth and to love God and our neighbour. So though we wouldn't cut any ice at the Ritz or Hollywood, you can just say of us that, as a set, we do our job and keep up to our ideals as far as we can, and that if any woman in there knew that her enemy was ill she'd visit him, or that a poor person wanted her, she'd hurry out at once. And we'd go, wouldn't we, to any parishioner who wanted us in prison, and we all do our best to help out-of-works with clothes or money, and so, I suppose, in a way we can feel that …" I grew embarrassed and finished up lamely, "… that we are hoping to hear some day, 'Inasmuch as ye did it to the least of these my little ones, ye did it unto Me'."

I cannot say what a fraud I felt when Mrs. Jay ran off to her bus in the Market Square saying I had helped her, really helped her, quite as much as Father Merrion. Especially, as a kind of impatience of this odd wasted day seized upon me and I broke out to Arthur on my return, "And oh, my dear, I'm so perverse that I feel I've a hundred theological unbeliefs in my head that I never had before; it always happens when people talk about pain and free-will! Do you know, I believe what would really do me good would be to go to a Quiet Day held by Aldous Huxley or Joad or H. G. Wells! I expect I should come home from that a militant Christian!" Arthur was most delightfully sympathetic, and said that excess of religious emotion often produced this effect on critical if untrained minds. "And I don't know what I'd do without you to laugh things over with," he added, "for I haven't felt much like laughing to-day." At one o'clock punctually, he told me, Mr. Weekes had appeared in the vestry with two of the sidesmen to present an ultimatum; that unless Mr. Strang resigned his curacy and left Stampfield they would be obliged to give up their sittings in Saint Simon's. Fifty-nine members of the congregation had signed a notice to the same effect, and this was presented to Arthur with silent hostility.

"I made no reply," said Arthur, "except to ask them all to come to the service when I would give them my decision in our church. They meant, of course, to come in any case, and the church was packed. All through the first hymn I couldn't help noticing that Mrs. Weekes was whispering to her husband (you know her demure murmur that hardly sounds or shows). By the time the troops of Midian had finished prowling, the poor old fellow was looking like a convicted criminal, and I knew that Strang's illness had done its best. But I didn't suppose anyone else knew much about it, as I went up to the altar and offered up all our prayers for him, there, to mark the urgency of the crisis. I prayed for Herbert Strang who was dangerously ill, and then I got up into the pulpit and preached."

"Oh, Arthur, what about?"

Arthur rose and walked about the room. "About? Oh, well, I gave them a good deal of Aristotle on the danger of democracies; I rubbed it in how the weakness of the Allies is the public gossip and cavilling and criticism of each other in the press and in ordinary speech. I told them that we in the Church should look upon Christ as our dictator, that we should segregate ourselves from grumbling in voluntary concentration camps of silence. I said that no views expressed by any free Englishman could be as subversive or detestable as the malicious gossip of his critics. It was rather a hot sermon, Dick would say, I fear, as I felt so intolerably angry to think not only of that poor fellow, Strang, but also of the hateful pettiness and spite of this place in the last few days. I have never in my life felt like ranting and scolding before, and it was a most curious sensation," said my husband, thoughtfully.

"Oh, don't give way to it, darling," I cried. "At least, only once more, so that I can hear you doing it, and then for ever after you must hold your peace! But what happened afterwards?"

"They all came round to the vestry—the previous deputation, I mean—and they made me more ashamed of myself than I had ever been before in my life. How can people say that human nature is disillusioning? Or is it that it's because these men are essentially Christians that love and mercy come as naturally, or more naturally, to them than prejudice and hostility? Mr. Weekes said that of course their protests were withdrawn in view of Mr. Strang's sad illness, and in ten minutes they were all arranging a private subscription list to cover all the medical expenses for poor little Strang. I can't tell you how touched and pleased I was. I told them straight out I wasn't worthy to be their priest, and they rejoined …" Arthur threw back his head and laughed at the memory.

"Oh, what?"

"That they'd always known I was on their side really all the time! You see women can't have the monopoly of unreason-ableness!"

"No, indeed! But what darlings they really are. I knew Mr. Weekes would have to knuckle under anyhow. And what then?"

"I went to the Strangs …"

"Without lunch?"

"Do you know, I did forget about lunch," Arthur confessed. "But really, that meal yesterday would last me for weeks. As a matter of fact I only realized it when I discovered how hungry I was at tea-time."

"Well, I'll get supper, and then run to see her," I said, rub-bing my stiff knees.

"You won't get supper," said Kate, beaming at the doorway. "For I've got it for you, and a surprise and all." (Kate's surprises are, alas, too often sausages and onions, and so it proved on this occasion.) "But don't you go to Strangs, Mum. They say he's as bad as can be, and two nurses, so what'll be the good?"

But I did go, of course; how could I leave that poor little thing alone till I had seen how she would face the night? I only wished I were brave about the black-out and could feel, as Arthur says he does, a delight in the new eerie darkness of our strange little town—Stampfield of the Dark Ages, as he calls it.

' I stumbled up the steps of the bungalow with nothing in my mind but my old nurse's tales of Jack the Ripper, and hope I did not show my relief too obviously when I met Dr. Boness in the little passage.

"Ah-ha, in at the death!" he said. He is the kindest man in the world, but under his sister's influence he uses very odd ex-pressions. Even he was conscious of it this time, for he amend-ed his words hastily—"I mean to say here in time to quiet that poor little woman and make her take the dose I've left her and go off to sleep. Mrs. Weekes has kidnapped her baby, with the kindest intentions, but Mrs. Strang's left with nothing to do and has broken down altogether. And I can't stop, for I've got to go and sign poor old Mrs. Hodge's death certificate."

"Oh, she's gone," I said, with relief. Death does seem more of a triumph than anything else for the old and lonely in these unhappy days; and however modern one may try to be in one's ideas about Heaven, in my mind at once I saw Mrs. Hodge, young and fair, wandering where,

> "Quiet through the fields, all crystal clear,
> The stream of life doth flow."

"But tell me, how is Mr. Strang?"

"Not too good, but we'll pull him through," said Dr. Boness as cheerfully as ever. "I'll look in when you've settled Mrs. Strang and give you a lift home. We can't have you running into a motor in the blackout, Mrs. Lacely."

Poor little Mrs. Strang was lying on the sofa in the drawing-room, a heap of blankets on the floor. The nurses and her husband fill the two bedrooms, and she was camping out here in spite of Mrs. Weekes' offer of hospitality.

"They all said I should go, but I couldn't, could I?" she asked, feverishly. All her defiance and anger had disappeared, and she only looked like a woe-begone pretty child. She was too tired to rebel against the doctor's orders any more, and looked at me with trustful eyes when I promised he wouldn't die while she was asleep: I would tell the nurses to wake her. So often in great misery some preoccupation like this obscures the main issue, I know. She could not think what his death would mean, only that he must not die without the comfort of her presence. I made up the uncomfortable bed and gave her her dose with the sort of soothing words you use for a child.

"Your husband came and prayed with me," she said, a little shyly, "and he was so definitely marvellous that I won't say any more, or I only just begin to cry again."

I said that was very sensible, and I would just say my own evening prayers by her nice warm fire till the doctor came for me, and this exactly satisfied her sense of the proprieties. "You'll pray for him, won't you," she said, sleeping with her tears already, "because you know he is so definitely marvellous." As I felt I should, after all the fatigues of the day, disgrace myself by sheer hysteria if she told me anyone else was definitely marvellous, I sank on my knees (still very stiff) by the lowest arm-chair I could find. Certainly I was praying for victory now, I realized dreamily, for victory over death. Isn't that the victory we all are praying for, in spite of all human experience? And why do we do it when death is the only escape from fear, and our old haunting dread for those we loved individually has grown into the real definite terror of the War. Oh, lucky Mrs. Hodge, I thought, even as I prayed for Herbert Strang ("And why, I wonder, my love, should we use Christian names for those who are mere acquaintances just because we are in church?" my grandmother used to ask), until my muddled thoughts faded into a dream of flowers and rivers and trees where Rossetti angels "evermore do sit and evermore do sing". I cannot say that a motor-horn even in a dream should suggest angelic voices, but Dr. Boness's call to me fitted in quite nicely.

"Home, John?" quoted Dr. Boness to me inevitably, and I smiled dutifully. Do we ever really care very much what happens to us on the way, I wondered, as long as we reach home at last?

Arthur had been called out, I found, to visit a dying man at the other end of the parish, so I crawled upstairs to bed, feeling a quiet night infinitely more desirable than a quiet day.

VIII
SATURDAY

THERE WAS a terrible bustle this morning.

Kate is an indefatigable worker in a crisis, but her energy takes odd direction. It was very noble of her to rise at five and wake me by washing out the hall, and what she always calls the Gents' Cloaks, but I could not see why the entire basement should also be scrubbed all over again, as it was only done on Wednesday, and it seems most unlikely that the Archdeacon should penetrate there.

"Him?" said Kate, "no, but I won't have Mrs. Sime saying I don't keep a clean kitchen!"

This unfortunate consideration meant that I had to do Dick's room for Archdeacon Pratt myself. I hate to put visitors in Dick's room, but I didn't dare to risk the black-out in the spare-room, as we have just had a new air-raid warden appointed to this district, and he is unlikely to have sunk into the easy-going ways of Miss Boness, who said candidly that if the Germans were fools enough to bomb Stampfield in the snow she'd let them. We are, I imagine, as safely situated as any town in England, but like every other place, we bitterly resent this imputation, and point out either that Hitler knows that nothing would wear on the nerves of England like the destruction of our breweries (Gold's Entire), or that we lie in a straight line between London and Manchester, and would be a dumping ground for his unused bombs. Arthur got himself into such disgrace with dear nervous Miss Grieve by pooh-poohing the idea, that we affect now to share the common terror, and fall over pails of sand in the house, like all good patriots, though I firmly refuse to spend 15s. 7d. on a stirrup pump.

I tried to harden my heart as I swept and dusted Dick's room, reminding myself vigorously that he would soon be here for a week's leave. But what use is only a week with someone who was once that absurd little creature in a minute cap and blazer at a child's school, a round-faced, very solemn, captain of his cricket XI in his preparatory school, and an incredibly noble and earnest young VIth Former in his last house group? This I told myself was sentiment, and turned severely to the book-case; but if all the mothers all over the world united their feelings as they dusted every country's equivalent of *Peter Rabbit, Just William* and, even more pathetic, the first signs of highbrow taste, in T. S. Eliot, Auden, and Huxley, how could wars go on any longer? Again I rebuked myself, only to relapse into maudlin sentiment over the discovery of the key of Dick's roller skates (lost tragically four years ago) in a drawer of his shaving-mirror, under a pile of May Week programmes. The Archdeacon must put up with dust, I decided, unable to endure these memories any longer, and was positively relieved to hear the front-door bell. I had to go down to protect Arthur from interruption, as he was either making out lists of services, or writing his sermon, or, indeed, as was still more probable, deep in *The Guardian* or *The New Statesman.*

Mr. Elgin stood at the door with a note outstretched in his hand.

"But you are coming to tea this afternoon," I said, in dismay.

"Yes, yes, but I wanted to let your husband know my future plans first!"

He looked so starved and miserable that I could not imagine that his plans included an engagement to Miss Croft. As Arthur appeared, starting out to the Strangs, I stopped him to read the note at once. I had telephoned just before breakfast, to hear there was no change, and that Mrs. Strang was still asleep, so there was no urgent hurry.

"This is what comes of your match-making!" said Arthur, most unjustly. "Elgin is handing in his resignation!"

"Oh, but why?"

"He says—what is it?—that owing to changes in the circumstances of his friends and unhappy gossip, he feels he will do better work elsewhere."

"Oh dear, that means that people have been talking, and he's afraid of being accused of hanging up his hat in Miss Croft's hall!"

"Incurable romantic!" said Arthur as he hurried away; but Kate's remark as I started out strengthened my theory.

"Such talk!" she said, looking at Mr. Elgin's envelope, "of Miss Croft's fortune, and how she'll be a match for the highest in the land!"

Of course, if the story of the legacy has swollen to this, Mr. Elgin may well feel uncomfortable, and I felt a little nervous about my tea-party, as I hurried out, and down to the Market Square to leave Arthur's watch at the mender's, and to see why the grocer hadn't sent up yet.

Outside the corner of "Ye Olde Teapot", Mrs. Weekes waved at me imperiously, and ordered, rather than asked, me in to Miss Croft's for a cup of coffee. I am sure that in ordinary life she would think this an undignified proceeding for one of her household magnificence, but the story of Miss Croft's legacy had only just reached her, and she was naturally anxious for first-hand information. Unluckily most of the *élite* of Stampfield had been fired by the same determination, and it was with the utmost difficulty that we squeezed into one half of an Olde Cosie Corner and obtained two cups of very milky liquid. Miss Croft herself was obviously in no condition to gossip. In the window was a notice: "Retiring Sale. This business will close shortly." On a shelf above us were Lincoln Imps marked down as low as ninepence half-penny; Barnstaple ware was going at a gift, and a heap of little notices in passe-partout frames about "Lovesome spot. Green Grot"; "I shall pass through this world but once …" and "Glorious morning faces", were offered at a penny each, as if Miss Croft were renouncing her philosophy and her business simultaneously.

"I'm sending every cake that's left to Miss Grieve's Cake and Candy Sale," she hissed to me, "and I am never going to look at Chocolate Fudge again!"

Mrs. Weekes kept her eye on every movement of the proprietress with obvious interest, but her conversation with me dealt primarily with the Strangs.

"Their little Pamela is too sweet", she said, "—her father's eyebrows, poor little mite!"

"But he isn't worse, is he?" I felt nervously that only the curate's demise could make Mrs. Weekes, of all people, speak so affectionately of those militant pacifist eyebrows.

"No, no, I was coming away just as your good husband looked in. Dr. Boness hopes for some real change to-morrow. I fancy he must have been going about with this 'flu on him for days, and it's his heart that causes us all such anxiety." Mrs. Weekes added firmly, "This quite explains that unfortunate sermon. A sick man is not responsible for his opinions, and he was a very sick man, Mrs. Lacely!"

"Yes, of course, he should have given in long ago. How is poor little Mrs. Strang?"

"Still asleep, quite worn out. I hope to persuade her to come to me for the night. It was very good of you to look in last night, I am sure." But from her manner I could tell that Mrs. Weekes felt I had been poaching on her sick-bed preserves.

"That will be lovely for her," I agreed. "I can't get round to-night anyhow, as my maid's away for the week-end, and we have the Archdeacon for the night."

"That maid of yours seems to spend more time out than in," pronounced Mrs. Weekes with some justice. "Did I hear you say to Lady Cyrus that you were expecting your boy on leave, Mrs. Lacely? I hope to have Ida very soon."

"Yes, any time now," I answered vaguely. "Did Lady Cyrus's girl know Ida at Roedean?"

That, I hoped, was a safe draw from a subject on which I felt a consummate hypocrite; but Mrs. Weekes, munching an eclair, unperturbed, while the frantic little assistant took down a papier mâché vase from the shelf just above us, pursued her inquiries mercilessly.

"I never knew anything about your relatives till I met Lady Cyrus. Somehow one always imagines that a clergyman's wife is the daughter of a clergyman!"

"They often are," I pointed out.

"And I know Miss Boness told me once that your grand-mother had an old-clothes shop."

"She hadn't," I said, unable to hide my smiles. "I may have said she looked as if she came out of one, for she did. But that was because she wouldn't part with her maid, and poor dear Smith was blind for the last twenty years of her life."

"Blind? Then how did she cook?"

"I mean her own maid," I explained a little impatiently, because I hadn't really the time to discuss my grandmother's staff just then.

"A lady's maid? She kept a lady's maid?"

"Oh, everyone did then," I said, a little infelicitously per-haps to Mrs. Weekes. "But my own mother didn't," I added, in the vague hope of making things better.

"Birth counts as well as money," was Mrs. Weekes' oracular reply.

"I think education matters most of all," I said, referring to Ida, and hoping, when I'd said it, that Mrs. Weekes would not take it personally. Fortunately she didn't, for she only shook her head and said one might have too much of *that*. On the whole, however, I felt that Serena had done me a good turn in the Weekes' estimation, and that if Miss Boness were to challenge me about gossip again, I would just tell her how she had spread a libel about my poor dear aristocratic-looking old grandmother!

I was just back from my jobs in time for the lunch which Kate almost put into our mouths in her haste to be gone off with Jenkins. Arthur shut himself up in his study with his ser-mon and I had a little happy leisure in the drawing-room, planning to read till tea-time, after I had washed my gloves

and mended our clothes, when I remembered the Cake and
Candy Sale.

It was a great temptation to shirk my duty and stay at home,
in charge of the house, though as a matter of fact nothing happens here as a rule on Saturday afternoon as everyone has just
got his wages and is for the moment in funds. But when I went
to broach the subject, pointing out speciously that I didn't like
to leave him in charge of the telephone, all Arthur did was to
look up and say that would be all right, and I must run along
and enjoy myself!—a picture of this particular form of entertainment which left me speechless. For the solitary advantage
of the War has been to discourage the bigger Bazaars and Sales
of Work which form so large a part of a clergy wife's duties
in ordinary days. I admit that I feel now, that if only peace
came I would serve, even in the parcel department, of a Bazaar
opened by royalty every day of my life; but meanwhile I do my
best to find some consolation in the close of this fearful form
of charity. Everyone was indeed, a little inclined to criticize
Miss Grieve for her lapse into our old peace ways, but as she
said, she had laid in extra sugar before the war began, and it
wasn't as if her entertainment did any *real* good to Hitler.

The one thing to be said for any entertainment in Miss
Grieve's house is that it is crowded. The drawing-room is so
small, and her possessions so numerous, that a very few people make a wonderful show. She moved into her present little
house in a row of tiny villas, when she left the Bank on her
father's death, with the unique distinction of not parting with
one piece of furniture belonging to those Better Days save
for one vast sideboard which almost broke down the neighbouring houses in its efforts to get inside. Her drawing-room
is dominated by a vast, round rosewood table, spread to-day
with war-sandwiches and war-cakes, Chamberlain cheese-
cakes, Gort's goodies, Winston waffles, at two-pence each, and,
in the gaps between a big rosewood tallboy, bureau and chi-
na-cupboard, festoons of crinkly green paper were draped over

card-tables laden with sale goods. At one of these Miss Boness severely guarded the collection of woollies, night-dresses and work-bags which go the round of all our Sales, and probably date back in origin to the beginning of the century. These hardy perennials owe their existence to the fact that all Church workers have a Bazaar Drawer in which they thrust the unsaleable goods which they buy, out of sheer pity, from other stall-holders, and out of which they extract articles when they are called upon to send offerings to yet another effort. Dick says that at the bottom of my receptacle he once found a pair of what he calls "frillies", with a portrait of Gladstone stamped on one leg and of Lord Salisbury on the other; but this is sheer libel. As none of the articles here can conceivably be described as cakes or candy, I can only imagine that their owners felt a sort of nostalgia to see them on show once again.

Miss Grieve herself was superintending a more patriotic stall, and urged me warmly to buy a muffler for Dick, who abominates them, or a body belt or a set of khaki handkerchiefs with the Union Jack emblazoned in one corner. She also exhibited photographs of Gort and Ironside, home-made gas-mask cases of very tasteful and exciting colours, and some battery torches which were snapped up at a very early stage. A small girl looking utterly repellent in a miniature khaki suit was also inviting us all to take 6d. raffle tickets for a reproduction of an equestrian statue of Lord Haig, which depressed me to such depth that I bought some handkerchiefs blindly, and passed on.

"You've heard about Miss Croft, I suppose?" hissed Miss Grieve over my parcel. "So kind of her to come in for a little, as if nothing had happened!"

Miss Croft was at the little green booth between the desk and the fireplace, busy at some purchase from Joyce who was got up for this entertainment as a pierrot—I can't think why—and being very coquettish about a bunch of snowdrops with one of our basses who had come to provide "a little mu-

sic" later on. I hope we shall not have to rely, later on in the
War, on the purchase of "Produce" from such a stall as that of
Joyce and her mother. There were a few tightly-packed vases
of daffodils and primroses, a basket of oranges (3d. each), a basket of brussels sprouts (1s. lb.), and a bowl of eggs (4½d. each).
These represent hours of patient touting on Miss Grieve's part
to the local shops, I expect, just as I am sure she squandered
her whole reserve of sugar on the patriotic cakes on the table.
A little girl, looking very chilly as a buttercup (or daffodil?) in
a soiled yellow sateen, was trying to raffle tickets for a leather cushion with moccasin fringes which we have all seen for
years in similar circumstances. On the other side of the fire-
place Miss Croft was ensconced amidst a confusion of moth-
er-of-pearl chains, Benares-ware boxes, olivewood pin-trays,
praying-mats, and squares of native embroidery.

"The only thing I can't find is any candy," I owned to Miss
Croft, as she turned round to me with her snowdrops and
daffodils.

"That doesn't affect me, anyhow," she smiled triumphantly.
"Do you know what I'm doing? Buying the ugliest things
on every stall, things that have affected my aesthetic taste so
often, dear, at these little gatherings, and then I am going to
take them home and burn them!" Can it be that Miss Croft is
already becoming purse-proud?

Inquiries about Mr. Strang were heard in every corner.
Miss Boness, as the fountain-head of information, was very
reserved, though we all assured her, one by one, that if anyone could pull him through it was her brother. The point on
which I was catechized again and again was whether he was to
be prayed for in church; and as, whatever Arthur can do, this is
looked upon in Stampfield as equivalent to a death sentence,
everyone grew very serious and joined in panegyrics which
were almost obituaries.

"Such a kind gentleman," little Mrs. Leaf kept repeating.
She had ventured to this Sale, I think as a kind of patent of

gentility for her little daughter with the scholarship at the High School.

"It's always the best as are taken first," said the verger's wife, who always attends these gathering with a vague feeling, I think, that she acts as her husband's deputy in a church ceremony.

"When I think of poor Mr. Strang," Miss Grieve told me, "I find myself repeating that beautiful line 'Soon, soon to faithful warriors comes their rest'." In view of her recent attitude over poor Mr. Strang's pacifism I could only assume that she feels the curate's chances of recovery are very small. Miss Cookes also seemed a little ghoulish as she wondered if a gaudy joint-ed Indian wooden snake would please little Pamela, and thus distract her poor, poor little mother. I couldn't help pointing out that, if Pamela sucked it, poor Mrs. Strang would certainly have another invalid in the house, and I fear Miss Cookes felt that her own common sense, and the art of Indian Missions were alike called in question.

"How we'll miss that manly voice of his in the choir," contributed the bass (whose name always eludes me). And by this time I felt that I could endure panegyrics and frowst no longer.

"I'm afraid I must go," I told Miss Grieve, reminding myself, with shame, that if I have grumbled over the cold all winter I ought to enjoy the crowded heat of the Sale—but I don't! "I do hope you're doing well."

"A pound at my stall alone," said Miss Grieve, hopefully, "and I do trust the cakes will go well."

At this I had, of course, to add a rather poisonous-looking mauve sugar cake, wrapped up with almost undue anxiety for economy in paper, to my parcel of handkerchiefs, a bag of eggs, and a greyish-white woolly "boudoir-wrap" which by this time could almost find its own way to my bazaar-drawer, I imagine, so often has it returned there to emerge again in the last three years.

"Do you sometimes wonder", asked Mrs. Eardley-Gage, who emerged from the tea-room opposite as I gained the hall, "just what a gathering of this kind has to do with the hill-sides of Galilee?"

I was just going to say a word of defence for Miss Cookes' olivewood boxes and pin-trays, which profess to be made of Lebanon wood, when I remembered in time that, though the late Bench of Bishops liked *humour*, they disliked mere *flippancy*, as Mrs. Gage told me once severely.

"They do make some money after all," I suggested, "at the cost of a lot of self-sacrifice and work."

"It would be far, far better to give the money outright," said Mrs. Eardley-Gage, who alone of us, probably, is in a position to do this. "I look upon these bazaars and little sales as one of the real curses of our church. It's not all due to self-sacrifice on the part of the workers. They enjoy the fuss and gossip and self-importance of having a stall. They betray, indeed, what dear Bishop Hoby used to call the antimacassar mind."

I was wondering if I could make a little protest on behalf of the Marthas of the Church as we walked do the drive, when suddenly one of Mrs. Eardley-Gage's parcels broke from its inadequate moorings, and a whole spate of little pink, mauve and white sugar cakes rolled abruptly down on to the pavement. We were both of us so encumbered with parcels that salvage was almost impossible, and anyhow the puddles were doing their best to destroy these offsprings of the antimacassar mind at once.

"Oh, what shall I do?" said Mrs. Gage, looking like Saint Elizabeth badly caught out at shop-lifting. "I can't leave them here to hurt somebody's feelings!"

For once there seemed no dog or child in sight to help us, and I hope no-one else was, or they would have seen two comparatively holy ladies engaged in the undignified pursuit of shuffling several battered little relics into a convenient privet hedge. This must, I think, have broken down a certain barrier between us, as I found myself telling Mrs. Gage how much I wished, on Quiet Days, that I had a more disciplined mind, while she gave me an account of how she controls her mind in war-time.

"I never listen to the wireless, and only glance at the papers," she said. "Every day I try to meditate on our great Peace Aims, and at different hours of the day I pray for every country in Europe." (Are there not too many for this programme, I wondered, and began idiotically trying to count the Balkans on my fingers.) For the rest of the day she puts it out of her mind, and reads Pascal as she knits for the troops. She writes, too, to all her nephews, nice *jolly* letters, she said, looking more than ever like a disconsolate Botticelli, as she rescued a falling bunch of daffodils, "with only a few words at the end of each to bring back to these dear boys an atmosphere of the churches where they worship at home". What books, she asked, did I send my boy, and mercifully proceeded to a long list, so that I did not have to confess that a course of strict economy in household books had at last enabled me to send Dick the newest Agatha Christie.

"Aren't you coming out of your way?" she asked, as we neared the Old Parish Church.

"I must just look in at the Canteen. You know Miss Henly has actually got it going already? She is wonderful."

"I think it would have been better for her to have waited till my husband opens it with Prayer on Wednesday night," replied Mrs. Gage, a little stiffly. "I certainly shall not go before then."

I felt a little on the side of the devil as I kept to my intention and made for the parish room, for I cannot see why even an unblessed canteen is not better for our girls and their boyfriends than a wet Saturday afternoon in Stampfield. Certainly the omission was worrying no-one at the canteen, for the big, semi-Gothic hall was literally packed with young, damp, vociferous creatures, shouting for fags and teas and bars of chocolate. Miss Henly was in the centre of it all, her stentorian voice calling her nervous, conscientious sixth-form to their duties; bandying jests and remonstrances if the noise grew too

loud, her Carmagnole cap well on one side, her face beaming
with enjoyment. I should not like to say how much the youth
and noise and heartiness refreshed me after the genteel fussy
atmosphere of the Cake and Candy Sale. It was regrettably
enjoyable, too, after listening to Mrs. Eardley-Gage's attitude
about the War, to hear strangely varying views, far more candidly expressed. Hitler, I learnt, has consumed a whole Turkey
carpet since last September; Von Are has a stone the size of a
potato in his kidney, and,

"Talk of War Aims," a pleasant babyish-looking boy in the
militia said to me, grinning, "what I say about the Germans is,
'Drown the lot'!"

"That's right, Bill, but I'd keep 'Itler and his lot for a bit of
torture first, not half I wouldn't!"

"Tell you what I'd do," said a tall girl with a Jewish nose,
"I'd just split up Germany into the Twelve Tribes of Israel, and
put a Jew at the top of each."

An A.T.S. lounging at the bar, who, apparently, shares some
of Mr. Strang's views, said she would rather make peace as
it was such a phoney war anyway, and what about marrying
Hitler to Princess Elizabeth? This opinion seemed to be going
to bring her into just such popularity as the curate's, when her
boy-friend cut in to suggest that she should stow her gaff, and
didn't she know that Lord Haw-Haw hoped to make England a republic before all was done? This led to a great deal of
ribald laughter, and the singing of half a verse of the National
Anthem, for we are profoundly loyal in Stampfield, and under
the cover of that I made for the door, warmly congratulating
Miss Henly on the success of the idea.

"Only a mere beginning!" she shouted. "By Wednesday we
shall have dart-boards and some competitions going, I hope.
That's why I put off the Rector till then!" How much these
extras will appeal to the Rector, whose life in the shadow of
dead Anglican divines has produced an attitude of resigned

gloom and disapproval, I cannot imagine, but I felt refreshed and inspirited as I went home.

"Some of us," I suggested to Mr. Elgin and Arthur, whom I found in the drawing-room, "don't see nearly enough of the young and irreligious. It's all right for you, Arthur, as you're so often at the Works and your Boys' Clubs, but we parish hacks do feel we get out of touch with youth."

"You can have my choir-boys as a gift," said Mr. Elgin, gloomily. He had evidently been sitting alone with my husband for some time, in a state of nervous tension, as his boots had snuffled muddy figures of eight on my matting, and cigarette ash lay around him and on him in every direction.

"They look such angels in surplices," I protested. "Of course, I know little Jimmy Hay, but then think of his home!"

"I'm usually thankful to get a boy from a bad home," said Mr. Elgin. "Your best church families always put in boys without an ear and with bad adenoids. I've just been telling the Vicar that I really can't stand Tom Higgs any longer, even if he is a good influence and is going to be confirmed in April, not if his voice cracks on E again."

"Well, I hope you'll train his substitute before you go," said Arthur, equably. "I've been telling Elgin how much we shall miss his wonderful playing, my dear."

The door bell rang and I hurried down to admit Miss Croft. To my great discomfiture Archdeacon Pratt was behind her, and I hadn't expected him before seven at the soonest.

"I fear", said the Archdeacon, following Miss Croft and myself upstairs, "that I am a little early, as I promised to look in at the Old Rectory after tea. Mrs. Gage was so very kind as to ask me to stay there, but I told her I was already trysted to you, Mrs. Lacely." (I can only trust my face did not show my disappointment at this unnecessary loyalty.) "She's such a charming woman, isn't she, and so efficient. Everything in her house is so beautifully done, and yet she seems always so far above mere material considerations."

Any woman who said all that could, of course, have been nothing but a cat, but I knew this was merely the record of Mrs. Eardley-Gage on the Archdeacon's card-index mind, and endured it. I did, however, bear him a grudge for joining my tea-party, as it would be impossible to kindle a spark of romance in his presence. He could probably give the methods of courtship in every primitive nation in Asia and Africa, but we could never slip, under his eyes, into one of those comfortable after-tea dreamy silences which I had planned for the encouragement of sentiment in our middle-aged, diffident couple. But no-one could have been kinder or more ready to adapt himself to our visitors than the Archdeacon. He told Mr. Elgin, all about the organ which had been installed in his last parish church, and the chants which he considered most suitable for a small choir. When he heard Miss Croft murmur something about investments to Arthur, he turned round and gave us a comprehensive survey of the industrial market in war-time, not forgetting Swedish match-timber. He inquired after Mr. Strang and told us all about the new remedy for influenza hearts. He asked after Dick, and, without waiting for an answer, described the newest anti-aircraft gun to us, with a wealth of technical detail. It is extraordinary how such omniscience leads to a torpid state of depression in the listeners, and I was just thinking that if I were Mrs. Pratt I should some day put on his tombstone, "Quick in opinion, always in the right" when he got up and said that, as he knew it took just seven minutes to walk to the Old Rectory, he must be going, to arrive there at six o'clock. Arthur said he would walk along with him, and I slipped out of the room after them, as Mrs. Sime was pealing at the back-door bell for admission.

I was annoyed with her for coming early, as she counts her fee of tenpence an hour from the moment she crosses my threshold, and I had asked her to arrive at seven; but she was so jubilant as she came in, in her shapeless coat with its rabbit collar, that I forbore to mention the time.

"She's got him!" she announced, dramatically. "Lil's got him good and proper. They'll be 'long soon to see the Vicar about the Bangs." (This pronunciation of the words "banns" in Stampfield always gives an air of triumph to any marriage, and was particularly appropriate for the case of poor Lil.)

"Who is he?" I asked, full of pity for the victim.

"Why, Alf Byng, the same as she took up with at first. He wasn't much good and made off, as you knows, but now he's in the Air Force and back on leave, and says they may as well be hitched up and get an allowance for their kid. And they've always been true at 'eart through it all," added Mrs. Sime, as a sop, I felt, to film conventions.

Here again is a queer reaction of war on our little world! I cannot imagine that the Byng *ménage* would ever be a success in peace time, or that Lil will fulfil the Mothers' Union ideal of a Christian home-maker; but I feel sure that Alf Byng will beat her if she is faithless, and that an enormous family will satisfy her requirements. The tax-payers will suffer, but poor Mrs. Sime will feel respectable at last.

I thought I would give my guests a little longer to themselves, so I took the Archdeacon's bag upstairs and unpacked it, wondering, as any parson's wife would in these circumstances, whether her own husband would ever wear gaiters. Arthur would tell me here that I touch on a point which is a real argument in favour of the celibacy of the clergy. Never, he says, does any man in any rank of life, from mayor to viceroy, admit that he desires honours for himself. "It's only to please the wife" is the basic formula, and though Arthur does not imagine, naturally, that a Bishop-elect would accept his appointment in those words, yet it is clear that, if wives alone covet honours, celibates must be the most unoffending souls alive.

When, after these diversions, I went back to the drawing-room, feeling that my guests had really had time to settle the date of their wedding and future residence, it was a severe disappointment to find Mr. Elgin looking absently through a very old music-stand, containing little but my old Scarlatti and Dick's jazz tunes, and Miss Croft sitting by the fire looking at a copy of the parish magazine, which can hardly be said to deserve the attention of a confessed highbrow. They both looked sincerely glad to see me, and still seemed undecided as to which could escape first. By way of a digression I told them Mrs. Sime's news, and was horrified to see poor Mr. Elgin going as yellow as the keys of our old piano. An awful suspicion swept over me that the graceless Lil had thrown his name into the maelstrom of her scandals, and I longed to be Alf Byng myself and leather the wretched girl at once. The truth about this I shall never know, as Alf Byng's rather mercenary chivalry will sweep away all old scandals satisfactorily; but if there is any truth in my surmise it explains the poor man's tortured look. The very idea of such an affair, apart from any question of scandal, would be infinitely repulsive to a sensitive and lonely artist.

"It is too bad of me, though, to have left you here so long," I said, "and I fear I can't even ask you to supper!"

Had Miss Croft's imagination followed the same paths as mine, I wondered, when she said with a warmth which had been wholly lacking in her manner before, that she had to go back to the shop to help her assistant to clear up a little after closing-time, and if Mr. Elgin liked to share some cocoa and sardine sandwiches with them there, she would be delighted. And when Mr. Elgin, his colour resuming its normal pallor, accepted as warmly as if it were an invitation to the Ritz, and they went off together, I found myself suddenly rehearsing events in the manner which my dear old grandmother would have done: "If there had not been a war you would have had two maids and Mrs. Sime would not have come in. You would have said nothing about Lil, to relieve all our minds, and, indeed, Alf would not have married Lil. Very probably, my dear, these elderly friends of yours will now come together, and so Good has come out of Evil and every

Cloud has a Silver Lining." That was the way her mind always worked, but of course it was easier to make silver linings out of Victorian campaigns in the distant Empire than out of the thunder-clouds about now.

Dinner was quite a success. Mrs. Sime, feeling, I expect, that the days of her Obliging will soon be over now Lil is off her hands, brought up the courses from the kitchen in turn, and dumped the plates loudly on the hall-table to attract my attention. After that I saw the Archdeacon watch with fascination a grubby hand holding a dish appear at the door, and await delivery by Arthur or myself. He can card-index it as a Stampfield nature-myth, I thought! But the artichoke soup was really hot, and I trust the Archdeacon has learnt that stews are not stews but casseroles in war-time. The cold sweet had suffered from my economy in eggs and cream, but I left two apparently well-fed clerics to their coffee in the drawing-room. (Not even for the Archdeacon would I keep in Arthur's study fire as well!) I did not disturb them till I had hustled Mrs. Sime up enough over the washing-up, not to let it extend into a third hour. (Yes, these ways are mean, but life is more a question of means than ways now, as Kate says epigrammatically.) The two men had reached the ends of their pipes, and the end also, I trusted, of what Dick would call the Strang Saga. By the end of the week I am quite incapable of taking any interest in First Principles, but these, alas, were still exciting the Archdeacon's mind.

"I cannot conceivably understand", he was saying, and there are so many sides of human nature which no orderly mind can, "how you feel that the whole problem is finally settled by Strang's illness. Everyone is sorry for him and is trying to help his family, you say? Well and good, that is Christian charity. But the question still remains as clamant as ever whether a clergyman has the right to use the pulpit for his own political propaganda or no. That is a big question, and one which exercises many minds at present, and this is a test case. You must decide what line you are going to take on Mr. Strang's recovery."

"But won't that partly depend on Strang's mind?" asked Arthur.

"And Mrs. Strang's?" I added.

"I can hardly hope from what you have told me of this very prejudiced young man that a sharp attack of illness will change his views," said the Archdeacon, stiffly.

"No, but Christian charity will, I am sure," said Arthur. "Not that which gives, but that which takes. Strang will certainly be a humbler and more generous man, and the Weekes's who, after all, really settle the tone of the parish, look upon him as their recreation, if not their creation. When once that attitude is established, I don't believe any situation, domestic, nationals or international could occur which would not lead to a firm and lasting peace."

"Only you have to be very ill first," I murmured regretfully.

"Analogies", said Arthur automatically, "are not arguments! They should never have any weight attached to them."

"Still," said the Archdeacon, unconvinced, "it is all utterly unreasonable!"

"Of course," agreed Arthur, "but then what else is the greater part of mankind? Take an historic parallel. I know my grandfather told me once that he would never forget the illness of the Prince of Wales in Queen Victoria's reign. There wasn't the same open publicity about his life in the papers as we would have, perhaps, to-day; but every strict home in England looked upon him, before he had typhoid, as an utterly profligate and dissolute young man, without realizing, as we do now, the mistakes in his upbringing and the anomaly of his situation. It was no sign of grace in him that he lay dying of typhoid fever, but the whole interest of the country centred, said my grandfather, round his bed at Sandringham for weeks. And on his recovery his faults were forgotten and new rumours were discredited. He was the man who had been near death and was alive again, and that was enough for his critics. I don't know if this is an especially English trait or not—"

"Constitutional government?" I asked, feebly, and to my amazement the Archdeacon laughed heartily. People without much sense of humour feel safe with a pun, I always notice, and people who have a sense of humour, like Arthur, dislike them.

"But in any case, there it is. As Dr. Boness's last report was so encouraging, I venture to predict that in a fortnight or so we will give thanks for his recovery; that Weekes will send him and his family away on a good holiday, and insist on paying for a locum for me in Holy Week, and that by the third or fourth Sunday after Easter, Strang will be back with a whole new series of sermons on the Parables or the Epistles, without one controversial word in them from first to last. My wife will probably add that Mrs. Strang will eventually produce a little boy who will marry the quite hypothetical daughter of Ida Weekes."

"Oh, no, no, I shouldn't like that!" I said, feeling that even British Constitutional charity might go too far.

The Archdeacon was obviously not convinced, but happily it was eleven o'clock, at which hour he always likes a glass of hot water—"hot, but *not* boiled, please Mrs. Lacely", so that at five minutes past eleven he can go upstairs to bed. I had just got down to the basement when the telephone bell went, and leaving the kettle on the gas-ring, I ran upstairs.

"I know it's far too late, and I do apologize," said a voice which was so agitated that I could only just recognize it as Miss Croft's, "but I had to tell you just to whisper. Oh, I feel you'll understand—I didn't like to go to bed without telling you how very, very happy we are! Not a word to anyone yet, not a word of course, but oh, my dear. ..."

"But—but I can't hear," I had to say, after I had poured forth my congratulations and heard an indefinite murmur in reply.

"'My heart is like a singing bird,'" quoted Miss Croft, with great dignity, and after prolonged good nights on this basis, I rushed back at length to my kettle.

The Archdeacon had boiled water for once that night, but I hope he did not notice it. It was twelve minutes past eleven before he went up to bed, so that it is no use trying to come up to his conception of an organized household. Still, as I have a very warm invitation to the future home of Mr. and Mrs. Elgin—place and nature unknown, but there are to be *two* grand pianos in the drawing-room—I need not depend on Dillney for visits to the neighbouring country.

IX
SUNDAY

IN ONE OF my rather neglected Holy books upstairs is a passage urging the reader never to let worldly thoughts occupy his or her mind before they make their Early Communion.

It is beautiful advice, but how strangely it suggests the safe, orderly, comfortable homes of Victorian England! Author and reader alike so clearly envisaged that the early riser is called by a maid in good time, and bathes and dresses neatly in a set of clean clothes, washed and mended and laid out by invisible hands, before proceeding through the country lanes or empty, shining London streets, to a well-lit, well-warmed church.

I think Arthur has some little books nowadays for his working-girl Confirmation candidates, which do not imagine this environment, and I hope they are written by well and truly married parsons on a few hundreds a year, for how can you prevent worldly pre-occupations if you are without a maid, and going to return to provide breakfast for a household? I had done all I could the night before, by tidying and dusting the sitting-room, and leaving the breakfast things ready on a tray, but I was only too justifiably anxious about the condition of the stove when I crept downstairs early in the darkness. Our old-fashioned boiler is not so much independent as undependable, and on this occasion the bath-water had been cold overnight, but boiling at three o'clock when I happened to wake up and hear the well-known sounds of a fiery furnace below. This morning nothing showed but a heap of cold ashes! How often in the past I have told my maids that all it needs is a little common sense and clean flues, and how coldly I have accepted their excuses about draughts and the need of the sweep. Now I know by experience, when Kate is away, that I can do all that a stoker may in the way of making up the fire, by putting in the dampers at eleven, and leaving a nice steady glow, and yet in the morning I find desolation, and have to go out to get wood and small bits of coal from the cellar and struggle to start it, with equally bad effects on my nails and temper. This morning I muttered to myself, "Where their fire is not quenched", as an ideal of human attainment, and was far too late for any pause of quiet recollection (see Holy Book again) as I ran to church under the dull grey morning skies.

These reflections, and the Archdeacon's face as he saw nothing but one small ration of bacon (cold boiled, this week) and three eggs of doubtful quality, led me to a rather indiscreet criticism of the hours and nature of Anglican services.

The Archdeacon naturally dislikes criticism as much as he dislikes having his desk tidied; it disturbs his scheme of things.

"I can't help thinking", I said, "that some changes might be made. I imagine that the times were planned for an agricultural population which usually rose at five o'clock and felt eight o'clock a dissipatedly late hour of the morning. And those people who spent all their week-days in the fields must have revelled in a nice stuffy church on Sunday, whereas nowadays men and women who are shut up in stuffy factories and offices all week naturally want to spend their mornings in the open air. It's their only chance."

"Sundays", said the Archdeacon, giving up his egg and I didn't blame him, "should surely be a day of self-denial and spiritual exercise rather than a day of enjoyment."

"Oh, that sounds much more like a Jewish Sabbath," I protested. "Surely in the Medieval Church Sunday was a happy, jolly holiday with people dancing on the village green, though I must say the weather must have been very different then!"

"My wife is a critical rather than a constructive thinker, I'm afraid," said Arthur, carving the bread, for my toast had not been a success. "We never seem to agree on the ideal hours for church attendance."

"Well, to begin with," asked the Archdeacon, "where is the sacrifice of getting up a little early one day in the week?"

"The one day a knocker-up or siren doesn't wake you," I protested. "Arthur's mother used to say that the weak part of the English Church was that it wedded the Catholic Friday to the Puritan Sundays but the one great relic of the Puritan Sabbath is the conviction that you should lie in bed as late as you want to."

"Those young people seem to be up early enough," said the Archdeacon, austerely, as the sound of bicycle bells came in at the window. "These cycle clubs are early enough on the way! What is to prevent them from attending church before they start?"

"They've got to get breakfast," said Arthur, temperately, "and then my boys and girls tell me their dress isn't suitable."

"I should think not," said the Archdeacon, horrified, as a row of girls in dark shorts and long purple legs passed by, ringing their bells violently.

"Some of them were at the seven o'clock service," Arthur pointed out, "and I've an arrangement with Stead at Harley that they should be welcomed there if they get as far—it's a good stopping place for the moors, and after the service his verger's wife provides cups of tea for them very reasonably."

"Very good, very good," said the Archdeacon, "but I fear they probably feel absolved from any necessity to attend Matins. No, no, I cannot condone with the break-up of the dear old English Sunday, when whole families attended church at eleven o'clock together and found their happiness in their homes."

I just managed not to murmur, "Did they?" sceptically, while Arthur pointed out that many of them attended Evensong after all, as very few of the wealthier in the congregation do, and that nothing gave him more pleasure than to see whole armies of cyclists and hikers strolling in to see over our great churches and cathedrals, as they do every Bank Holiday.

"I know you do a wonderful work amongst the factory people," said the Archdeacon, sinking into an arm-chair at my request, and feeling for his pipe and becoming suddenly kind and human. "And it may be that there is something to be said for the nine or ten o'clock Choral Celebration so many of you younger men hold in your parishes; but one is so afraid that they may be a loophole for non-fasting Communions!"

He looked tired, and I was so ashamed about the breakfast that I held my tongue about my opinions on this point. They are entirely out of date, and ruled only by expediency; but it is so frequently the lot of a parson's wife to help a fainting girl out of Early Service and escort her on the way home, to the loss of her own devotions, that we may be forgiven if we feel that whoever first insisted on Fasting Communions—and I believe there is some doubt on the point—had some limitations as regards common sense. I always remember finding dear Dick, who was confirmed fairly young and evinced a curious combination of real childish faith and charming naturalness, in fits of laughter over a holy book sent to him by an aunt. "Look at this bit about not swallowing tooth-water by accident, he said. Don't you think it must make God laugh?"

When I tried to explain the beautiful conception of reaching the King's Court in reverence—and it was easier to feel in those days of a comfortable household—Dick involved me in a long hypothetical discussion of the probable hours of meals, and wanted to know if it would matter about the tooth-water if you swallowed it going to bed at one minute past twelve. Now I know that all I wish is that far, far more might meet at that service where Divine Love comes to the heart of each individual, and that it doesn't matter to me much how they have been employed domestically beforehand. But this, as I say, is only the view of one parson's wife, who thinks not only of those comfortably in the Anglican fold, but of all those young people outside who do want to find some religion but would think advice of that sort so strange as to be grotesque.

Anyhow I held my tongue and didn't shock the Archdeacon, until, as he and Arthur culpably refused to go off to the study, I really had to begin to clear the breakfast things. Then the dear little man was almost beside himself with contrition and leapt up to help me, though it was all I could do not to laugh as he pranced majestically round the room carrying an egg-cup and asking, "Now to what department do I remove this?" He refused to be appeased, even when at last Mrs. Sime rang the back-door bell and came up to the pantry to wash up. Later on, I laughed helplessly when I found, from the extraordinary condition of the bedclothes, that the kind man had obviously set about making his own bed. But the worst of it is that now Mrs. Pratt will discover that I had let Kate out yet again! No country woman with a reservoir of village girls to draw on can ever understand how weakly we cherish anything like a passable maid in a manufacturing town where they hardly exist. Arthur, dear innocent, had never realized the absence of Kate at all, and he was so overcome with penitence that I found him in the kitchen later, flinging coals on to the stove with the zeal and extravagance of a stoker, with Mrs. Sime in the background.

"I know I have read", he said, "in American stories, that it is the duty of the husband to look after the stove, the sacred warmth of the hearth!"

"Come, come, what about the Vestal Virgins?" I asked, while Mrs. Sime stared in speechless stupefaction.

"And that reminds me," said Arthur, putting down the scuttle. "What is this about Lily, Mrs. Sime? I do trust this new step meets with your approval, and that she is really determined to make a fresh start."

If Alf Byng were one of Arthur's friends, I am sure my husband would risk the undying hostility of the Simes by urging Alf against the step he contemplates. But Alf has been a stranger for so long, and our relief to have the immediate scandal of Lil removed is so great, that I imagine Arthur, after some very straight talk, will allow her first love to right the wrong, and to put up the banns. "For she's his wife, if anyone's, in Gawd's eyes," Mrs. Sime hastened to point out as I left the kitchen, hoping

that Arthur's return to his professional duties would save any
further inroads on our coal-cellar. When I next met him in the
hall, he was still so conscience-stricken that he urged me to go
and lie down at once, but by this time I was dressed for church,
and the Archdeacon was ready with his bag.

I had an inward struggle as to whether I should tell him that
a pyjama-string was hanging out or not, but I was so thankful
that he was catching a bus home, instead of returning to lunch,
and he had been so kind all morning, that I felt I could not bear
to convict him of any lapses from decorum or method.

There was quite a good congregation, I was glad to see, either to hear the Archdeacon's sermon, or to join in prayer for
Mr. Strang. Dr. Boness had rung up while I was below stairs
to give a guardedly hopeful report, and as Mrs. Weekes was
not in her pew I knew that Mrs. Strang was in good hands.
Mr. Weekes was pacing the aisle with the stealthy tread of a
first-class churchwarden and no hint of a suggestion that he
had even thought of seceding to the Old Church; Colonel
Greenley and Mr. Chubb were each settled in their pews. My
thoughts turned to Miss Croft, who was walking up the aisle
with a beaming face, and I realized with surprise that instead
of the severest Fugue of Bach, in which I should have expected Mr. Elgin to express his joy, we were being treated to a positively treacly bit of Mendelssohn, with the *vox humana* calling
out the melody.

"My favourite tune," whispered Miss Croft, as I made way
for her to share my seat to-day. "Peregrine is playing *his* favourite as a voluntary at the close!"

My shock of surprise at the name, which our organist has
hitherto guarded as a secret, was so great that I forgot all about
the last voluntary, though Arthur assures me it was a quite
cheerful gavotte of Bach's. Certainly the two elderly lovers had
solved the problem of give and take, I thought, as I disentan-
gled a floating wisp of Miss Croft's hand-woven black and
white scarf from my umbrella-handle. Her happy face, looking

ten years younger, and a note of gaiety which kept creeping into Mr. Elgin's accompaniment to the versicles, warmed my heart all through the service. It is extraordinary how even a commonplace love-affair touches and renews our hearts as we grow older.

> *"Yonder a maid and her wight*
> *Come whispering by;*
> *War's annals will cloud into night*
> *Ere their story die!"*

You couldn't exactly call Peregrine's beloved a lass, but nevertheless they were making the protest which all lovers make, against the drabness and death of the world, to prove that hope and joy do spring up eternally. I expect I should have included myself among the green things which I was calling upon to bless the Lord, but folly is often more inspiring than wisdom.

But I am bound to say that my happy thoughts about the union of divine and profane love in some unimaginable eternity faded during the sermon. I had meant to have a quiet doze so that I might only remember the kind little Archdeacon pacing about, puzzled with the egg-cup, but to-day, when I needed it so badly, sleep would not come. From the moment that the clear precise little voice rapped out the text, "These ought ye to have done and not to have left the other undone", I felt wide-awake with irritation.

What use is it, I asked myself, to scold the people who are in church already for not coming to church? What does the preacher understand about the life of an ordinary working man or woman? (And it's no use to quote that horrid verse of George Herbert's, for I'm sure Mrs. Herbert never wielded a broom in her life.)

The Archdeacon talked to us about the sacred rest of a Sabbath spent in God's House. To-morrow morning he can come down as late as he likes to a pleasant breakfast, and half of his work will be done in a warm, spacious study; when he goes off to his appointments it will probably be in a comfortable car. I admit that most of this respectable Sunday morning congregation have leisure in the week, or don't look upon Sunday morning as the one day when they can get out of this dark little town into the air among their fellow men and trees and flowers. But what sort of message is this for the world outside, and why that reiterated talk of going to church and coming to church? On Good Friday and sometimes on Sunday evenings in summer, Arthur and his choir process with the Cross round our mean little streets, and the sinners and publicans who lounge at the corners stop shamefacedly to listen. Don't we need much more of this, of the Cross in the world, than perpetual requests to walk inside into pitch-pine pews? Here I rebuked myself, remembering my Quiet Day, for presumption, and counted ten and tried to listen again.

The Archdeacon had reached the seasons of Church now, and was-asking how we had kept Lent? Had we been consistent in self-denial in food and amusement and, still more important, given more time to prayer and Bible-reading and church sermons? At this indeed I hung my head. My only preoccupation this Lent has been to make rations go as far as possible, and get good nourishing food into Arthur while I distracted his attention by my conversation enough for him to eat what was before him without question. "Lent," said a Presbyterian minister to me once, "was originally instituted to curb the Bacchic tendencies of a Mediterranean spring." Well, certainly as far as amusement goes, Arthur and I have had no temptation to go Bacchic in Stampfield, but I suppose my invariable custom of falling into an arm-chair over a novel, when I see a clear half-hour before me, is what the Archdeacon would call amusement. I have perforce done my fair share of Lenten Services, though with little attention, I fear, but with regard to reading! "You will find this Saint John intensely interesting dear," Arthur said on Ash Wednesday, and so no doubt I would have, if I had ever got beyond the third page. There was one long sentence in that which brought me up again and again, and most unluckily a little shelf of Jane Austen is always so temptingly at hand. I have a sad feeling that *The Daisy Chain* is really the most uplifting book I have got through in bed, and even in that I have always skipped the frequent and harrowing death-beds. "If this is your last Lent on earth," the Archdeacon suggested, "what account can you give of it?" Sleep was just creeping over me as I pictured myself retailing to an angel with the quick, reproving countenance of Archdeacon Pratt, how very difficult I found Morning Prayers when I tried to get odd jobs done first, "like dusting the drawing-room, you know", when I woke with a jerk to find that the Archdeacon was looking forward in the Church's year. Easter, he said, would soon be upon us, but was that a reason for relaxing our Lenten efforts? Should we not carry on our habits of self-denial and self-discipline into all the rest of the Church's year? This, I admit, does not seem to affect me very much after the sad result of my self-examination. I could resolve to follow up *The Daisy Chain* with *The Heir of Redclyffe*, of course, and buy rather more fish, as meat certainly will be awkward. But apart from my personal shortcomings, I always feel outraged with this appeal which I have heard in one form or another every Lent of my life. The listener must surely have a sense of having been lured into good behaviour on false pretences. It always makes me think of wise little Henry Fairchild who refused to learn the first declension in Latin because he foresaw that he would then eventually have to learn the whole of the book. Anyway, I think the Archdeacon must have mistaken the sermon, when he got one out of his drawer, as we are only about half-way through Lent now, and he went on to pander to our local self-consequence by suggesting that life nowadays was uncertain indeed, and who knew on what evening we might not hear the words: "Thou fool, this night shall thy soul be required of thee,"—which I could only interpret as an air-raid alarm. Do people only come to church to be offered their choice between sudden death and Lent for life, I wondered; because if so, you cannot blame the outside world for calling us joyless!

Then I rebuked myself all over again, as the Archdeacon came to a close and I decided to stay on in church for the Litany as a corrective for my critical thoughts.

It is only since the War that Arthur has read the Litany at this time. There is a pause before the sermon so that people can come in then, omitting Matins, and another after the sermon so that anyone can go out. ("Daddy's the most winning kind of jailer," says Dick. "He's always offering you chances of escape!") It is only in war-time, and said rather than chanted, that the Litany, I think, really comes into its own. In my childhood I was told to look upon all the petitions as requests for delivery from our spiritual enemies, but only the saints could possibly feel such urgency against the sins of sloth and greed and selfishness. To me it seems to bear the marks of a real and tangible enemy at the gates, especially in those agonized petitions near the close which you only appreciate properly when you are tired of droning out "We beseech Thees" to a dismal chant. I suppose critics say that it is instinct with a belief in a tribal god; but not many of us perhaps are our most sensible and superior selves in war-time.

"O God, arise, help us and deliver us for Thy Name's sake. O God, we have heard with our ears, and our fathers have declared to us, the noble works Thou didst in their day and the old time before them!"

"O Lord, arise, help us and deliver us for thine honour."

All those last petitions seem to me to unite us with all who have prayed in the past, and with the certainty that, at bottom, however weak or wandering we are, we pray to a God in Whom we do believe. It took me far away from our little parish of Stampfield and Mr. Strang's pacifism, and our local quarrels and gossip and the Archdeacon's family Sundays, to the long line of the desperate confessors and martyrs in every age who have faced despair and defeat, as we must face him at times, confident that we are, after all, at the foot of

> *"The great world's altar stairs*
> *That slope through darkness up to God."*

I WAS very hungry for lunch.

As Kate was away, Arthur and I had it in the kitchen. Kate has, luckily, a passion for white-washing, and as the paint is good it is really as cheerful as a basement kitchen can be, and Arthur and I feel particularly Darby and Joan as we face each other down here. I know some people would think it dreadful, but I think it dreadful to have a kitchen which isn't nice enough to eat in yourself. And it does save so much carrying and fetching, a special consideration, as darling Arthur, with all his broad- and absent-mindedness, has one odd conservative instinct. He is quite inevitably puzzled and depressed if he does not have roast beef and fruit tart in the middle of the day on Sunday. "The last vestige of Puritanism," I tell him even as I humour him, and indeed I cannot feel it a suitable prelude for the Catechism, which he takes in church afterwards, or for the Bible Class which I hold in our dining-room.

This Bible Class, I need hardly say, consists also almost wholly of grandmothers. It is a relic of the days when the Sunday School was one of the great forces of religion north of the Trent, and some of my old ladies have attended a Sunday afternoon Bible Class of some kind for fifty years. I often wish that I could have a class in our very good and up-to-date Sunday School—and I don't think the critics of the Church realize how well these are managed nowadays—as I never expect any new young member to join my class and face the Gorgon-stare of the old *habituées* who are quite as exclusive as members of the Grid: or of Boodles'. Long, long ago I feel, they have heard everything that any clergy-wife has to say about the Christian faith, and any such innovation as a suggestion that I should read them some scenes from *Pilgrim's Progress* is met with hearty disapprobation. It really makes very little difference what I do and say, and I no longer feel any nervousness, for the proceedings never vary. One elected mother, Mrs. Bebb for this month, clocks in on all the others severely in a large manuscript book, hoary with age, and extracts from each member the sum of one penny towards the Christmas, or—just now—the summer treat. This ceremony is nearly always followed by a rather acrimonious discussion as to whose turn it is to choose the hymn. A great deal of reminiscence goes on round this point. ("Ah, no, excuse *me*, Mrs. Dodds, it was Quinquy as you chose 'Peace, Perfect Peace', the day after your Bob got that clout on his jaw at the football." ... "Well, I may be wrong, dear, but I know I'm not; it was Quinquy Mrs. Sime asked for 'Blessed are the pure in heart'. I could tell you why, but better not.")

In any case it doesn't matter much, as we nearly always have "Peace, Perfect Peace", a hymn which rarely appears in church services now, and then most of the old ladies settle down to enjoy their quest of peace by taking a good nap. Meanwhile, surveying their quiet, tired old faces, I make some disjointed remarks on the Epistle and the Gospel of the day. Today we had the miracle of the feeding of the five thousand, and I always think it seems rather poignantly beautiful to people whose one idea of real enchantment is a long day out with a good picnic, and aren't in the least daunted by the idea of being one among so many. I cannot say that I provided, however, any such novel thought on this occasion as Mrs. Higgs, who said briskly in conclusion, "Those basketfuls! How they'd please the Food Control nowadays!" This was at the start of the discussion which follows my address, and I need not say that we all went rather far from the original story in an interesting discussion on waste, principally, I fear, the waste of our neighbours. The gossip meandered on so happily that my thoughts wandered, and it was only when I discovered suddenly that something like a battle was raging over the suggestion of Mrs. Bebb (whose sense of drama is doubtless fostered by her favourite literature) that we should all use our savings for a day at Buxton at Easter, instead of waiting till summer, on the grounds that by Whitsuntide we may all be blown sky-high.

"There's a want of faith for you!" said our verger's wife, reprovingly. "If Heaven can keep us till Easter, why not till Whitsun and make it Scarborough?"

"There may be no cheap tickets by Whitsun," suggested Mrs. Leaf, who hands over every penny grudgingly all the year, and annoys everyone at the treat by her parsimoniousness over ice-cream carts and the swings.

"The Lord will provide," pronounced Mrs. Sime, feeling no doubt that Heaven, having provided Lil with a husband, would certainly see to her life in an air-raid.

As we seemed in for a long discussion, I suggested that we should think things over this week, and after Sun of my Soul, sung loudly and very slowly, the old ladies rambled off at last, stopping at the gate for long cracks, for all the world like the Rectory ladies after their Quiet Day.

Arthur did not come in to tea—a bad practice of his on Sundays, as he usually gets a cup of strong, dark poison from some parishioner. There were two christenings to-day, and the parents do love to ask him back to their houses on these occasions and he loves to go. When I wonder whether all his patient work in the parish is appreciated, I remind myself of the stock of little Arthurs and Camillas who are growing up in Stampfield, and I know that his people really love him after all. I could wish, indeed, that our names did not figure so prominently in the future Mrs. Byng's family, but perhaps they will have a steadying effect on the Lil Miscellany in time to come.

It seemed rash to leave the house empty all through Evensong or so the Tempter told me, when the telephone rang and Miss Boness spoke to me, in a state of great excitement.

"Good news from the front, Mrs. Lacely! But first I must just say *have* you heard about Mr. Elgin and Miss Croft? Such a surprise! You could have knocked me down with the proverbial feather! Well, well, better late than never, I say, and journeys end in lovers' meetings, don't they? The journey to Leeds, I mean. When did you hear about it?"

"Oh, a little time ago," I answered, vaguely, for Miss Boness hates to be a minute behindhand with any information. "But what's the good news?"

"Dear Mr. Strang! My brother has just been in and he says that things have taken the most favourable turn. Of course, he won't say we're out of the wood yet, but he does say that we're really toeing the line now. So much so that when I said shouldn't the dear Vicar let the congregation know at once, he didn't actually forbid it. The relief and joy will be so great, won't it? I don't suppose any curate was ever loved better than Mr. Strang!"

"I could slip round with a note, of course," I said, doubtful-ly, "if Dr. Boness really thinks—"

"He says it won't do any *harm*," replied Miss Boness, as if Dr. Boness regarded any church interference a little doubtfully. "And Mrs. Weekes has just rung up to say that Mrs. Strang is so relieved and happy that she insists she'd like something said about it. My brother says 'anything to soothe her', for she's been in a dreadful state, you know. Adela has been marvellous with her, of course, and she is very anxious that Mrs. Strang should have her own way, too. So if you could, dear Mrs. Lace-ly? I'd go myself, but I was just in the midst of sorting out old paper and rags for the Government, and one almost feels national work must come first, 'My country, right or wrong', you know."

Certainly, I thought, I can manage to get a note sent up to Arthur in the chancel, by the verger, with less fuss than Miss Boness would have created. In her present frame of mind she would have been quite capable of stopping at the lectern and announcing it herself! The choir was just concluding an an-them, which seemed to me rather a curious commentary on the events of the week: "O, where shall wisdom be found?" they boomed as I found my usual nook behind a pillar.

The church was very full; the silence as Arthur stood up to preach was intense. And then everyone looked at his neighbour as my husband gave out: "We have joined in prayer already for our friend, Herbert Strang, who is dangerously ill. I am very glad to tell you now that, though there must be anxiety for some time, the Doctor reports that our prayers are answered, that his condition has improved greatly during the day, and that we have every reason to hope he will be spared to us. I know that you all will remember him both with thanksgiving and with prayers to-night before the throne of God."

I am in the happy, and perhaps not unusual, position of liking my husband's sermons. Arthur's mother once declared cynically that the reason why clergymen's wives had such large families, with such long gaps between them, was probably because they wished to avoid evening sermons for as long as they could, on the happy pretext of looking after their children, "to let Nurse out for church".

"It doesn't matter whom you sleep under," was Dick's comment once, when I said I enjoyed Arthur's sermons, and no doubt one does get drowsy when one knows one's husband's line of thought too well. But just now he has been giving the simplest form of addresses at Evensong, by relating briefly and entertainingly the life-stories of famous men. Ten years ago he heard this done by the headmaster of our greatest public-school, and, as Arthur said, a life-story, especially if the moral isn't pressed home, really does interest everybody. I don't know if these addresses were called Arthur's Bed-Time Talks, as the originals were, but I always find interest in them. To-night Arthur told the story of Henry Carey and all his efforts and disappointments in India, and the opposition of the Government and the East India Company. He spent years, Arthur told us, in teaching himself the language before he made one convert, "and it is, perhaps", he added, "because it is so difficult for any of us to grasp a new language, a different mode of thought from our own, that we are tempted to con-

demn and obstruct would-be missionaries to-day". That was
his only reference to the burning question of the week, and
I doubt if anyone but myself noticed it. For everyone was so
evidently looking forward to hearing the latest news and discussing it when church was over, that Arthur, I gathered, curtailed the closing years of Carey's life a little drastically. (He has
that knack of understanding the feeling of an audience which
helps the audience, I think, to understand him.) The last hymn,
which had been chosen, I like to think, by Mr. Elgin with reference to his own feelings, was "Now thank we all our God",
and the Stampfield congregation all shouted it out as if their
relief and gratitude about Mr. Strang were a personal victory.

"And so it is," said Arthur, when we both reached home at
six o'clock, the day's work over for us both at last. "Everyone
rejoices everywhere in the victory of life over death. I don't
mean that this was all people felt about Strang. There was a lot
of remorse for past unkindness, and a good satisfying sense of
drama in such a sudden attack and recovery; but at the bottom of it all is our human triumph over our one great mutual
enemy—death. It's that", he added sadly, "which makes wars
so absurd and intolerable—they are the reversal of the human
instinct. But it's that, too, I suppose, which makes the Easter
message of the limits of death's victories come to us with fresh
triumph every year."

The poor dear looked quite worn out, and I was just deciding to go and get supper ready very early, for my efforts
at strong mutton broth are crowned with success by now,
when I had a presentiment. A car swung round our corner
and stopped suddenly and violently at our gate, and I felt my
blood running up to my head and down to my toes as I gasped
out, "Arthur, I know it's Dick!"

And there outside was a small open car, with Ida Weekes
at the wheel. And on the pavement, holding the door open
for Ida, and smiling up at the house heartily, stood Dick. The
evening sunlight fell on them both; and though I suppose to

the passer-by they would have seemed a very ordinary couple of young people in khaki, getting out of a small, uncomfortable and dilapidated car, to me they seemed young Greek heroes for beauty and youth incarnate, and some mysterious elixir which was filling up the horrid hole in my heart and bringing life back to me again. Because, you see, like all mothers, I never see my son leave the house now without wondering if I shall ever see him again.

"Brace yourself, Mums!" said Dick, hugging me as I tumbled down the steps. "Hullo, Daddy, here's Ida! Come in, everyone, because we haven't got long, I'm afraid."

"I knew it was you," I said, as I kissed dear, tall, pretty Ida.

"I should think so, with the noise her casserole makes!" laughed Dick.

"But where's your bag?" I asked, disappointed, "Have you really not come to stay?"

"Not now, I'm afraid! We started off overnight and we only got here an hour ago, and we must be back by six a.m. to-morrow. But don't worry, Mums! I'm getting leave in three weeks, and after that I'm going on a course for three months, and I'll probably wangle more leave after that."

"How good of you to bring him," said Arthur to Ida. His very cordiality showed that he was wishing a little that we three could be together without anyone from outside. I don't say that men are the jealous sex, but they are certainly less adaptable about new situations.

"She jolly well had to come," said Dick, seizing Ida's arm. "She had to soften her parents' hearts while her penniless wooer laid his heart, and fifty-nine pounds, seven and sixpence at her feet."

"Oh stop, you silly boy!" cried Ida. "Dear Mrs. Lacely, I hope you don't mind! I hope you don't think I've been enticing him! No-one to look at him would think he'd reached the age of consent!" (Like all her contemporaries, Ida has a large vocabulary of unsuitable phrases at her disposal without, I am sure, any clear idea of their meaning!)

"He's legally responsible for himself, anyway," said Arthur, smiling now that he was slowly (for how slow the quickest men are!) beginning to understand the situation.

"Yes, rather, but we've come to get your consent and what not," said Dick. "We've got her people taped all right, and now we've come to see you about getting hitched up in April. You can make a good cheap thing of it for us, with special reductions, can't you, Daddy?"

No-one can tell how heavenly it is for a proper, sedate, elderly parson and his wife to look at youth and happiness, and hear such silly conversation and gaiety. In spite of all the Freuds and Havelock Ellises in the world, I do not believe that mothers feel anything but joy when their sons come to them on an errand like this, with a girl the mother knows she can love. They have agony enough when their sons choose what seems a false goddess, or when the right goddess looks haughtily away. But every mother for all time has always wanted her son to have the best of life, and what better can there be than a happy marriage? I suppose it's only in war-time that we accept quite such sudden decisions without any need of adapting ourselves; but now when every moment is precious, how can we grudge them one? And to find Ida clinging to me affectionately and patting my back, while she told Dick not to be so crude in his remarks, made me slightly hysterical with happiness and pride.

"What do your people say, Ida dear?" asked Arthur, a little doubtfully. "Isn't all this rather a shock to them? And you know it can't be the sort of marriage they might well expect for you."

"Here, Daddy, what about the gallant Defender of his Country?" protested Dick.

"I was a bit nervous about Mummy," said Ida with her delightful candour. "She always did seem rather to feel I was marked down for a Prime Minister."

"Well, I'll take the job if it's offered me," interrupted Dick.

"But on Friday I got a marvellous letter; you know how hard her writing is to read—about how she'd never known till she met some one, I imagine, called Lalicypro, or something like that …"

"Gosh, what company you keep in Stampfield!" said Dick, pulling Ida down on the arm of his chair.

"… who seems to have fed her up with no end of respect for your high degree, dear Mrs. Lacely. Indeed, I don't know if I dare to marry into your family now I gather that your father or some ancestor was a boy friend of a Duke who looked like Welly Willy."

"Oh Ida, don't be so absurd!" I said, laughing quite normally at last. "What has my grandfather having served under Wellington got to do with it? Why he might have been a corporal for all she knew, and he was only a Major!"

"Well, anyhow, all that Lali-whatnot said went down so well that I pipped off a letter by return saying that I meant to marry young Prince Stampfield, and then we followed it up by coming on here to-day. And you know, seriously, darling, the real truth is that, as Daddy says, he doesn't respect or love anyone as he does you, Mr. Lacely, and that if Dick's like him he asks for nothing better. And you see when the War's over he'll want someone just like Dick in his business. None of the rest mattered really in the least, only it came in rather handily with darling Mummy who does so like a bit of varnish to the name."

"Why did you never tell me I was a long-lost duke, Mums?" asked Dick, who was gazing at Ida as if she were the soul of wit, so that I longed to hug them both again. "Out with the strawberry leaves!"

"I can find you some strawberry jam," was all I could suggest. "You have come for supper, haven't you?" (More milk in the soup, four eggs with the finnan haddock and, thank goodness, most of the tart is left, my mind registered automatically.)

"We couldn't! We've been eating since five o'clock at home, and they would give us a sort of stirrup-cup of champagne and poached eggs."

"Besides, we must get off," said Dick. "But only for three weeks, darling," he added, squeezing my hand, "And then you'll have to lead the blushing bridegroom up the aisle with *sal volatile* and smelling salts. Mummy, do tell Ida she must come the proper bride! If I'm to be dragged to church at all I've always thought I'd like to march up the aisle with a walking tent!"

"I can show you my veil, Ida," I said eagerly, "if you'd have it? I happened to get it down the other day to look at it."

"Oh, Mums!" cried Ida, and the name threatened to upset me all over again. "I bet that was the very first time Dick mentioned that he was walking out with me!"

They were all laughing at me when to my amazement Kate marched into the room, erect and big and blooming in her new spring "costume".

"Hullo, you old sinner," cried Dick, "out again as usual?"

"Not when I heard you was back. I came straight home to congratulate you both, my hearty, I'm sure." She put out a very tightly-gloved hand, beaming all over.

"But, Kate, how did you hear?" I gasped, as the young couple welcomed her greetings.

"Why, we got back by the two o'clock bus from the Pictures, and I met the kitchen girl from Weekes's," said Kate, scorning my surprise. "So I told Private Jenkins, you can come in or not as you like, I said, but I'm going back to see they get a good supper for once."

It was only Kate who cried when Dick and Ida drove away a few minutes later. She was so disappointed not to feed them, and only consoled herself by waiting upon us hand and foot, and I can't say I was sorry, for emotion is exhausting when you are over fifty, and I was thankful that Mrs. Weekes had sent a message to say they would look in to-morrow morning, for I don't believe I could even have telephoned that evening. Arthur and I were glad to sit and talk each other into composure, and what mother in the world has any right to complain over a good-bye to her son when she is to see him again in three weeks, and knows that he is to get his heart's desire?

"And yet, perhaps," I said, when at length I got up to go to bed, "perhaps I'm only taking it all so happily and calmly because I still happen to be in love with you, Arthur. It does make a difference!"

"Isn't it," said Arthur, looking over the top of his spectacles, "one of the justifications of our profession and of the unselfishness and humility which we try to practise in our lives, that most clergymen do love and are loved by their wives?"

By a strange accident my errant engagement-book was lying by the arm-chair in the dining-room when I went in to say my prayers. I took the pencil and wrote down (though was I likely to forget it?)—"Mr. and Mrs. Weekes to call on Monday." Thank goodness, I thought, the Magdalen Committee is not till twelve o'clock! And then I turned over the leaves, with all their jottings of X.Y.Z. Union, N.V. Council, G.F.S. Com., Y.W.C.A. Club—all the humdrum yet somehow inspiring work of the parish I hate and love so well, till on Monday three weeks I wrote down proudly, "Dick and Ida's Wedding Day".

THE END

FURROWED MIDDLEBROW

Printed in Great Britain
by Amazon

77002097R00119